SPANK!

Edited by DL King

PHOTO BY STACIE JOY

Spank!

D. L. King (editor)
Published by Logical-Lust Publications, © 2010

ISBN: 978-1905091-80-5
Paperback version
Published by Logical-Lust Publications © 2010
Additional editing by Rachel McIntyre
Book layout and typesetting by jimandzetta.com

Cover design by Helen E. H. Madden, pixelarcana.com
© Logical-Lust Publications 2010
Cover photos © Stacie Joy 2010 thepixeltrix@gmail.com
Cover models: Deity and Max

Acknowledgements

I'd like to thank Deity and Max for allowing their very charming derrieres to grace the covers of *Spank!* Thanks to Steven for his spanking expertise in creating some memorable handprints on our models beautiful behinds, as well as "holding the light" (sorry, Peter). A big thank you to Sean (penboy7.com) for allowing a group of thoroughly depraved individuals to use his home as a make-shift photo studio. And, of course, a big thank you to the many talented writers whose spanking-hot stories you will find inside.

Preface

I have this favorite porn film. In it, one of the characters keeps repeating a line, over and over. It gets silly after a while and, like *The Terminator* line, "I'll be back," those in the know seem to repeat it in both likely and unlikely places. Sitting down to write this preface, I immediately thought of it—but changed slightly, to better fit the context.

I know spanking.

And I do, you know—know spanking. Other people who *know spanking*—or love spanking—or just gravitate toward spanking, can never quite get enough. It may well be an acquired taste, but once acquired, either as the spanker or the spankee (or perhaps both), it is never lost. The authors of these stories can tell you that. And they will.

If I've done my job right, this book will get you hot and bothered and give you ideas. It's a compendium of the art of spanking. There are curious bottoms, naughty bottoms, well-tempered bottoms, good-natured bottoms, boy bottoms and girl bottoms. There are shocked and surprised bottoms, pouty and annoying bottoms. There are married and single bottoms. There are ingénue and "old hat" bottoms, as well as the requisite number of experienced and first time hands. I think you'll find there are bottoms and hands to suit all tastes. But I should let you be the judge.

D. L. King
New York, 2010

It's a spanking—it's supposed to hurt!

For those of us who like to spank and be spanked, this phrase will inevitably be uttered, sometimes seriously, sometimes in jest. But it does happen to be my philosophy about a good spanking: It may turn me on; it may be romantic; it may make me crazy with desire before, during or after the event—but a good spanking is supposed to hurt.

And a good spanking story, one that holds my prurient interest (why else would I pick up a book of erotic stories?) is supposed to make me believe that the spanking hurts, or, even better, to make me ride the pain or the power right along with the characters.

The protagonists should be believable. The tops should have good reasons for dishing out the spankings (even if they're "just" sexual reasons); the bottoms should deserve the spankings, and at the end of it all they should care about each other. Oh, and an extremely hot, strong, authoritative top helps.

The stories in *Spank!,* edited by D.L. King, have managed to cover all those bases well, each in its own unique way, with the characters, settings and plots ranging from the sexual to the serious to the surreal.

I simply loved "Elementary, My Dear Sir," in which a widow, recently acquitted of murdering her husband, is attracted to the inspector who had brought the charges against her. He doesn't believe she's innocent and attempts to get her to confess. What elevates this story is the narrative, the details of its Victorian surroundings, and the awakening of the dormant romantic feelings between the inspector and the strong-willed female protagonist. But what really slammed it home for me was the powerful way he spanked her, followed by his taking charge.

"The inspector's hand descended upon her ass with the coppery strike of a hammer against an anvil. Pain exploded through Rowena's body. She closed her eyes, tears stinging the lids. The fire along her rear burned then dissipated until it was a dull throb. She waited for the next blow. 'Inspector?' His hand descended again.... 'Do not speak until I give you permission.'"

Because I tend to get off on mild humiliation scenes, I also liked the modern yet anachronistic "Slippering." In this "politically incorrect" tale, a wife is punished by her husband in front of his male friend. "You're not going to hurt her, are you?" the friend asks, to which the husband replies: "'I'm giving her a short, sharp lesson in the error of her ways...Of course I'm going to hurt her.'"

And of course the friend must rush home and see if his wife is willing to try something similar.

I want to feel the heady rush of power that comes from taking charge; such as in "The Trumpet of Destiny": "I began to really enjoy myself. I had never spanked anyone before: let alone someone of my own sex.... 'You, my girl, are going to get the spanking of your life.'... I let her have it. She squealed, writhed, wriggled, danced on her heels and begged for mercy."

Or I want to feel the suffering that leads to sexual release, such as in "Just a Spanking": "Pain rips me apart. The simmering tightness in my pussy comes to a sudden boil, welling up and spilling over into the emptiness."

When a scene in a story gets me breathing heavily, I'll return to it over and over (my copies of *The Claiming of Sleeping Beauty* and *Carrie's Story* still fall open at certain key pages), but picking up a new book, especially an anthology of short stories, is like walking into a spanking party where you haven't met everyone yet. You may already have your favorite players and you won't abandon them, but then you will see a stranger across the room and you simply *must* find out what he or she is all about.

When I bottom I know the spanking's going to hurt. It's supposed to hurt. I simply have to take it anyway. I simply have to dive in because at its core it's what turns me on. You may not like *every* story in *Spank!*—such are the variegated desires of those who share this fetish—but I'm pretty sure you'll be turned on.

Pick a story at random or start at the beginning. Dive in.

Cassandra Park
New York, 2010

Contents

Acknowledgements

Preface - D. L. King

It's a spanking—it's supposed to hurt! - Cassandra Park

Just a Spanking by Lisabet Sarai _____ 15
Apple Bottom Hard Cider by Kathleen Bradean_____ 24
Anthropology by Donna George Storey _____ 41
Anything but Ordinary by A.D.R. Forte _____ 52
The Royal Montague by Cervo _____ 63
Elementary, My Dear Sir by Anna Black _____ 76
The Accidental Spanker By Sean Meriwether_____ 94
Necessary Roughness by Beth Wylde _____ 105
The Good Soldier by Sacchi Green_____ 116
The House on Oxford Street by J.Z. Sharpe _____ 129
Finally by Jessica Lennox _____ 142
Fit to be Tied, Bound to be Gagged by Allison Wonderland ___ 148
Thin-Skinned by Jean Roberta_____ 158
Slippering by Lee Ash_____ 173
A Well-Red Bottom by Maggie Morton _____ 185
Just Rewards by Tara S. Nichols _____ 194
Sugar by Sommer Marsden _____ 205
The Trumpet of Destiny by Roxy Katt _____ 214
Richard's Reward by D. L. King _____ 227
What Jackie Gives Me by Evan Mora_____ 238

About the Authors

Other anthologies from Logical-Lust Publications

Just a Spanking

By Lisabet Sarai

To GCS of course

"Could you get off on just a spanking?"

The message arrives as I'm halfway through grading an exam. I'm tempted to ignore it, but when I see the *From:* address, I don't dare. It might be instructions. It's not often that he tests my obedience while I am at work—he normally respects my professional identity—but he has been known to make exceptions. I vividly recall delivering a two-hour lecture on web application architectures with a fat purple plug stuffed into my ass. I couldn't sit. I couldn't walk around. I had to stand still, trying to concentrate, hoping that my cunt juices weren't soaking through my skirt.

The memory is enough to make me wet. Hell, just seeing his email address quickens my breathing. That's the effect he has on me, from four hundred miles away.

"If you were the one giving the spanking—of course," I shoot back, mostly relieved that he's not asking anything difficult. I need to get these finals graded by tomorrow.

His reply arrives in less than sixty seconds.

"Don't be glib. And don't try to flatter me. Think before you answer. You'd be naked, but I wouldn't touch you at all, except

15

to whack your ass. No tweaking your nipples. No fiddling in your cunt. And no bondage, either. Just the sting of my palm slapping your butt, as hard as I can, again and again. Would that be enough to make you come?"

Would it? It's an intriguing thought experiment, which is of course why he has brought the subject up. I doubt that he'd be able to resist touching me, though. I know that my taut, fat nipples are magnets for his fingers. He loves to tease me, to frustrate me and make me beg, but despite his Dom persona, he's not immune to my influence.

"Don't you think that it would be a bit boring? Sort of anti-climactic? After all the things we've done?" I know that he's sitting in his office, staring out at the bay and remembering all the pervy games we've played over the years. As am I.

This time his response is less rapid. "I think of it as pushing your limits, in an elegant, minimalist sort of way. Just a spanking. Simple pain, not agonizing but unrelenting. No toys. No kinks. Just my hand on your butt."

"No kinks?" I add an emoticon to the message so he'll hear my amusement. "Since when is spanking vanilla?"

"For us it is," he replies. I can imagine his voice saying this, rich and dark and full of that secret knowledge of my soul, the power that melts me every time. My nipples tighten and my clit swells. I don't know how to answer.

"Next weekend," comes his next message, without waiting for my response. I swallow hard at the delicious menace that he can communicate even through the sterile medium of electronic mail. "Be prepared."

We manage to meet at least one weekend a month, despite the distance and the demands of our regular lives. Sometimes I fly up to visit him. Sometimes he comes down to see me. Either way, as soon as we are together, we're swept into some alternate existence where every sensation is magnified and every emotion has the weight of revelation. The so-called real world simply evaporates. For me, for those two magic days, his voice, his fingers, his cock are the only realities. Plus the implements of pain and pleasure that he uses so imaginatively as an extension of his will.

He meets me at the airport with a kiss tender enough to reassure me that I'm more than just his slut. His lips wake every inch of my flesh. By the time he releases me, I'm flushed and tingling all over. After that initial embrace, however, he doesn't touch me at all.

He leads me to the parked car. I remember him taking me once in a sweltering parking lot, his fingers crammed into my cunt while he whispered all the indignities he planned to inflict on my poor body. As that part of me fluttered helplessly around his hand, I knew that he could ask anything of me and I'd obey. Now he is asking something new, a kind of restraint that I find more difficult than any bondage.

I am dressed as he requires, short skirt with no panties, silk blouse with no bra, and my favorite lace-up boots. I fidget on the seat as he drives up 101. The plastic is sticky against my bare skin and getting stickier by the minute. He stubbornly keeps his eyes on the road.

I part my thighs. The car fills with the ripe scent of my pussy. His nostrils twitch but otherwise he ignores me. My nipples feel huge and hungry as they do when he winds them with rubber bands. I try to keep still. Each whisper of silk across my breasts makes my cunt clench and weep.

He opens the car door—a gentleman Dom—and helps me out. The brief contact of palm on palm makes me shudder with want. I follow him up the stairs to his apartment, watching his strong buttocks shift in his trousers as he climbs. I think about how they tense and relax when he fucks me. I'm panting by the time we reach the third floor, but not from exertion.

The door swings open. He steps aside, gesturing for me to enter. Normally he'd have me pressed against the wall, knee in my crotch and hands under my blouse, before the lock clicked shut. Today he simply stands beside me, a half-smile on his full lips, as I survey the familiar room.

He has already set things up. In the dining area, the table has been pushed out of the way. Two of the chairs face us, side by side, flanked by the ottoman that normally sits in front of the armchair. That armchair is the usual location for his spankings, but I can see that tonight will be different. He's trying to minimize my contact with his body. Clever man.

"Strip," he orders, as he has so many times before. My heart somersaults in my chest, as it always does. He seats himself in the middle chair to watch me remove the few clothes I'm wearing.

I can feel the weight of his eyes, tracing my curves, lingering on my swelling breasts. I move as slowly and sensuously as I can, working to arouse him, to undermine his resolution not to touch me. His pants are loose. I can't really tell whether his cock is hard, but his lips are parted and there's a flush on his cheeks.

"Behave yourself, Becca," he warns. "No teasing, or you'll get the cane after I'm finished with your spanking. In fact, you're guaranteed the cane if you're not naked in ten seconds."

His threat has the desired effect. I tear off my blouse and a button goes flying into the corner. I don't care. I stand naked before him, awaiting his instructions.

He makes me wait. Heat shimmers through me. Blood pounds in my ears. I study my toes and listen to my breath. Fear and excitement comingle, until I can't tell one from the

18

other. My bratty determination to make him touch me fades away, although my clit still throbs and my juices trickle down my thighs. All I want is to please him. I'll wait forever if that is what it takes. Indeed, a part of me would rather wait than know what comes next.

"All right, Rebecca," he says finally. "Kneel on the footstool and stretch your body across my legs." I look up to find that he has placed one of the throw pillows on his lap. I understand that he wants a barrier between my body and his possible erection. Plus the cushion is too soft to provide much friction. Obviously he has planned this carefully. I would not have expected less from him.

I am awkward as I clamber onto the ottoman and spread my body across his lap. The ottoman is the perfect height. When I bend at the hip, my belly rests on the cushion and my ass is in the air, just to the right of his body. I rest my chest on the chair to his left, cradling my head in my crossed arms. I'm not uncomfortable. I feel stable and well-supported.

"Thighs together. That's right. Bring your knees closer to the chair. Good." I comply as promptly as I can. The shift raises my butt higher. I'm totally accessible. Completely vulnerable.

It's delicious.

Usually he warms me up when he's about to spank me. He will stroke and knead my buttocks, then pinch me hard just as I am starting to relax. More often than not he'll slip a blunt finger between my cheeks and swirl it around in my pussy. He'll tell me what a pervert I am, to be so wet at the mere thought of being beaten. I'll be torn between embarrassment and pride. I know that this is one reason why he wants me.

Tonight, though, the only warm up is more waiting. He doesn't touch me, though I can feel his eyes like ghostly fingers on my exposed flesh. My cunt feels heavy and swollen, pressed against the cushion. I shift my position the tiniest bit and pleasure sparks from my clit to my nipples and back again in a maddening cycle.

"Be still," he orders. "No squirming around. No humping the pillow. This is a spanking, pure and simple. You may yell or cry as much as you want. But I don't want you to move. That will spoil it."

There's menace in his voice, and promise. We are about to embark on a new adventure together.

"Do you understand?"

I'm sure he feels me tremble as I nod, but he doesn't chide me. Instead he brings the flat of his hand down hard on my ass.

"Ow!" I'm startled more than hurt. The sting races like a wildfire from my cheek to my clit. The swollen nub compressed between my thighs is a red-hot coal. "Ouch!" Before the echoes die he lands another blow, sharp and precise, on the opposite mound. Brief pain flares before pleasure drowns it.

Smack! Smack! Each slap builds the heat. I barely have time to suck in a breath before he hits me again, his open palm walloping me with all of his considerable strength. He varies his targets, whacking one cheek, then the other, with an occasional fiery blow to the back of my thighs. Otherwise, he gives me no respite, just pummels my ass again and again and again.

Before long I'm yelling each time he connects. My skin feels raw. My whole ass burns. Fire spikes wherever his hand lands, a sudden jump in background heat. I try my best not to shrink from his slaps, to fulfill my part of the bargain.

Real pain has long since overwhelmed the teasing sting of the first few spanks. Still, I'm turned on by the process, perhaps more by the thought than by the sensations. There's a buzzing in my pussy, an itch that's amplified each time he strikes. I arch my back the slightest bit, pressing my pelvis against the disappointingly puffy cushion.

Of course he notices. He reads my body like no one else. "Naughty slut!" he exclaims. Sharp blows rain down on my battered ass. "Be still! Don't disappoint me."

Guilt smothers the pain for an instant. I tighten my thighs, struggling to relieve the torment at my center.

"I guess I'll just have to hit you harder," he says, and follows through on his promise.

Thwack! Slap! Even he couldn't possibly have the strength to keep this up. Agony stitches across my lacerated flesh every time his hand finds its mark. He's a terrible machine, determined to prove that he can spank me into complete submission. Just a spanking. I can hear him laugh to himself as he thrashes me, unrelenting, glorying in his power over me. Bent over, I can't see him, but I know the demonic glee that is transforming his face. I've seen it before. Intoxicated by his control, he spanks me harder still.

I stopped yelling a while ago. Now I'm whimpering, my eyes squeezed shut, tears leaking out the corners. I'm drifting in a haze of pain. The snap of his flesh meeting mine, the reek of my soaking cunt, the constant bolts of raw sensation sizzling through my body—these have become my world.

I can't take any more. I'm sure that I can't. I worry that he'll do real damage. What about the rest of the weekend? I'll be destroyed. Our precious time together will be wasted. Doesn't he see? Doesn't he know?

In all the years, we've never had safe words. They weren't necessary. He always seemed to intuit exactly how much I could take.

I wonder now whether I've deluded myself. He seems far away, lost in his own dream of domination. But I can't bear the thought of trying to stop him. Of disappointing him.

Something changes. He lays into me as hard and fast as before, but I feel his attention turn to me. "Trust me, Becca," he says in that velvet-dark voice, even as his palm blisters the back of my thighs. "Relax. Let go. Give yourself to me."

Do I really hear his voice? Is it my imagination? Is it telepathy? My fear shrivels. The tension coiled in my chest unfurls. The pain floods through my limbs, washing my doubts away. I open my mind and hope that he can sense the change, my new willingness to endure anything he wants to inflict upon me.

His palm is a thunderbolt. Pain rips me apart. The simmering tightness in my pussy comes to a sudden boil, welling up and spilling over into the emptiness. I convulse in his lap, shaken by exquisite pleasure. He's still spanking me but now each blow just takes me higher. I come again, writhing against him, hoping that he'll forgive me for moving.

I lie there, my limp body draped across his thighs, for a long time. He strokes my hair and plants kisses on my ravaged ass.

"Well, now we know," he says. I twist around to look at him. He's got that manic grin that means he's especially pleased. I feel warm all over. "You *can* come from just a spanking."

"I told you." I laugh, knowing that for the moment I have permission to be a tease. "You should have believed me."

"I believe in the scientific method. Never trust a claim until you've tested it."

"I'm sure that your objectives were purely scientific."

"Of course." Gently, he helps me up to my knees and then to standing. It hurts to move. He kisses me and the pain melts away.

"Anyway, I'm hungry. Go take a shower and I'll take you out for sushi. I figure that it will be easier for you to sit on one of those cushions than on a chair."

"Yes, sir." I'd rather stretch out with him on his bed and cuddle, but I know better than to argue. Halfway to the bathroom, I turn to look at him. He's watching me, no doubt appreciating the fiery red hue of my buttocks.

The satisfaction I see on his face makes me want to do it all over again.

Then I notice that his trousers are wet at the crotch. I turn away before he can see my triumphant smile.

Clearly he can get off on just a spanking too.

Apple Bottom Hard Cider

By Kathleen Bradean

Lord knows it wasn't her singing, which one of her rivals described as, "A bitch in heat." Or her sense of fashion, which kept her on *TMZ*'s worst dressed list. Or even her copycat late-night antics that led one record executive to dub her "Me Too Mya." What she lacked in class, she almost made up for with brash balls. (A flash shot of her emerging from a low-slung sports car, wearing only a micro mini and a pair of six-inch canary heels, laid to rest the rumor that she might have been born with a pair.) Chuck Ferguson could have overlooked all of that if there were a chance in hell that he'd ever get a word of praise from her. But no. On or offstage, she was a demanding diva, and he never got it right. The only reason he'd put up with her so long was Mya's (just Mya, no last name) biggest asset: the plushest bottom that had ever graced the backside of a dance club queen. While it assured (how Chuck loved using any word that started with *ass*) and inspired many a late-night wank session, it wasn't enough anymore. She, and it, had driven him to the brink.

He stared out the window of the limo. Only one more night, then he could resign as Mya's manger—although she would assuredly (hah!) fire him before her birthday party was over. Fine. He had a freshly scrubbed Disney Channel star waiting in the wings for his guidance. For once, he'd have a client who would do as she was told.

He was going to miss seeing Mya's fine booty stuffed into a pair of jeans, or hugged by those short knit dresses she liked so much. But while other managers felt that sex with the talent was a perk of the job, and even demanded it, he'd never so much as patted that legendary derriere. He didn't dare. Mya was a good six inches shorter than he was and, except for her bottom, skinny as a rail, but she had a way of keeping him on a tight leash.

He flexed his hand. Lately, he'd wanted to do more than pat Mya's tush. Mya needed a good, hard spanking, and he needed to be the one who gave it to her. He dreamed of sinking his teeth into that juicy apple bottom. Unfortunately, that long overdue spanking would have to be delivered by proxy. The parents of his next popstar princess made it clear that his squeaky clean reputation was the only reason they'd allow him to manage their darling daughter. One picture of his hand raised over Mya's bared bottom, and they'd fire him.

Mya sprawled against the dark blue leather seat of the limo as it crept down Sunset Boulevard. "You luv mommy, yes you do," she told her Chihuahua.

The tiny animal was blinged and bedazzled in Mya's signature color: Mya magenta. The dog's eyes begged Chuck for help. He knew exactly how it felt.

She shoved the dog into the magenta purse-sized carrier she took everywhere with her. "This better work, Chucky."

When he didn't immediately rush in with assurances, she kicked him with her studded black leather hooker boot. He turned away from the window but said nothing. Behind her outsized sunglasses, no doubt her eyes had narrowed. Before, that would have made him coo in soothing tones while he fixed whatever it was that had her panties—if she ever wore them—in a bunch, but he was done with that.

She tilted her head and pulled off the glasses. Even through the darkened windows of the limo, oncoming headlights made her squint. With the earpiece of her sunglasses clutched between laser-whitened teeth, she batted her eyelashes. "Chucky-wucky."

Oh god, not the baby voice.

He glanced at his watch and then peered out the window. "We'll get there at twenty-five 'til midnight. Most of your guests should have arrived by then."

"Should?" She tugged at the hem of her dress, but it shrank back over her thighs.

He shrugged. "Hierarchy of fame. When you're pulling twenty mill a picture, you can show up late for your own funeral."

"But it's my birthday."

To be exact, it was the third anniversary of her eighteenth birthday, but he wasn't going to let that little tidbit hit the press until he was safely away from her.

"We can only pay them to show up. We can't force them to arrive before you."

"Pay?" she screeched.

"You didn't really think all these B-list types came just because we invited them, did you? This is a play date, a pay-to-play date."

"You mean I gotta pay people to come to my party? Didn't anyone come just 'cause I asked them?"

The truth was that they'd only had to pay a few people's appearance fees, and those were the kind of people who brought an energetic party entourage with them. Like extras in a movie, their job was to fill in the scene but not overshadow the stars. Most of the guests were coming because they seemed to like Mya, but he couldn't resist the chance to hurt her.

"Some gossip bloggers will show up anywhere there's free booze. And, of course, there's the winner of your contest."

Ah, the contest. That, Chuck admitted, had been eighteen strokes of pure genius. It was the only reason he stayed with Mya through the release of her latest record. So many times, as she'd belittled him, he'd been tempted to walk away. Every time, he closed his eyes and imagined the scene that would finally play out tonight. She thought she had his balls in an iron grip, but he was about to show her who was boss.

Mya squirmed. "Yeah, about that contest…"

Oh no. She wouldn't. She couldn't. He swallowed his alarm and played the part that came naturally to him. "Sweetie. Darling. It'll be all right. Trust me." He patted her hand.

Her upper lip curled.

"We've talked about this. Your fans are in a feeding frenzy as they fantasize about being the first to tap that forbidden fruit when it finally becomes legal. Of course, that's why we've been playing up the virgin angle so hard. That's why we delayed the release of your record to coincide with your birthday. This is it. This is your time."

"I get that. What I don't get is the whole birthday spanking thing."

He'd told her this about a thousand times. It was pure bullshit, of course, just an excuse to get his revenge, but he tried to sound as if he knew what he was talking about. "It's symbolic of taking your virginity. We had thousands of entries for the honor of giving you a little birthday spank in front of your guests. Like I said, your fans all want to be your first."

She frowned more. "Yeah, but..."

Chuck leaned forward, his hands clasped before him. He widened his eyes. "It's never been done before. No more 'Me Too Mya.'"

She glared at him. He'd never dared call her that to her face before.

Before she got angry and took it out on him, he rushed in with soothing assurances. "No one will ever forget this night. You'll be the top internet search for weeks, maybe even months. More hits than Britney even. Your new singles get more radio airtime. Everyone will be talking about you. Lady Gaga will choke with jealousy. Justin Timberlake might do a duet. Madonna...Well, you get the picture."

"He's not a creep, is he? The contest winner. You didn't pick just anyone."

"Believe me, sweetheart, I took extra special care in choosing just the right man for the job. But of course we told everyone it was a random drawing."

She sat up. "Oh! Maybe we should have a girl do it! Lesbian stuff gets lots of attention."

"But you're not a lesbian."

She rolled her eyes. "Of course not, stupid. It would be pretend lesbian. You know. For the cameras. Guys dig that shit, as long as the girls are hot."

"I don't happen to have a spare fake lesbian lined up to spank you tonight."

"Well, you should. Do I have to think of everything?" Mya leaned over her Chihuahua. "Isn't that right, Pookie? Mama is paying ten percent for what? I could have spent that on a mani-pedi for you instead. Yes I could. Yes, I could."

"Don't worry. This will be a night to remember."

Mya rolled her eyes and went back to nuzzling her dog.

Chuck looked out the window to see where they were. He could see the club's neon sign half a block down. A punk kid on a skateboard wove between an old lady with a bag of groceries and a gay couple on the sidewalk. Traffic moved slowly. Mexican men in red jackets waved cars toward valet parking lots.

He pulled out his phone. "We're here. Yeah, grand entrance time. Thanks, Mike." His stomach clenched. Mya never seemed to get nervous about anything. She drummed her long nails on her thigh. He was always tense enough for both of them.

The club's red carpet was a couple yards away. Paparazzi pushed against a black velvet rope on the sidewalk, cameras ready. How they always knew where to be was still one of the great mysteries of Hollywood to Chuck.

Mya smeared a fresh coat of gloss over her lips. "You should have booked a date for me." She slammed her hands into her lap and sighed. "You always make me go to these things alone. People are beginning to wonder if we have something going on."

"What? Us? No. Everyone knows I'm only here as your manager. Nothing else."

"Uh-huh. Then stop staring at my ass with your tongue hanging out, and stop steering straight guys away from me." Mya climbed over Chuck to get to the door. "Oh, and don't forget Pookie." She dropped the Chihuahua's carrier in his lap.

"You can't bring a dog into the club."

"He's a service animal. I tell waiters all the time at restaurants." Mya rapped her knuckles on the limo partition. "Hey, jerkwad, stop moving already. We're here."

The limo lurched forward as the driver stepped on the brakes a lot harder than he had to. Mya almost went sprawling on the floor of the limo, but Chuck wrapped his arm around her tiny

29

waist and held her up. As she struggled to balance, her dress rode up. The bare skin of her bubble butt rubbed Chuck's nose. He fought back the almost overwhelming urge to make motorboat noises.

She squirmed out of his arms and into the seat near the door. "Oh Chuck, if only you were a man."

A bouncer from the club, six feet six of solid steroids in a T-shirt two sizes too small, yanked open the door. Flashes went off. While Mya flashed them back, Chuck got out of the limo on the traffic side and headed into the club.

A spotlight hit Mya as she entered the club. She ignored D-list celebs, wriggled fingers at the Cs, air kissed Bs, and threw her squealing self into the arms of the A-listers. While she worked the scene, Chuck moved through the crowd. People glared at him. It was amazing how many of the guests he'd worked with, and how many still held grudges. The rest, mostly singers looking to make it to the big time, posed and smiled. He'd have time to network later. Right then, he had to find the real special guest.

Daddy Dom wasn't hard to spot. The bald ex-Marine stood alone at the back of the dance floor. The Hollywood crowd seemed to sense that he wasn't someone to be treated with their usual disdain. Their distance was almost respectful instead of the usual open rudeness. He leaned against a small stage, veined forearms crossing his broad chest. Even though he wasn't as bulked up as the bouncers, Chuck would have bet on Daddy Dom in a fight.

"Thanks for coming." Chuck offered his hand and winced as Daddy Dom gripped it. He wished he could have left Mya's dog in the car. The carrier was so magenta, and sparkly.

Daddy Dom looked over Chuck's head. "I want to talk to her."

Chuck turned to watch Mya shaking her moneymaker on the dance floor. "I don't think that's a good idea."

"I didn't ask you for your opinion. I won't spank her unless I've talked to her first. Bring her to me."

"She's busy."

Daddy Dom shrugged. "Suit yourself. I'll be leaving now."

"Wait." Chuck put his hand on Daddy Dom's forearm. Geeze, the guy was solid muscle. Even the thick veins that ran down his arm were hard. Daddy Dom looked down at Chuck's hand. With a weak smile, Chuck pulled it away. "I'll try to talk her into coming over."

As he shifted the dog carrier to his other hand, he considered asking Daddy Dom to hold it for him, but decided the answer was probably no.

Chuck worked his way through the crowd on the dance floor. Mya was in the middle, surrounded by pretty boys. "Excuse me, sorry, coming through."

Her dress rode up enough that a shadow of her under cleavage showed.

He put his hand on Mya's shoulder and leaned close to her ear so that he could be heard over the music. "The winner of your birthday spanking contest would really like to meet you."

She kept dancing, jiggling her ass across his crotch as her arms swayed over her head. For a delicious second, his hardening cock was trapped in the cleft between mounds. He swallowed.

"I'm busy," Mya said.

He swore she squeezed her buttocks on purpose while bumping back against him. He wanted to shove her head down and dry hump her right there.

31

"He said he'd leave if he can't talk to you first."

Her shoulders slumped. She spun around. "Isn't this the kind of shit I pay you to handle?" She stomped off the dance floor, muttering obscenities.

Chuck suppressed a smile. He hoped she mouthed off to Daddy Dom. This was going to be good.

"Mya, I'd like you to meet..." Chuck realized he shouldn't introduce the guy as Daddy Dom and give away his plan, but he had no idea what Daddy Dom's real name was. He'd found the guy online. On Daddy Dom's website, a picture of a sorority sister type with her mouth twisted into a red O of rapturous agony convinced Chuck he'd found his man.

Daddy Dom kissed Mya's hand. "I'm Daniel." He didn't speak loudly, but he made his rumbling voice heard over the music.

Mya fluttered her eyelashes. "So you're the lucky winner."

"I'm honored to be here. And thank you for taking time to talk to me. I know you want to enjoy your party, but I like to know a lady before I get intimate with her."

Mya giggled.

"I see the rumors of your charms haven't been exaggerated." Daddy Dom glanced at her backside. "I love a lady with real curves."

"Such a flirt!" Mya tore her gaze from Daddy Dom to scowl at Chuck. "I'm sorry. Are you still here?"

"I, um..."

"Daniel seems like a perfect gentleman. I'm sure I'm safe in his hands."

Chuck pulled on his tie. "Yes, but—" If Mya and Daddy Dom started comparing stories, things could get ugly for him.

"Scoot, Chucky. I got this." Mya turned her back to him.

No matter what happened, Chuck felt he could be proud of the party he'd thrown for Mya. He'd delivered on every demand of hers, no matter how unreasonable. The metallic balloons were Mya Magenta. Not fuchsia, not rose. Magenta. It took three months to find the right shade. The DJ kept the crowd moving on the dance floor. The flowers were wired with LED lights so they looked like something out of the movie *Avatar*. Each guest had a goodie bag with her signature perfume, her latest CD, and a box of Mya chocolates that were supposed to be shaped like apples, but looked more like a peach, or, to be honest, her bottom.

Chuck rocked back on his heels. Now that the cake (a towering replica of her latest album cover) had been cut, his moment had come. He rushed up on stage and motioned for the DJ to turn down the music. It was warm in the club, but not hot enough to explain the beads of sweat on his temples. For the first time since he'd plotted Mya's humiliation, he had a moment of doubt, but it was too late.

"Where's our party girl?"

A bright light shone down on Mya.

He held out his hand. "Come up here. We have a little surprise."

Mya's narrowed eyes counterbalanced her fixed smile as one of her rivals (the same one who called her a bitch in heat) sang Happy Birthday. Afterward, they did that little hug-pat thing as if they were dearest friends.

"And we have another special guest. Mya's been a good girl this year, so she's getting a birthday spanking."

The guests clapped hard. That's what they'd been waiting for all evening.

"First, let me introduce the lucky winner of Mya's birthday spanking contest." Chuck waved Daddy Dom onto the stage. He tugged at his tie again.

Daddy Dom waved to the crowd and sat down on a chair. His long legs spread. Several of the women, and most of the men, in the audience whispered and pointed. After letting them get a good look at him, he moved the chair so that his profile was to the crowd.

"And now, Mya."

She strutted across the stage, stopped at Daddy Dom, and purred hello. Daddy Dom took her hand and helped her settle over his lap. She faced the audience, with her feet pointed to the back of the stage. People laughed as she struggled to keep her tits in her dress.

Chuck moved back. "Help Daniel count," he urged the audience.

This was going to be good. She was already wriggling. With her head hanging off Daddy Dom's thigh, the swell of her bottom rose high. The crowd wouldn't be able to see Daddy Dom's hand smack her ass, but they'd be able to hear it. Even better, they'd see the look on her face.

Chuck kept his hands off his swelling cock. He leaned forward, eyes on her face, waiting to see that look of dismay when the first spank landed. She probably expected a pat. He'd told Daddy Dom to really give it to her.

People lifted their phones, ready to take pictures that would be instantly sent around the world.

Mya's comeuppance, for the record.

Daddy Dom leaned over Mya and whispered something. She nodded. He lifted his hand.

Smack!

"One!" the crowd shouted as flashes went off.

Mya pouted prettily as she reached back to rub her bottom. The crowd laughed. Chuck frowned. That wasn't what he'd told

Daddy Dom to do.

Daddy Dom whispered to her again. She moved her hand.

Smack!

"Two!"

Chuck fumed. Daddy Dom didn't even bare her bottom!

Smack!

"Three!"

By the tenth one, Mya squirmed. Even though he was upset at Daddy Dom, Chuck was mesmerized. The pace picked up. Daddy Dom lifted his hand higher each time. As it landed on Mya, her bottom quivered. Each slap sounded louder. Chuck's cock pressed against his underwear. He slid a hand into his pocket and stroked it. He was stone rigid at the thought of how warm and pink she must be under her dress. It would feel so good to slide his cock over her hot ass.

"Eighteen." The crowd clapped and hooted.

"And one to grow on," Daddy Dom said as he let his hand fly.

Crack!

Mya yelped and jumped to her feet. She rubbed her butt.

Chuck had to keep his cock under control. Everyone was looking at him. "Uh, how about that! Mya! And a special thanks to our contest winner—"

Mya grabbed the microphone out of Chuck's hand. She licked her lips and dragged straggly hair out of her eyes. "Did you enjoy that?"

Chuck looked at the audience. "Uh..."

"Not them. You. Did you enjoy watching me get spanked, Chucky?" She grabbed his hard-on. "Feels like it."

Guests who had turned to go stopped their friends. Everyone turned back to the stage.

Mya's long nails wrapped around the microphone as she paced the stage. "You know, it's my birthday, and I think I

35

should get a little gift too. Don't you think?" she asked the audience.

They yelled agreement.

"Now, most of you know my dear manager, Chucky-wucky. He hasn't been happy with me lately." She pouted. "But instead of being a man and confronting me, he put together this little scheme to spank me. But was he man enough to do it himself? No!"

The crowd booed. Chuck stepped back. A big hand landed on his shoulder. He gulped as he looked up at Daddy Dom.

"Lucky for me, he hired this professional dominant." She gestured to Daddy Dom. "Daddy Dom here doesn't think it's right to spank a girl without her consent, so we had a nice little talk, and he let me in on Chucky's plan. It seems Chucky likes watching a girl get spanked. Daddy Dom says that Chucky spends hours wanking to the pictures on his website. Isn't that right, Chucky?"

Chuck's face went bright red. His pulse pounded against his collar.

"I say turnabout is fair play. What's good for the diva is better for her gutless manager. So here's the deal, Chucky. Either you let me get in a few licks of my own, or I call the parents of your newest little virginal protégé and let them know what you've been up to."

Mya settled into the chair and patted her thighs. "What's it going to be, Chucky?"

He didn't have a chance to say no. Daddy Dom gripped his arm and dragged him over to Mya. Before he knew it, he was over her lap and someone tugged down his pants.

Chuck couldn't look up. He could feel the heat of the party guests as they crowded the stage. He breathed through his mouth. No matter how many times he licked his lips, they felt dry.

"Is this how I do it?" Mya asked Daddy Dom.

"A lady should never hurt her hand," Daddy Dom said. "So use this paddle."

Chuck tried to look over his shoulder, but someone pushed his head down.

"You've been a naughty boy, Chucky," Mya said.

He was going to die of embarrassment, but he was going to jizz his pants before that happened.

"By the way. Where is my Pookie?"

Chuck tried to remember when he'd last had the dog carrier.

"Men's room," someone shouted.

"Ooh, Chucky, did you make my sweet little girl puppy look at your nasty cock while you were pissing? You're going to pay for that, you pervert."

SMACK!

Chuck screamed.

SMACK!

He fought to get away, but Daddy Dom held him down for Mya. He couldn't breathe. White-hot pain exploded across his butt. Each slam of the paddle made it worse. His hard-on jabbed into her thigh.

"Someone's bottom is getting pink. Or should I say, Mya magenta!"

The audience went wild.

Between the heat of their bodies, Mya's scent rolled over him. He imagined her pussy getting slick.

SMACK!

Tears rolled down his face, a face he'd never be able to show in Los Angeles again.

"He's humping my leg like a dog in heat. Nasty boy!"

SMACK!

He flared his nostrils and pulled in her sweet, juicy fragrance. He could feel the heat of her through his pants. His balls tightened. Chuck's head lifted. The crowd was only a couple feet away, and they were all watching him. Their expressions were a mix of gloating, amazement, and lust. For the first time ever, he was the center of attention. The shame was intoxicating. He tried to grab his cock, as if that could stop the inevitable.

SMACK!

He spurted inside his pants, his mouth forming a perfect ring as he shouted, "Oh!"

Chuck was sure his ass was bruised.

Mya and Daddy Dom kissed goodbye at the door of the club like old friends. Daddy Dom gave her the paddle as a gift, and told her to put it to good use. They turned to Chuck and laughed.

The end of the party was like watching crime lords line up to kiss the ring of the new godfather. Even the A-listers paid their respects to Mya before leaving. That wasn't the way people behaved in Hollywood. Chuck didn't get it, but he was too humiliated to do anything but stare down at the huge wet spot on the front of his pants.

The walk from the door to the limo was a nightmare. It was two in the morning, but there were people walking down Sunset. He was sure that they, and every driver passing by, knew he'd been spanked. Worse, they could see how much he'd liked it.

He clutched the Chihuahua's carrier as he gingerly lowered himself into the limo. He'd been told if he lost the dog again, he'd get another spanking.

Mya sprawled against the seat and stared at her iPhone. "Ten thousand hits already."

"Your spanking video?"

"No, idiot. Yours. And wow, look at my iTunes downloads. Cha-ching!" Her long fingernails tapped against the iPhone as she scrolled through her messages. "Holy fucking shit! I've been asked to perform at the AMAs!" Mya leaned forward, her eyes gleaming. "You know, I should fire you, but I think you're good for my career."

Chuck groaned.

"Aw, Chucky-wucky. Don't be like that. Things are going to be great between us now that we have this night behind us. Behind." She snickered. "All this time you've been lusting after my ass, and you didn't even get to touch it after Daddy Dom got it all warmed up. Poor thing. If you're very, very good, one day, I might let you kiss it."

Chuck wondered if he could get a download of his spanking. While she'd been paddling him, it was terrible, but flashes back to it now were turning him on. The weird thing was that he wasn't angry at her. He knew he deserved the humiliation she'd meted out. That's what he got for forgetting his place.

Sitting there, gloating at him, she was magnificent. The rush of love and awe that surged through him made him shake. From the curl of her lip as she watched him, she knew exactly how he felt.

She slipped her hand between her thighs. Leaning forward, she trailed wet fingertips over his lips. His cock swelled again as the aroma rushed over him.

"Don't you dare lick that until I tell you to." She grinned as she settled back to watch him. "I think that I like this new relationship." She spread her legs.

Chuck stared at her slick bush. Just a taste. That's all he

wanted.

She kicked his shin with her spiked boots. "You're supposed to say, 'Me too, Mya.' Although, now that I think about it, it should be, 'Me too, Mya, ma'am.'"

Chuck nodded dumbly. Of course. That was it exactly. She understood him better than he knew himself. He slid onto his knees.

"Thank you, ma'am."

"Oh, Chucky. It'll be all right. Trust me." She patted his head and let him rest it against her thigh as the limo glided down Sunset Boulevard.

Anthropology

By Donna George Storey

I was drawn to Andy from the moment I met him. No doubt part of it was his sky-blue eyes, his mischievous smile, his large hands that looked like they could finger pussy for hours. But I think the real attraction was his profession. Andy was an anthropologist with a specialty in Indonesia. I'd been to London and Paris, but I've always nursed a yearning to explore someplace really exotic, even a little dangerous.

A month after we started dating, Andy asked if I wanted to go to a potluck party given by a fellow grad student in his department. It would be a chance to meet his friends—an interesting bunch, he promised—plus the food was guaranteed to provide a sensual education. Anthropologists always brought fascinating dishes they'd picked up from their world travels.

I said yes right away because I loved being with Andy, and I was tired of my usual English department get-togethers: pub-crawls and ironic Jane Austen teas.

The first five minutes of the party, however, were nothing to write home about. Andy and I handed over his homemade *nasi goreng* to our hostess, Natasha, who cordially informed me I could leave my coat in her bedroom while she got me some wine.

At that moment a new guest sauntered in, a leggy redhead named Penelope, who brought a dish of cilantro-and-cabbage dumplings she'd learned to cook in Shanghai. Perhaps it was because I was the exotic newcomer, but Penelope took an immediate liking to me. We went off to the bedroom together, chatting as if we were old pals.

I was about to toss my coat on the bed with the others, but Penelope's Chinese silk jacket wrinkled easily, and she suggested I hang mine up as well. As she reached for the door of the freestanding closet by the bed, I marveled at her anthropologist's boldness. Opening a stranger's closet without permission was definitely courting danger. Who knew what secrets lurked within?

But even I never expected the vision that greeted us as the door swung open.

"Wow," Penelope breathed.

My jaw dropped.

For Natasha's cabinet was indeed bursting with secrets. Or perhaps the better word would be "implements." Two black leather paddles. A bouquet of riding crops. A square wooden board with a handle that looked like a pizza peel. An enema bag. Fur-lined handcuffs. An assortment of leather straps, masks, and studded collars.

"Oh, you've found my toy closet," our hostess said from the doorway.

I jumped guiltily.

In contrast, Natasha's smile was so innocent we might have stumbled upon her childhood collection of Barbie's.

Then I noticed Andy standing behind her, his leather

jacket draped over his arm. He, too, smiled benignly at the array of sexual playthings. Cultural relativism—surely the best defense in any awkward social situation.

I'd apparently mistaken Penelope's response for my own dismay, because she immediately launched into a nostalgic tale about the sexual predilections of a former boyfriend. He liked to give her enemas and was especially intrigued by how her abdomen got all swollen from the fluid. He'd rub his hands all over her belly, pressing lightly to make her squirm. Afterwards, he always wanted anal sex.

Natasha nodded. "The two often go together."

"I've never been spanked, though," Penelope added.

"Would you like to be?" Natasha asked.

Penelope thought for a moment. "Why not?"

Natasha smiled. "That can be arranged."

My own belly contracted in sympathy, fear mixed with a decidedly sexual tingle of the taboo. I was half-expecting the spanking to occur on the spot, which presented a dilemma. Should I stay and watch or run screaming back to Jane Austen?

Instead, Natasha and Penelope began to discuss their statistics class, while Andy pulled me away to meet a friend. I'd almost convinced myself the whole thing was a dream until half an hour later, when I spied Natasha leading Penelope back into the bedroom.

She closed the door behind them.

Andy and I were seated on a nearby sofa, swapping travel tales with a fellow Southeast Asia hand, but my attention was focused solely on the hushed, but tantalizing, sounds floating through the door. I heard Penelope's voice rising in a question—I caught the words "bed" and "panties"—followed by a long stretch of silence. Had the spanking begun?

I nodded politely as the man droned on, but my eyes instinctively shifted back toward the bedroom. Then I did hear a *thwack*, then another and another. I cocked my ear for a cry or maybe pleading to stop—or go on—but I only heard a soft murmuring, then another few *thwacks*. A few minutes later, the door opened.

Penelope emerged, looking slightly flushed, but no worse for the wear. "It feels like my butt just ate Indian food," she announced.

A few of the guests laughed, but the rest didn't even bat an eye. Apparently anthropologists were not easily shocked.

"Any other takers while I have the paddle out?" Natasha called from the doorway.

Andy arched an eyebrow at me. I gave him a no-fucking-way-in-hell frown.

But later, loose on wine, I got up the nerve to give Natasha what I thought was a provocative goodbye. "Thanks for the sex party."

"Oh, that wasn't a sex party," she purred. "If you're interested in a sex party, come back next Saturday."

Later, in the car, Andy said my eyes popped open so wide he was sure she'd smacked *me* on the ass.

In fact, my bottom was still smarting. English lit types might lead pedestrian lives, but we have good imaginations. "That was certainly an education for me, but you seemed to take it all in stride."

Andy shrugged. "Oh, I knew Natasha worked as a dominatrix on the side. We all do what we can to supplement our measly stipends."

"Have you ever been to one of her sex parties?"

"No. Would you like to go?"

My stomach fluttered with the same confused feeling—fear and desire all tangled together like a couple making love. I'd never been to Thailand or Borneo like Andy. The wildest thing I'd done in my timid little life was give him a blowjob in the shower last week while I rubbed his tush crack with a soapy finger.

"If you really wanted to, I suppose I could go along and watch." I was aiming for cool, but my voice came out small and scared.

Andy glanced over at me. "I'll be honest with you, Julia. One of my old girlfriends was into mild BDSM. She couldn't come unless she was on top, and I was spanking her ass and calling her a naughty slut. I enjoyed it, but that's because I liked to make her happy. My deepest desire now is to do whatever it is that makes *you* happy."

I sighed. "It all just seems so foreign to me."

"I know what you mean. The first few weeks I was teaching English in Jakarta, I was scared to death. But I'm glad I stayed. Traveling to a new place always stretches you, physically, mentally...and sensually."

The twinkle in his eyes definitely made me wonder where he might take me from here.

But Andy didn't mention the spanking party again. I was the one who couldn't get it out of my mind, especially when we made love. Entwined in his arms, I imagined I was back at Natasha's apartment, shamelessly opening the door to watch her spank Penelope's ass. Afterwards, she smeared the now-blushing buttocks with chutney in languid, circular motions—a twist of fancy that was both absurd and strangely arousing. I saw myself taking her place, my body draped over the bed so Andy could snake an enema hose into my anus. I pictured him holding his inflamed tool to my cleansed opening, licking his lips in anticipation. But instead of fucking my virgin hole, he began to spank me across the ass with his boner, now brick red and massive like a knight's long sword. *Whack, whack.* I cried out with each blow and then gradually the sobs turned to pleas. *More, yes, more.*

Even out of bed, I found myself making excuses to brush my buttocks against Andy's crotch or bend over in front of him so he couldn't help but gaze at my ass. I purposely acted sassy so he'd call me a naughty girl. But I just couldn't get up the courage to ask him to spank me.

Then one day I happened to find myself at the local costume shop. The selection of slutty outfits for women was impressive, but I immediately reached for the schoolgirl costume. Maybe actions would speak louder than words?

I handed him the bag with no explanation, a blush creeping over my cheeks.

"Is this a present for me?"

I nodded.

He pulled out the package adorned with a smirking female dressed up in a plaid skirt and white blouse. His eyebrows shot up. "Thank you, but I'm afraid it's not my size."

I tried to laugh, but all that came out was a nervous cackle.

Andy studied my face. It took but a moment for the light to switch on in his eyes, but then again his job was the study of humankind. Grinning, he leaned close and whispered in my ear, "I can tell you're turned on by this, Julia. I can smell your wet pussy. Are you a naughty schoolgirl who gets hot and bothered by the idea of getting a good spanking?"

I inhaled sharply.

"I thought so. We'll need a safe word, so I'll know if I should stop. What should it be?"

"Anthropology." I'm not sure why that word popped into my head, but it seemed right.

He chuckled. "So it is. Now tell me what you did at school that deserves punishment."

He probably expected I'd have to make something up, but actually I did have one naughty secret in my own closet, a transgression from my undergraduate days when I worked at the campus library. Bored out of my mind, I'd sneak off to the quietest corner of C-Floor, shove my hand down my pants, and bring myself to a muffled orgasm while the shelves of books looked on.

I'd never been caught, and I'd never told anyone. Until now.

"I...I hid in a quiet corner of the library, and I...I played with myself," I stuttered, my face flushing scarlet.

Andy clicked his tongue. "This calls for some serious intervention, Julia. Go change into your school uniform in the bedroom. Take off your panties too. Because of course, you weren't wearing any when the librarian caught you masturbating in the stacks and sent you to the principal's office for a good talking-to."

At first I doubted I could even stand up, my pulse was pounding so hard. But the sudden gush of desire drenching my panties brought me to my feet. Naughty as I felt, I didn't want to leave a wet spot on his sofa. I shuffled back to the bedroom, trembling like an addict desperate for her fix. I was still shaking as I tried on the middy blouse. The plunging neckline didn't even cover my bra, so I stripped everything off, wincing as the cheap cotton chafed my stiff, sensitive nipples. The plaid miniskirt fastened around my waist easily, but it was so skimpy it barely covered my ass. The white thigh-highs only seemed to accentuate the problem.

Looking more like a stripper than a schoolgirl, I walked slowly back to the living room. I hoped the next part of the trip would be easier with an experienced traveler at my side.

Andy had moved over to his desk. His eyes glittered as he took in my short skirt and exposed cleavage. "Hello, Julia. Mrs. Beckwith informed me there was an incident in the library this afternoon." Though he was still in jeans and a T-shirt, his voice was all dressed up in a stuffy suit and tie.

I bowed my head. "Yes, sir."

"In fact, I'm told you were found back among the English literature classics with your hand between your legs doing something unspeakable. Is that true?"

My first impulse was to deny it. Which was ridiculous, because I wanted what was coming. The sooner, the better.

"Yes, sir," I whispered.

Andy's lips tightened with disapproval. "Perhaps you can tell me why you were so horny you couldn't wait until you got home to do your dirty business?"

"I...I was thinking about my boyfriend, sir."

"I see. Do you let him touch you between your legs?"

My cheeks felt scorched, and another flood of wetness coated my naked thighs.

"Well?"

"Yes."

"Well, this is a *very* serious matter, Julia. The disciplinary policy of the Academy no longer includes corporal punishment, but I must make an exception in this case. When the flesh errs, the body itself must be reprimanded. Come here and bend over."

I walked to him and placed my palms on the edge of his desk. As I leaned over, I noticed the unmistakable lump in his jeans. I pressed my lips together to hold back a smile.

Andy tucked the hem of my skirt up into the waistband, baring my ass cheeks to the air. "Are you ready to suffer the consequences of your misdeeds, Julia?"

I whimpered assent.

With no further warning, Andy's palm met my buttocks with a satisfying crack. The stinging afterglow spread from my ass through my cunt and belly like a warm wave. He smacked me again. I cried out.

I hadn't invoked the A-word yet, but to my dismay, he stopped.

I waited, my ass burning, wondering if he was going to make me beg for more.

He cleared his throat. "How thoughtless of me to neglect the most important part. According to school policy, in order to truly learn her lesson, the student must be engaged in the offensive behavior while she is being punished. Therefore, I want you to diddle your clit while I continue to discipline you, Julia. Do you understand?"

"Yes, sir." My voice cracked, but I obediently dipped my hand between my legs. My clit was so hard and big I could swear it was dangling down between my legs like a small, satiny-pink cock. Andy waited until I got a good strumming going before he spanked me again. I gasped. The dueling sensations, shooting simultaneously from my clit and ass, made me forget everything else in the whole wide world.

Andy slapped me harder, once, twice, three times. He began to aim the blows directly on my asshole. I wiggled my ass like a puppy and begged, "Please, no," but I was nowhere near invoking the name of his exalted profession. In fact, I was in heaven.

"What are you thinking of now, Julia?"

"My boyfriend fucking my wet, swollen cunt," I choked out, my finger jiggling faster between my slick folds.

"Do you want to get fucked right now?"

"Yes, sir, but..." I faltered, my throat tight with shame.

"But what?"

"Could you fuck my asshole instead?"

Andy clicked his tongue again. "You do have a dirty mind for such a prissy-looking miss. Did your boyfriend ever take you back there?"

"No, sir, never."

"Too bad. If you were a naughty slut who got her ass fucked every day, I'd do it right now. But the first time requires special preparation. If you're a very good student this time, for our next session I'll bring an enema kit and some lube so I can punish your spanked, pink asshole properly."

I moaned again, but it wasn't from disappointment. His filthy words and the "confessions" he'd forced from my lips were sweet enough chastisement for now.

"Then fuck my wet pussy, sir. Please." I opened my legs wider and tilted my ass up.

Laughing softly, Andy probed my vagina with the head of his cock, then buried himself in all the way to the root. He ploughed me slowly, in and out, all the while maintaining a steady rain of blows on my buttocks. In this position, I felt every inch of him, his girth stretching my hole tight, the knob of his dick tickling my cervix. I was so sopping wet his cock made sloppy, slurping sounds with each thrust.

"Tell me what a bad girl you are, Julia. Tell me how much you need to be punished."

"I'm bad. I play with myself in public. I bring dishonor to the Academy."

"That's right. You are a bad, bad girl. And now you must learn your lesson. Come on my cock, Julia. Milk your principal's prick with your horny, schoolgirl twat," Andy panted.

Then he reached around and pinched my nipples through the flimsy blouse. It was the last straw. My cunt spasmed around him, and I screamed, "Fuck me, fuck me, oh, yes, anthropology!" before I realized my mistake, but he kept slapping my ass anyway, the blows weakening as he grunted and shot his spunk into me.

For the longest time we stayed that way, floating together, cock in cunt, sweat and laughter, sweetness and spice all mixed together like a foreign elixir.

Later, when we'd wiped up and were sitting hand-in-hand on the sofa, I told Andy I thought I might be able to handle going to one of Natasha's sex parties after all.

"Really?" Eyes twinkling, he pulled me down over his lap and smoothed his big, warm hand over my bare buttocks. "I'm sure the other guests would agree your ass looks pretty in pink. But I have to warn you; fieldwork involves more than just showing up and watching. A serious anthropologist has to spend a lot of time preparing and practicing."

"I'll try to be a good student," I promised, pressing my mons against his thigh. Soon Andy and I would be off on another journey to some new and distant land that was really not so far away at all.

I had a feeling I was going to like it there.

Anything but Ordinary

By A.D.R. Forte

"What's the fascination?" he asked.

"Erogenous tissue and endorphins," she said. "The vibration from the blow travels through the flesh to the clit and other sensitive parts. And the pain causes the body to produce..."

"Endorphins. Emotional release. Yeah, I get what's in it for the spankee. What's the fascination for the spanker?"

"Control fantasy. Control complex. Giving fantasy..."

"You sound like a fucked-up textbook."

"Thanks, but you asked."

She looked up, over the top of her book, a biography of Patton.

"I think my question was more about the aesthetics."

She shrugged. "I don't know about the aesthetics. I've just read about this stuff."

He stood and went to the lunchroom window. The jagged ridge of the mountains outside was glazed in shadow, black spikes against the orange-red dirt below.

I'm a real estate agent, he thought. *I sell glorified dirt.*

He wanted to be more like the guy in the expensive suit today that he'd shown four different million-dollar ranch properties to. The suit had been concerned there wasn't a good room to use as a dungeon. A dungeon?

Ordinary guys didn't dabble in dungeons unless they were total heels. He didn't want to be a heel or a freak.

"I wonder why nobody's invented a spanking robot?" she mused from behind him.

"Too impersonal."

She laughed. He heard a rustle of movement and she was at his shoulder, Patton in hand, looking out at the desert afternoon.

"Thought you didn't know anything about 'weird, freakish shit,' Steve."

"I don't." He smiled at her. "But I've worked with you long enough."

She laughed again.

"You wish." She tucked the book under one arm, picked up her coffee, and turned to head back to the office floor.

"See ya later," she flung back over one shoulder.

When she was gone he looked at the doorway for a long while. Too young, too brilliant, too fascinating for him. He thought about her bright pink fingernails, her spiky hair, her pointy-rimmed glasses, the sandals she wore even in winter— such winter as they had out here. If he could have dared to consider the aesthetics of spankings, she would have been the woman he'd want to learn from.

"Yeah. I wish," he said softly and shook his head. At his hip, his phone buzzed impatiently and he took it from the holder with a sigh.

Too eccentric to notice an ordinary guy like him.

Saturday evening. Across the room he saw his phone blink,

ringing on silent, but he was on the treadmill. And if it was a client, he didn't want to answer, not tonight. Tonight he wanted to shut out the reality of over-enthusiasm that was his stock in trade.

He wondered what happened on the inside when the outside didn't match. When the gilded exterior got too heavy, did it implode on the emptiness beneath?

Morbid. Morbid and self-absorbed.

He pressed the up arrow on the control panel and the speed of the track increased beneath his feet. If he had time to throw himself a pity party, he obviously wasn't running fast enough.

No clients tonight. No girlfriends either, not even lawyer girl with the long blonde hair. Tonight he wasn't selling his smile for either money or sex.

He pulled off his sweat-drenched T-shirt on the way across the room. T-shirt balled up in one hand, he checked his messages. And checked the solitary voicemail again, and again, not believing what he'd heard.

"I've emailed you the directions to my apartment and instructions. If you can make it, I'll expect you at eight. Be right on time."

She hadn't identified herself, but he could close his eyes and conjure up the faint, creamy scent of her vanilla perfume, the startling blue-grey of her eyes. He looked at the time, panicked, but it was only a quarter past six. He'd be there. On time.

He found her door tucked behind a giant potted palm. *A doorway to a paradise of earthly delights,* he thought cynically. But when he opened the door and walked in as the email had told him to, he stopped. Sparse in its lack of furniture, except for the antique bookshelves and armchairs beside them, the tiny table tucked into a corner with a vase of wildflowers, it was her. Nothing like he'd been expecting: no incense, no neon, no bright colors and new age paraphernalia. He felt ashamed he'd even thought her capable of such kitsch.

Slowly, still looking around, he bent to take off his sneakers and socks as instructed. He left them at the door and stepped onto the spotless carpet, one foot in front of the other until he reached the middle of the room where he turned to face the far wall that should have been a breakfast nook, but was crammed instead with shelves of books. He waited, hands loose at his sides. Empty. No thoughts, no feeling. Nothing.

Until he saw her.

Her hair was soft around her face, spikes gone. She looked softer, vulnerable. He'd never seen her like this before.

She put a finger to her lips, reminding him of his instructions, and the babble of words he'd have used to try to fill empty space died before they got face time.

Standing behind him, she reached around his chest to unbutton his shirt. She lifted it off, and his undershirt. He let her, automatically pulling his arms free because she was shorter than him, not thinking about the fact of *her* taking off his clothes. Even though somewhere, his mind, his body couldn't ignore it.

Hands slid down his chest, rings pulling at hair, fingernails pinching his nipples. She'd skipped the bright nail polish that had graced them up until Friday. He thought her bare fingers looked sexier than ever sliding across his skin. Massaging, playing, touching *him*.

With her hands still resting on his stomach, he felt her rise up on tiptoe, felt her clothing brushing his back, the heat of her body underneath them. A promise of soft female flesh. Then he shivered.

Her tongue circled the knob of bone at the top of his spine between his shoulder blades; he felt her lips on his skin. Wet, slow, her tongue probed each segment of spine, working downward, a silver trail of her saliva marking him. He felt dirty, used, and his dick was jutting forward in eager anticipation, hurting in the confines of his pants. But as he'd been told, he stayed still.

Though that was damn hard when she was licking, or rather tongue-fucking his backbone all the way to the waist of his pants, where she could go no further. Then, kneeling behind him, she unbuckled his belt. She unbuttoned his fly. She pulled the pants to his ankles. He lifted one foot, knowing what he needed to do, when to move to help her. One foot and then the other.

Of course, she would take his boxers off next. He was ready for it. He wasn't ready for the sound of scissors chewing their way through cloth at his thigh. Over his ass-cheek, through the elastic waistband. He didn't move.

So he'd go home commando. There was no thought of resisting or protesting.

The material fell away. He heard her sigh.

"Your ass is amazing." She reached out to touch the admirable part. Part of him, he reminded himself, as she pinched and caressed. "It's so firm and tight. And not pasty or pale." She paused. "Steve. Do you tan in the nude?"

And when he wondered if he was even capable of speech, she added: "You can answer."

He cleared his throat. "I don't tan. Grandmother on one side is Mexican. Whole family's Sicilian on the other."

She laughed. "And a little German mixed in. So you're all natural." One finger stroked the crack between his cheeks. "No wonder you're so beautiful."

Beautiful. He hadn't thought of himself in those terms.

Something clinked behind him. She rubbed oil or lotion, something liquid, into his skin. Starting with his ass. She massaged his thighs and calves and stomach with it. He looked down at the glisten of his hair and skin as she ran her hands up his torso to his neck. He closed his eyes as she massaged the muscles between his shoulders, thumbs rubbing lotion and heat into him. Easing tension away that he didn't know was there.

Was this intimacy? This lack of fear when she explored his body, fingers probing between his legs, rubbing the space behind his balls, teasing the sensitive opening to his ass—places he didn't let women touch. Didn't let anyone touch.

She cupped the head of his straining dick as she rubbed it with oil, laughing behind him as it spilled a little white cream into her palm. Treacherous appendage. She rubbed her fingers together, rubbed his precum into her skin. He heard her inhale and knew she held her hand to her nose, breathing him in. His stomach tied itself in knots.

"Move your legs. That's it."

He felt the touch of air on oiled skin between his legs as he widened his stance. She was sitting or kneeling behind him again. He didn't dare turn around to look.

"I love looking at you from here," she said, answering his unasked question. "Down here I can see the swell of your balls between your legs. I can look at the curves of your ass, the length of your back. You look..." she searched for words. "You look male. Posed. You make me think of sex and heat and mating."

He took a deep breath and nodded.

She took the belt from his pants. From the corner of his eye, he saw her pull it free. It was so hard to stay still when anticipation bubbled through his veins. He needed to feel something. Make something happen.

But she was moving restlessly behind him, making dissatisfied noises every now and again.

"It has to be perfect," she said. "I have to be in the right place."

He refused to fidget, only letting his fingers press surreptitiously into his thighs now and again. His only concession to impatience.

"I know I can make this so good for you. I'm worried about getting it right." She finally went still. "It's like having a really pretty cake. You're practically drooling to taste it, but you want to put off the moment before you cut it. Make it just right."

Yes. Yes he knew just what she meant, except he didn't have the power to end it. He knew the tingle of wanting slithering through his skin, doubled and tripled because the moment of release wasn't his to choose.

"Are you ready?" she said. He nodded. He closed his eyes.

He felt the force of the blow, but it didn't hurt. He thought that before he felt the after-sting, but it was nothing. She was using backhand blows he guessed, because she was right behind him. Three or four blows on the same cheek until it tingled warm all over. A few more.

Was he aroused by physical sensation or just the idea? The sound of leather—his own belt—on his naked flesh.

But she'd moved, shifted a little to his right and now he felt the warm stinging blows on his right ass-cheek. Heat filled his ass, and his thighs as a few blows landed there. Not by chance. He knew better than to think she was leaving anything to chance.

The sound of breathing and blows filled the room until she stopped.

"Oh. Your skin is red all over. It's flushed. I..." Her voice was light, as full of wonder as a little girl's. He felt her fingers, feathers brushing his tingling skin.

"But it looks as if it's not quite right. It doesn't fit with the rest of you."

Probably because I'm just the real estate guy, he thought. *I don't get this; I can't make it any fun.* But she hadn't sounded surprised.

"But then, it's only the first coat layered on," she said, and he heard the glint of eagerness in her voice.

She put one hand on his hip and he felt her breath hot on his lower back. She was right behind him, close enough that he felt her body heat again. He was enjoying this, her proximity, what he'd decided was surely intimacy...

He gasped. Flinched. The force of the belt on his right cheek seared through skin and flesh. That hurt. Her hand was firm on his hip, holding him steady as he shuddered and told himself he could bear it. But it was the relentlessness, blow after blow, not ending, not easing, that was killing him. His ass tensed even though he knew that made the pain worse. Try as he would, his muscles wouldn't relax, his mind wouldn't stop yelling at him to move, move away. But there was pride at stake.

When she stopped, he almost sobbed. Almost. Before he caught himself.

"You're trembling," she said, out of breath and pleased. "And your skin is so red now; the blows fall white on it. It's so amazing, in such a twisted way."

He wanted to say, *I know. This hurts like hell.* He only nodded. He'd asked for this, he'd wanted to know, and she was doing it for him, for his sake. He wanted to kiss her.

She took a deep breath, stretching, flexing her arm. But her other hand, oh god, she'd reached around to stroke his dick again. Not that he needed that. How it had remained hard he didn't know. He should've gone soft by now, lost it to discomfort, but he was harder than ever. Erogenous tissue. There was no accounting for it.

He moaned, because the instructions had only ordered him not to talk after all, and moved into her hand. Fucking it. She rubbed him faster, fingers on his oiled flesh noisy. His hips bucked, but he knew he wouldn't come. Not yet, not without more. And well before that, she stopped.

She shifted again behind him. Considering and studying, he thought. Finding the right position to begin again. And when she did, he all but screamed for her to stop.

He realized now that she'd been holding back, measuring her strokes. Now she gave her full strength to each blow, and he ground his teeth as she drove the breath from him with each hit, wondering how she could inflict such pain on him. Fists clenched at his side, he rocked on his feet with each blow and he heard her warning him not to run away. Telling him to breathe.

Breathe? Why breathe? Oh. Because his head was spinning and he was about to pass out.

He didn't realize she'd slowed down. Didn't know her hand was on his hip again, steadying him, until he found his own balance again. Pain filled him up. Sweat trickled down his body, crawled down his forehead to burn his eyes. His mouth hurt because he was grimacing, his jaw clenched against the pain.

Inside and outside, he was solid. Lust-filled pain. Not empty.

"You're welted," she said, softly. Like a lover telling secrets. "The skin is purple here and there."

Her fingers showed him *here* and *there*, probing at the

wounds so that unintelligible grunts escaped the trap of his teeth and he shook his head from side to side. Begging her silently to stop.

"I've done this to you," she said. "And it makes me wet. My heart is racing; my clit is throbbing. I want to comfort you. And...and I love seeing you like this."

There wasn't any regret in the words.

Eyes closed, he shivered against the pain as she wrapped her arms around his waist and laid her cheek on his battered flesh. He tried to picture them. He standing, bruised and beaten into the humiliation of admitting pain. She kneeling, embracing him with the appearance of submission.

Anything but ordinary.

She unclasped her arms after an age, after his shivering subsided and the sweat cooled and the pain turned into a thick, omnipresent ache shot through now and then by a stab that made him hiss and wince. She sat back on the floor, cross-legged, and handed him his clothes, piece by piece. Watched him dress like a mother coyote overseeing her cubs' first stumbling attempts at independence.

"Should I drive you home?" she asked as he leaned against the wall, eyes closed in agony, to put his shoes on. He shook his head as he took the glass of water she insisted he drink.

"No. I'll be fine."

He looked up, found blue-grey concern searching his face.

"Really. I will."

"Steve..." she breathed.

"You were magnificent."

He put the glass down on the floor because there was nowhere else. He took her face between his hands and kissed her deep, stealing her breath. She slid her arms under his, around his back, and his tormented, unfulfilled body felt every inch of her soft curves. Breasts, stomach, hips, pussy. Beauty.

"Drive safe. Call me when you get home."

"Okay," he promised. It was all he could manage.

She closed the door behind him, and he limped back to his car. First thing when he got home would be a warm shower like she'd told him. While he jacked off. And an ice pack after that.

The stars were thick in the desert night. Same stars as yesterday, same stars that would be there tomorrow. He'd still be selling dirt and dating hot, bitchy women who liked his money far more than they liked him, and his amazing ass hurt so badly he could barely walk.

But he couldn't stop grinning.

Damn, this stuff was good.

The Royal Montague

By Cervo

The strange thing is that what I remember most is the earring. You'd think it would be the pain or the embarrassment. There I was, over his knee, with him sitting on what had been my old sofa. He had been spanking my bare butt really hard for almost ten minutes when I happened to glance under the couch, between swats, and saw my earring right there in the dust bunnies.

I was yelping and wiggling so much that I had no chance to ask him to let me fish out my earring. It was a diamond post. It was a very, very small diamond, but it was part of a pair I had gotten for graduation, and naturally, I wanted it back. But how could I ask for my earring in the middle of getting spanked? I couldn't catch my breath much less talk because he was spanking me so hard. He wasn't paying the least attention to my yelping, pleading, and crying so why would he stop to listen to some whining about an earring?

How did I lose the earring? I don't know. More importantly, why was I in his apartment, over his knee, getting a really hard spanking? I'll get to that.

I love Montague Street. It's in Brooklyn Heights. I loved it

63

even more back when I moved into my first apartment over a more-or-less, sort of French restaurant. Back then, the building was a dump—but a really nice dump—with big radiators that clanked and banged and worked most of the time. My room in our apartment had even bigger windows that hardly kept out the cold the rest of the time. As an assistant copy editor for a publisher in Manhattan, and with two other roommates, I could almost, just barely, afford it.

We could only see a little slice of the East River from our bay window, but the street was full of interesting, crazy people. There were musicians and painters and some very old people who had been there, they said, "before the whole street went to Hell." It didn't look like Hell to me, but who was I to judge? I only knew about Minneapolis in those days. One winter in Minneapolis will let you know what Hell is really like.

But back to my spanking. I hadn't been spanked since I was twelve when I threw my math book, *Fun with Numbers*, into a ditch full of scum. Since then, there have been lots of spankings. I have a real thing for getting spanked. I just do. It's a little embarrassing, but it's true. I mean you can't just blurt it out at parties and on dates, but it's a big part of me. I like having my bare butt under a guy's nose while he spanks me silly. So I might as well get spanked if I want to...But I didn't know that back then. Let me get back to how I learned.

I moved.

One of my roommates got pregnant and the other one went to Poland. I was left with the rent, which I couldn't afford on my own. Luckily, I was able to move in next door with two other girls. My new room had the bay window in the front just like my old room had. I had to share the bathroom and kitchen, but I had my own entrance because the apartment had two doors from the hallway. So I could pretend I had my own apartment.

A guy took over my old place. His name was Winston Depue, which sounded pretty cool to me. He was very tall and slender, and you could tell he was always thinking about something. He had a lot of reddish-brown hair, a long, angular face, and he had these big hands. The best part of him was, and still is, his hands. They had long, gracefully shaped fingers and were not too boney or too soft. They were so handsome and just so sexy. He wore jeans and tweed coats and he smelled like some kind of herb, sort of like dried flowers—but very masculine flowers—or maybe hay.

Anyway, I discovered that Winston Depue spanked a lot of girls. They came and went, came and went, some of them rubbing their bottoms on the way out. He seemed to be spanking someone almost every day and most nights. I thought maybe he was some kind of professional spanker at first, but most girls don't have to hire some guy to get spanked if they want to. I find you can usually talk guys into spanking you pretty easily.

Anyway, I could hear him spanking them even with the drapes closed. His sofa was backed up under the bay windows. If he had just left the curtains open a little, I would have gotten a great view of the fun. The sound of it was really hypnotic. Spank, spank, spank, spank, spank, spank, over and over again with squeals and crying underneath. Mmm hmm.

One lovely spring night I was sitting by my window enjoying the sea breeze and some cheap wine. The garbage had been hauled away that afternoon and there had been a long rain, so the dog smell was not really noticeable. Most of all, there was the usual spanking sound coming right through my bay window. It was this very steady, sharp smacking.

I was a little drunk from the wine, just pleasantly fuzzy, and the sounds fascinated me. I kept hearing that sharp, hard smacking and lots of crying and whimpering. The windows were so close I could have crawled out my window and into his apartment. I guess he didn't notice that he had left the side window open, because his big velvet drapes were closed. Well, not quite closed. I could see light and movement.

So I poured another glass of wine. I tried to politely forget the sounds by reading *The Times* Book Review, but that was too creepy, so I decided to steal some of my roommate's chocolate chip cookies from the kitchen, where you couldn't hear the spanking. Instead I went back to the window, taking the half-gallon of wine with me.

I leaned out the window and slipped my fingers between my neighbor's drapes. They seemed to spread open all by themselves, and I could see right down onto the seat of the sofa that was right under the bay window.

There was this girl getting a wicked spanking. Her skirt was flipped up and her panties were down around her ankles. She was across my neighbor's lap with her face pointed away from me. Her pussy was practically in my face. She was too busy getting spanked to worry about that. Her bottom was amazing. It was huge! I wondered if that was because it was swollen from all that spanking. The rest of her was not that big, but her butt looked immense. It had a nice shape, but it was so red. I mean really, like black cherry red.

By now the whole block could hear the spanking, and I could clearly see his hand landing over and over on her bottom. People stopped eating supper to look out their windows to find where the sound came from. Pedestrians were stopping to look up at his window. A guy in a leather jacket started taking bets. One old guy following his wife looked up when he heard the sound. Then his eyes wandered down to his wife's behind, and he smiled as though he was remembering something nice.

People stopped, smiled, and chatted. They nudged each other with their elbows and chortled. I guess it was so loud that the spanking was infectious. The crowd was getting sort of giddy, like the spanking was some sort of event to celebrate spring. It was for me, so I poured myself another big slug of wine just as I noticed a patrol car slowly inching up Montague, through traffic, toward our block.

I couldn't stop myself. I leaned across from my window and pulled aside the drapes.

I yelled, "Hey, Mister, you think you oughta keep spanking that girl? Her butt looks really swollen or was it always that fat?" It broke the spell. People quickly moved down the block after that. Needless to say, Mr. Depue turned his head toward me with his hand raised for the next spank and gave me a totally dead, fisheye-stare. He was really mad in a sort of reserved English kind of way, but he was not nearly as mad as the girl with the fat, red bottom getting spanked. I guess the "fat" remark was what did it.

I guess I realized how mean it sounded then, and anyway, she turned out to be really cute. It was just that he had a pillow over his lap and it really pushed her butt way up in the air, so it looked huge from the angle at which I was "introduced" to it.

She got up, yanked up her panties, stuck her arm out the window, gave me the finger, and stormed out of the place. I felt just awful, especially since she didn't have a fat bottom. I wanted to apologize to the girl for yelling about her butt, and naturally I wanted to say I was sorry to Mr. Depue. The truth was I was jealous. I mean if you wanted to get a good spanking, it might as well be from some tall, mysterious, lanky English guy with big handsome hands, right? Jealousy is one of my weaknesses.

Mr. Depue slammed down his window, and then sort of

glared at me with his arms folded. I suppose he was really mad in a cool, sophisticated, tall, masterful sort of way. So I knew I had to take myself next door like a good girl, ring his bell, and say my piece looking right up into his big eyes. I finished half a glass of wine and did just that. Well, right after I adjusted my hair and eye makeup, brushed my teeth, put on a little scent, changed to heels—and then higher heels—stole a shot of my roommate's vodka from the freezer, chewed a Tums, and made sure my white cotton blouse was still starched, crisp, and neat over my pale peach bra. I unbuttoned my shirt just enough. I also checked to see that the pleats in my skirt were nicely pressed and that the skirt was as short as I had thought. It was surprisingly shorter than I remembered, but I wore it anyway. Then I went over to introduce myself and apologize.

The front door of the building was open, so I tiptoed up to the second floor. That's hard to do in heels on marble steps, I can tell you. I could see they had cleaned up the hallway since I left. My old oak front door had been stripped, varnished, and waxed making it look very grown-up. On the door, just above my eye level, was a brass plaque that read, "W. Ste. John Depue, PhD, Therapist."

Now that plaque was very impressive for a girl from Minnesota, and all I could think about was how tall you would have to be to put that plaque way up there on the door. My heart, which was already beating really hard, tried to jump out of my cleavage. Fortunately there's enough of it to prevent that. A therapist? A doctor? A *cute* doctor?! A cute *English* doctor who spanks girls? I didn't want to seem like a ditz, so I slowly got myself under control. After a few minutes of just standing there breathing, I knocked on the door.

Nothing happened. I waited a minute or two because I didn't see how he could have gone out so quickly, and then I used my ring to knock on the door again. Then I got nervous and started banging my ring against the door about twelve times in a row.

The door flew open and there was Mr. Depue, only now, he looked seven feet tall, and a big lock of soft brown hair was nearly covering his left eye. The rest fell in lovely, but very masculine, tresses around his face. He was breathing hard too, and I could tell I had distracted him from doing something really intense.

"I'm sorry," I said.

"So am I," he said and then, "will that be all?"

"I live next door," I said.

"Astounding. Anything else I should know?" He wasn't sneering though. He was just being colorful and witty. Cute. He was every bit as cute, profoundly and truly cute, as I had ever imagined a guy could be.

"I came to apologize," I said.

"Is this some sort of sorority thing? A prank? Are you some frat boy's girlfriend? Did some perverse boy put you up to this charade? Some clod from a fraternity where they stand in a row holding each other's penises and yelling, 'Heave!' until everyone vomits at the same time?"

"No..."

"...Because that sort of thing is really too ritualized for me. In England we just get drunk and throw up in the road. It's more natural. We have public schools and remnants of the Church of England if we want class-driven perversity, deviant rituals, that sort of thing. Will that be all? Or does this also involve magazine subscriptions?" He started to close the door.

Well, maybe not that cute right then. He was being pretty snotty, but he certainly was still very pretty, so I gently held the door and said, "I interrupted you...before...just now...and I am really very sorry for it."

"You did, eh?"

"Yes, I noticed through an opening in the curtains that you were spanking someone...a girl."

"Ah yes, the opening that I saw you open with your charming little paw. That one I think in fact, no?"

"Um, yes, I opened the opening to help you...to warn you."

"Very decent of you. Super. Do go on."

"Your window was open and everyone could hear you...uh...spanking away...so I thought you'd like to know the whole block heard it, especially me. I shouldn't have, but I opened the curtains a little so I could see. I wanted to help you, because I saw the cops."

"The cops? I believe I, or you, should be saying 'jiggers' at this point, shouldn't we?"

"Jiggers?"

"As in, 'Jiggers, the cops!' I have no idea what it means, but I thought Americans said that at the approach of the constabulary."

I had a feeling all that was a snotty trap, so I just went on with, "But I guess I embarrassed the girl. The girl you were spanking."

"By yelling about the size of her bottom? Do you really think so? Why should bellowing about her rump embarrass her, do you think?"

I let my eyes drift down to my feet. "It sounded mean, but I didn't mean it to be mean. I just wanted you to know about the cops. I went about it all wrong, I know. I was very foolish and I am...I'm very sorry. So please forgive me if you can, and I won't bother you ever again."

"Well, let's not make rash promises or go to wild extremes. Perhaps you had better come in."

"You think so?" I said.

"Yes, immediately. Do come along." He opened his arms wide to usher me inside as he pushed back the door.

I didn't say a thing for once, not a single dumb thing. I just followed him inside. I slowly stepped over the threshold, went to the center of the room, and looked around. I suppose I should have been scared, but I wasn't. He was so cute, and he had these really broad shoulders. And he had a really nice little, round butt. It moved very nicely when he walked back to his desk. I could smell his aftershave or cologne or something faintly in the room. It was like warm leather or maybe just very cute guy.

My old living room was now a calm office with heavy oak furniture and low light. The only thing left from when I had been in residence was the ancient overstuffed sofa. It had been there when I moved in and it was so heavy it was nearly impossible to move. I guess he liked it as much as I, which made me like him for liking it.

He sat down at the desk and said, "I suppose you are curious about all the spanking, is that it?"

"Yes, the...um...spankings. You seem to give a lot of them right over there on my old couch. To all sorts of girls."

"That's easily explained. I am a certified Percussion Therapist."

"You are?"

"Yes, it's an offshoot of Transactional Analysis. Goes right to basics. Leaves out the blather, and gets right down to the problem at hand."

"With a lot of spankings?"

"Yes, very liberating, a good spanking, if properly given."

"How do you—?"

"Know? I have no idea. I'm not a theorist. I'm a practitioner. I picked it up in California—very popular in San Francisco.

Two-week course, certified, signed, and ready to practice. Came back here to set up shop to help nervous young ladies overcome a wide range of phobias and set goals."

"You learned all this—about spanking—in two weeks?"

"Well, I am English you know, and I had a PhD in English literature, so I am quite familiar with different sorts of pain...It came to me quite naturally."

"Oh," I said in as small a voice as I could manage. My mouth was very dry now, and I felt odd standing there in front of him with him seated at the desk, and I with my apology still unaccepted.

"In fairness, I have to concede that you did interrupt my session. It will take some time to rebuild the necessary bridge to a proper spanking relationship. I accept your apology I suppose, but I wonder, do you think you would feel better if I spanked you? Happy to oblige, you know. We can start immediately."

"Now?"

"No time like the present to face the music. Hmmm...mixed metaphor there, and you don't exactly face it, do you? Still, I think you see my point. We could have a drink afterwards if you like."

"Well I do feel very ashamed so I suppose—" I said, and I let my eyes come up just enough to meet his. In the light from the desk lamp I could see that they were very big eyes, and very, very pale blue.

"Well then, as we used to say at school: It can't be helped. It must be done. So down with your knickers, and out with your bum. Step over to the couch, please. You needn't bother to sit down. I'll be right with you."

He pulled open a drawer on his right and took out a leather paddle that was even bigger than his hand, "Don't worry about that. That's for the punishment phase. We won't get there for a bit. Got to warm you up thoroughly first. By the way, what is your name?"

"My name?"

"Yes, your name. What is it?"

I was not sure if I should tell him my real name so I said, "Daisy Buchanan?"

He looked at me while he squinted one eye almost shut and turned his head sideways. I giggled. It was just nerves, but I giggled.

"Denise Filbert. I'm from Minnesota."

"Well then, Denise," he said as he crossed the room and paused next to the couch. He took hold of my chin and lifted my eyes to his. "I am going to give you a spanking for your own good. Would you prefer English or American spanking?"

"What's the difference?"

"American consists of a few swats and an endless amount of talk. The English approach involves a very long and moderately hard spanking with a cuddle after. Very little palaver. It's my own personal technique. I call it the Royal Montague. Catchy, eh?"

"English, I think, but not too long," I said, thinking I was plain crazy to say it.

"We'll see. I'm just going to slip off my jacket, roll up my sleeve, and we'll get things underway, shall we?"

Then he sat down and gently took my hand. He very, very patiently eased me forward until I was right in front of him and then he slipped his hands inside my skirt and found the waistband of my panties. He tugged them down very slowly until they dropped below my hips and landed around my ankles.

"Lift up," he said.

I raised each foot while I rested my hand on his shoulder. He slipped off my heels and gathered my panties to inspect them. They had "Tues" embroidered on the hip. It was actually Wednesday, but I hadn't done my laundry. I almost confessed that to him, but before I could, he eased me, ever so gently, over his knee so I was lying across his lap on what had been my old couch. He rested his hand on my bottom for a little while. I sighed because it really felt very nice. After a few minutes, he carefully raised my skirt and pinned it to the back of my shirt.

He pressed one hand down on the small of my back and then the other one lost contact until it returned with a loud "Smack!" that covered both of my cheeks. He really did have very big hands. During the pause that followed, a long painful wave of sting surged all the way through me from my bottom to the top of my head and out to my fingers and toes.

I was too surprised to breathe and just said, "Oooooooooooo-oooooooooooooooooo."

He gave me eleven more swats like that with a pause between them, until I was yelping after each one. My butt was as hot as a griddle and throbbing already.

After that, he really got down to giving me a spanking. It seemed to go on for two or three days, but it was really only about ten minutes. It seems very short now, but it was all I could take then. I was crying, begging, kicking, and promising to be good forever during the whole thing. I tried to wiggle and twist away from his hand, but he was so strong that it was completely hopeless.

"Now I think you're ready to be punished," he said, and I almost fainted. He rested his hand on my naked rear and leaned forward to pick up the paddle from the floor. I could easily feel that he was enjoying himself, but I squealed at the sight of the paddle. No matter, he applied it thirty times at an even pace until I was limp over his knee.

"Now, don't you feel better?" he asked.

I said, "Owwwwwwww," and went on crying. He gave me my cuddle, which by then I really thought I deserved. Later, he was very sweet and got down on his knees to fish my earring out from under his sofa for me. That gave me a whole new and very nice view of him.

That night we did go for that drink at the classy bar in Armando's Restaurant across the street. He sat on a barstool while I stood next to him. We were about the same height that way, so it wasn't so bad. Somewhere along the line, he leaned over and kissed me behind the ear. I love to be spanked, but I absolutely adore being kissed in back of my ear...and lots of other places too. He's still kissing me even though, very often, I can't sit down to enjoy it. We go home for that.

Elementary, My Dear Sir

By Anna Black

"In here, ma'am?"

Lady Rowena Fairchild stared at her maid's stout reflection in the brass-framed mirror on her dressing table.

"Yes, Mary. Bring Inspector Maxwell in here."

Mary's near-sighted eyes skeptically regarded her mistress and her plump lips twisted in what was clearly a sign of disapproval.

Rowena brusquely waved for her to go.

Mary did so, closing the bedroom door behind her.

Rowena sighed and looked at herself in the mirror. Her blonde hair hung heavy and loose about her slender shoulders. Blue eyes, a bit shadowed from lack of sleep, took in the pale green dressing gown she wore.

It was late in the morning, but Mary had not yet opened the heavy burgundy drapes. The gas lamps in the bedroom tinted the rose-patterned walls and heavy furniture in a warm, intimate glow.

Rowena was well aware that it was the height of impropriety for a woman, especially a widow, to receive any caller, much less a man, in her bedroom.

But ever since she was arrested and put on trial for the murder of her husband, Lord Edmund Fairchild, propriety was more of a luxury for Rowena than a necessity.

And now the man who had investigated her husband's murder and arrested her for it was paying a social call.

She reached for the sterling silver and cut crystal bottle of perfume on her dressing table. It had been a gift from her barrister in celebration of her acquittal. She opened it and applied some of the heady fragrance to her body. She closed it and placed it back on the table.

A small smile curled about her lips.

Someone knocked at the door.

"Come in, Mary."

The door opened and Mary stepped into the room. Behind her loomed the figure of Inspector William Maxwell.

Rowena looked at him in her mirror.

Inspector Maxwell was not much older than her own twenty-six years. According to her solicitor, the inspector's rise through London's Metropolitan Police Force had been nothing short of meteoric.

Tall, broad-shouldered, with thick dark hair, and chocolate colored eyes—that should have been as warm and invitingly soft as a fur wrap but instead were sharp and cunningly cold—the inspector was a fine specimen of the male species.

It was a shame, therefore, he was as cold and dispassionate as any man she had ever met.

He held his black derby in his hands, his long fingers holding firmly onto the brim. He was, as always, impeccably dressed in a charcoal-colored wool sack suit. Gentleman, he was, but he never failed to make Rowena think of some caged jungle creature.

Controlled, inhibited, constrained, and yet, if the cage were to open or the bars to disappear, what lawless savagery, long repressed, would eagerly leap forward.

Rowena rose from her chair and turned towards him.

His eyes widened when he saw how she was dressed, but no other expression showed on his handsome if rather ascetic features.

"You may leave us, Mary."

Mary glanced doubtfully between her and the inspector.

"Go, Mary. It is Inspector Maxwell after all. I will be perfectly safe with such an esteemed member of London's police force. I can assure you of that. And please take the inspector's hat."

"Yes, ma'am."

Mary took the derby from the inspector, dipped a quick curtsy, and then left the room, closing the door firmly behind her.

Rowena and Inspector Maxwell regarded each other from across the blue and red carpet of her bedroom. All during her trial, she had been mindful of his glacial presence in the courtroom as he waited for all his hard work concerning the investigation of her husband's death to culminate in her conviction.

However, instead of a guilty verdict, the jury had come back with not guilty.

Even now, weeks after the trial, Rowena could still hear the riotous shouts and cries that erupted in the courtroom at the Old Bailey at the jury's pronouncement. And she recalled that at that moment she happened to turn and catch the eye of Inspector Maxwell.

His dark eyes had burned with such thwarted fury it had sent a violent chill down her spine. And, not surprisingly, in light of her proclivities and the savagery of his blistering gaze, a moistening in her quim.

She had not seen nor heard from him since that day.

"Would you like a refreshment, Inspector?"

He glanced disdainfully around her opulent bedroom. "If you had wanted to offer me something to drink, Lady Fairchild, you should have thought to welcome me in a more appropriate setting."

Rowena smiled as she walked over to him. "I wasn't talking about something to drink."

He frowned but, as she expected, chose not to respond to her coquetry. Instead, he stared at her as if she were some puzzle he was compelled to solve or some exotic creature he yearned to dissect in order to ascertain its secrets.

"Very well," she conceded. "If you didn't come to pay a social call, why are you here? Have you come to arrest me for some other crime I didn't commit? Embezzlement? Treason? Pickpocketing, perhaps?"

His mouth tightened, which was a shame because he had such kissable lips. "But you did commit the crime I accused you of, Lady Fairchild. You did kill your husband."

"I was found innocent of that charge, Inspector. As you yourself witnessed."

His handsome face flushed at her reminder. "That is true. But the guilty have sometimes gone free."

"Just as the innocent have been imprisoned. Or executed. Fortunately, in my case, a travesty of justice was averted."

Inspector Maxwell shook his head. "A travesty did occur, Lady Fairchild." He took a step closer to her. "I don't know how you did it but somehow you beguiled that jury into finding you innocent."

"Beguiled them?" Rowena laughed. "I fear you give me far too much credit."

"You were once an actress. Therefore, it is not beyond the

realm of possibility that you somehow used the skills you practiced upon the stage to equal effect in that courtroom."

"Really, Inspector. To suggest that I, a mere woman, was capable of confounding a courtroom full of such learned and erudite men." She smiled and shook her head. "Impossible. No, I was found innocent because I am innocent."

"I refuse to believe that. My investigation was quite thorough."

"Indeed it was. You questioned not only the servants and all of my late husband's friends and relatives, but also my friends, relatives, and just about everyone I have ever known or had contact with in my life."

"It was crucial to my investigation to compile as complete a dossier regarding the accused as I could."

The accused. He meant her.

"In order to establish motive?" Rowena said.

His dark brow lifted. "Among other things."

She ticked off on her fingers. "Motive, means, and opportunity. Is that not the criteria used to establish whether someone has committed murder?"

"Yes, Lady Fairchild. Among other things. You possessed all three."

"As you stated to in court. My motive for murdering my husband was greed. My opportunity to kill him was the fact I was with him the night he died and my means was—"

"Poison. As I stated in my testimony."

"Which, of course, neither you nor anyone else found any evidence of."

"You obviously used some kind of rare or unknown poison."

Rowena laughed. "Rare or unknown? Come now, Inspector. Although you were successful in influencing the grand jury to indict me on such insubstantial evidence, it was brought out in court that my husband died while having intimate relations with me."

He nodded. "That was your testimony."

"Testimony, may I remind you, supported by Edmund's physician. My husband was not only an elderly man, he had a weak heart."

Inspector Maxwell's dark eyes sharpened. "But there was one other infirmity your husband possessed that both you and his doctor neglected to mention in court. Lord Fairchild was impotent and incapable of having sexual intercourse with you. Therefore, he did not die as you stated he did."

Rowena blinked in surprise. "How did you find that out? Dr. Meriwether would not have told you."

"It doesn't matter. What matters is that it's true." Inspector Maxwell took a step towards her. "You killed your husband, Lady Fairchild. Why will you not admit it?"

"Admit what not's true?"

Rowena laughed but there was a raw edge to her laughter as it upset her to think on poor Edmund and how the inspector refused to believe she did not murder him.

"Is that why you came here?" she said. "Hoping I would confess to something I didn't do in order to ease your own guilty conscience?"

Now it was Inspector Maxwell's turn to look surprised. "My guilty conscience? What do you mean?"

"It is not my husband, the manner of his death, or whether or not I was responsible for it that has you so obsessed."

She moved close enough to him that she was certain he could smell her perfume. "It's me."

His nostrils quivered as he scented her. "What? You're mad."

"Mad?" Rowena gazed up into his dark eyes. "I'm not the one who's mad. It's you. Because of your unbridled desire to see me brought to justice. But it's not by the law or through the courts that you want to see me punished."

She lifted her face until her mouth was just inches from his. "You want to do it," she whispered. "Don't you?"

Inspector Maxwell's only response was an arched lifting of his eyebrow.

Rowena knew she was taking a risk being so frank concerning his behavior towards her. But, blast it all, he was sorely testing her patience. She could not help but admire his intelligence, as it was quite formidable, but she had assumed he possessed what she liked to think of as common sense.

"You're clouding the issue, Lady Fairchild."

"Really? And what issue am I clouding?"

"Your guilt, of course," he said flatly. "You hope to distract me from it with your feminine nonsense."

Rowena sighed. "How many more times must we go over that? I was found innocent of the charge you brought against me."

"We will go over it as many times as it takes for you to admit your culpability in the matter."

"I won't do that."

Inspector Maxwell put his hands behind his back, which served to emphasize the broadness of his shoulders and the slimness of his waist. "Your husband was incapable of having sexual intercourse with you. Therefore, he could not have died in the manner you testified to in court."

She sighed. "My husband was embarrassed regarding his inability to achieve an erection. And if you recall, Inspector, I did not say he died while having sexual intercourse with me. I said he died as a result of heart failure due to an act of intimacy between us."

Rowena bit her lip. "Although, I must admit, I do feel some

responsibility for what happened."

Inspector Maxwell moved close enough to her that the wool of his jacket brushed against the silk of her dressing gown. His burnt almond eyes were fiercely alert and he brought to Rowena's mind her late husband's hounds once they had caught the scent of a fox.

"What do you mean?" he asked.

Rowena gazed up at him from under her lashes. "As you well know, my husband was not a healthy man."

"He was seventy years old, Lady Fairchild. Forty-four years your senior and certainly not physically capable of keeping a wife as young as you sexually satisfied. Especially in light of his impotency."

"That is true. But he was far kinder and more generous than any man I have ever met."

A smirk creased the inspector's lips. "Of that I have no doubt. Especially in relation to the generous part."

Rowena ignored his snide reference to his theory that she had not been content with the gifts and luxuries, the manor and title, Lord Fairchild had showered upon his young wife. That she had, in fact, murdered her husband because she had become greedy and wanted it all.

"It's true my husband was not a vigorous man and that he had lost the ability to satisfy me in the ways deemed suitable for a man and woman. But we had found other ways to give each other pleasure."

Inspector Maxwell's lip curled and initially Rowena thought it was with disdain. But upon closer inspection, she saw it was trembling. He stared down at her, his dark-lashed eyes boring into hers.

"My husband and I," she went on, her voice just above a whisper, "engaged in...activities that pleased us both."

"What activities, Lady Fairchild? For you certainly did not bring them up in court."

The inspector's breath moved across Rowena's face and she could smell and nearly taste the scotch mints he must have partaken of earlier.

"No, I did not. I was thinking of my husband's reputation."

She hesitated, needing to draw out this erotic *pas de deux* between her and the inspector for as long as possible.

His face tightened. "Go on. What did Lord Fairchild do to you?"

Rowena lowered her head and released a heavy sigh. "He liked to tie me up and whip me."

She waited two hard beats of her heart then looked up at the inspector.

He only stared down at her, but a muscle along his strong jaw clenched.

"Continue," he said, his voice low and husky.

"Unfortunately, that proved too strenuous for him." She cleared her throat. "So he took to spanking me instead." She licked her lower lip. "Especially when I'd been naughty." She smiled at the recollection.

Inspector Maxwell glared down at her but she noted his breath had quickened.

"He would place me over his knee, pull down my undergarments, and spank me on my bare bottom. He would do it until I had spent myself. The night he died...he overexerted himself and suffered a heart seizure."

Rowena lowered her eyes. "I blame myself. He'd had a difficult day and I should have insisted he rest that night."

"I find it hard to believe that a man like Lord Fairchild would be involved in such perversions."

Rowena raised her eyes. "What? Why? Because you and

others saw him as the embodiment of the perfect gentleman?"

"Exactly."

"Please tell me you're not that naive."

Inspector Maxwell frowned. "I am not. I am well acquainted with what goes on in establishments owned by the likes of Eliza Barrett, for example."

"Acquainted with her, are you?"

Eliza Barrett owned a couple of brothels in London that catered to prominent businessmen, politicians, and even the occasional aristocrat. Her specialty lay in fulfilling her clients' desire for flagellation. She had even designed rooms for them to indulge in sadomasochistic activities.

Revulsion twisted the inspector's handsome face. "The woman is a fiend and should burn in hell."

"I do not disagree with you on that, Inspector."

Eliza Barrett's alleged practice of drugging women and abducting children to force them into prostitution was, in Rowena's eyes, the epitome of evil. As a child growing up poor and parentless on the streets of London, she'd barely escaped being kidnapped and forced to work in such houses herself. Lord Fairchild had once admitted to her that, before they were married, he had paid a visit to one of Eliza's brothels. But even he had not been able to stomach what had gone on there and had not returned.

"No, Lady Fairchild, I am not acquainted in the way you are insinuating with Eliza Barrett or her ilk. But for you to stand there and state that a man of Lord Fairchild's reputation would indulge in such depravity in his own home? I refuse to believe it."

"Depravity? Is that what you think Edmund and I did?"

"Yes."

"And you have never indulged in such *depravity* yourself?"

Inspector Maxwell stared witheringly down at her.

"Or, perhaps," Rowena went on, her voice shaking with both anger and excitement, "you have dreamed of doing such things? To me perhaps?"

He grabbed her arms and shook her. "You brazen hussy! How dare you!"

Rowena's cunt tightened and inwardly she smiled. He was so close to the edge.

"Are you an honest man, Inspector?"

He tightened his hands about her arms, his eyes blazing. "What do you mean?"

"Are you honest?"

"As much as one can be in such a corrupt world."

"Then be honest and admit you have those feelings for me."

He released her arms. "You are obsessed with yourself, Lady Fairchild, as I have discovered many in your former vocation to be."

Rowena nodded. "Theater people can be quite narcissistic, but we are also students of human nature. The fact that you chose this time of the day to call on me suggests you hoped to find me thus attired. And I suspect you also knew I would invite you up to my bedroom."

He shook his head. "I am here because I am an officer of the law who was forced to bear witness to a travesty of justice. You murdered your husband, Lady Fairchild. I know it and so do you. Truth and justice. Those are my only concerns regarding you."

"Are you willing to test that?"

He only stared at her.

Rowena stepped away from him and walked over to her claret-colored ottoman. Once there she kept her back to Inspector Maxwell. She took off her dressing gown and let it fall to the floor.

Underneath it, she wore only her corset as it was the only piece of undergarment Mary had managed to help her on with before Inspector Maxwell had come calling.

Her bottom was bare as were her legs. She hadn't even had time to put on her garter or stockings. Her hair spilled down her back, the ends of it just brushing the upper curve of her buttocks.

When her husband was alive, just presenting herself to him in this manner had kindled his desire.

Delilah. Salome. Lilith.

He'd whisper those names in her ear when he finally put his hands on her.

Inspector Maxwell, however, was nothing like her husband, who had embraced the pleasures of the flesh as eagerly and enthusiastically as he had embraced life. However, there was no doubt in Rowena's mind that the inspector wanted her as much as she wanted him.

She'd known that the first day she met him. Even when his sole purpose had been to see her swing from the end of a noose, she had felt his lust for her. Lust he had been unable to acknowledge, thus leading him to channel it into his ruthless persecution of her.

But she had not been found guilty, had not swung from a rope, and his hellish appetite for her had not been sated.

And now, here she was, offering to him the very thing he reviled yet desired beyond all reason.

Rowena smiled. How utterly delicious.

The skin on her bare buttocks tingled as she waited for Inspector Maxwell's response. But he had not moved from where she had left him when she walked over to the ottoman.

She felt his eyes on her. Like lashes from a whip across her naked skin. She stood there, trying not to shiver, trying not to let him know she was starting to feel anxious.

She heard movement. Shoes moving across the carpet. However, she could not tell if he was coming toward her or leaving.

Fearing she may have miscalculated, she waited breathlessly for the door to open and close behind him.

Instead, she felt the stirring of air that meant someone had moved up behind her. Her heart pounded.

He put his hand on her bottom.

Rowena almost climaxed right then and there. Her mouth opened and she drew in a hard, sharp breath.

The inspector slowly moved his hand over the curve of her ass, his fingers lightly trailing across her skin. She had not realized that merely the anticipation of his touch could heighten the pleasure so.

His long fingers moved along the crevice of her buttocks then down, down to her quim. She bit her lower lip.

He leaned against her and fondled the wet hairs and lips of her cunt, the wool of his coat and trousers scratching her bare ass. His breath moved heatedly against her neck, then over to her ear.

"Tell me, Lady Fairchild."

He pushed his fingers deep inside her.

She gripped the back of the ottoman, her body shuddering. "What?"

"Tell me what really happened with your husband."

He slowly moved his fingers in and out of her cunt.

"I told you." Rowena threw her head back, her hips rocking wantonly against his hand. "I didn't kill him but not a day has gone by that I wished I had insisted he go to bed instead of..." She groaned when the inspector's fingers pushed hard against a particularly sensitive part of her cunt.

"Instead of indulging in the perversions you knew would kill him," he said.

"No, no, that's not true. I didn't know...Oh, God...I didn't know. I swear. I loved my husband. With all my heart. He was kind to me when so many were not."

Maxwell pressed his body tightly against hers. His fingers were now determinedly fucking her and she heard and felt his labored breath.

She was close to her climax, but this wasn't how she wanted to experience it. And in her heart, she knew it wasn't what the inspector wanted either, pleasurable as it was proving to be.

"You think I'm guilty." Her body shuddered as his fingers in her cunt drove her nearer and nearer to orgasm. "Nothing I say convinces you otherwise. Punish me then," she begged. "Punish me."

Maxwell jerked his hand out of her cunt. Grabbing her arm, he sat on the ottoman and pulled her across his lap.

Rowena pressed her cheek against the ottoman. Her cunt throbbed from the closeness of her climax.

"You are guilty, Lady Fairchild."

"Yes, I am," she whispered. "I am guilty."

"Say it!" he demanded.

"I am guilty of loving my husband so much that I could not say no to him."

She waited. Nothing happened.

"Go ahead, Inspector. It's all right."

"I want to hurt you, yes. Very much so. But I also don't want to."

Rowena was surprised. It was the first time since she'd met him that he'd ever expressed any concern regarding her welfare.

She turned her head and looked up into his eyes. "Don't

worry. I can take whatever you choose to inflict on me."

He slowly rubbed his hand over her rear, his smooth palm pressing hard against her flesh. Rowena heard his heavy breathing, felt the tightening of his leg muscles beneath his trousers. She moved her body along his thighs, like a cat rubbing against its master. Then she turned her head and pressed her cheek back against the ottoman.

The inspector's hand descended upon her ass with the coppery strike of a hammer against an anvil.

Pain exploded through Rowena's body. She closed her eyes, tears stinging the lids. The fire along her rear burned then dissipated until it was a dull throb. She waited for the next blow.

"Inspector?"

His hand descended again.

Rowena yelped, her bottom wriggling under his hands.

He pressed his lips against her ear. "Do not speak until I give permission. Do you understand?"

Rowena nodded, her heart pounding.

He struck her again, his hand leaping from cheek to cheek, the flesh burning under the assault, the pain drilling straight into her cunt. She jerked against his thighs, her lips quivering against the nubbed fabric of the ottoman.

"Oh, god!"

Maxwell stopped. "Did you say something, Lady Fairchild?"

"No, Inspector. I didn't—"

His palm slammed onto her rear.

"No, sir! Oh, no."

The pain was now so intense Rowena's instinct was to get away but, even as the pain slurred through her body, her cunt was aching with her need to climax.

"Admit your guilt, Lady Fairchild."

"I have." Tears trickled along her cheeks and onto her lips. She licked at the salty taste. "I loved Edmund and I wish he had not died. I mourn him every day."

"I'm not talking about Lord Fairchild."

"Then what—?"

His hand fell hard onto her right cheek, followed quickly by another and then another.

Rowena cried out, squirming against his legs. What did he mean? His frustration regarding his failure to prove her guilty of having murdered her husband? Wasn't that what this was all about?

"Inspector?"

He struck her rear again, and the heated throbbing of her buttocks was becoming unbearable. The stinging blows came again and again, the inspector's hard palm moving quickly from cheek to cheek.

Rowena rubbed her cunt against his trousers, no doubt leaving a wet spot on them.

"Oh, God, Oh God!"

She moaned as her orgasm gripped her, waves of bliss undulating fiercely in her womb. She dug her fingers into the ottoman and bucked her hips, riding her climax the way she rode her horse, her thighs tight and hard.

Maxwell gripped her hips. He leaned over and kissed her burning ass and the touch of his mouth on her heated flesh made her come again.

Afterwards, Rowena lay exhausted and limp across the inspector's lap as she struggled to regain her composure. Once she had, she pushed herself up until she was sitting next to him.

Maxwell looked over at her, the feral lust in his eyes brutally pure. Then he smiled and those chocolate drop eyes of his warmed. He put his arm about her shoulder and pulled her against his side.

She smoothed the front of his pristinely white shirt with her fingers. "Inspector?"

"Yes?"

"You do believe I am innocent of my husband's death."

He looked down at her for a long moment. Then he curtly nodded.

"Then what did you mean about my guilt?"

"Your guilt?" His hand moved along her bare thighs then slipped around to her still stinging buttocks. "Oh, yes. That."

He lowered his head, his lips brushing across hers. "I wanted you to admit your guilt regarding me."

"Regarding you?"

"You've wanted me from the first moment you met me."

Rowena smiled. "Guilt such as that is easy enough to admit." She looked up at him from under her lashes. "What about you?"

He frowned. "What do you mean?"

"Didn't you feel guilty for wanting me and yet doing all you could to prove I was responsible for my husband's death?"

"I was doing my job."

"Your job. Yes, of course."

Rowena moved her hand along his thigh and up the front of his trousers. His cock was long and thick beneath it. She gently squeezed it, impressed by its length.

He made a low sound in his throat. "But yes. I will admit. I did feel some guilt."

"Then you should be punished for it, don't you think?"

He stared at her, his face impassive, but she saw the dark eagerness leaping in his eyes like flames at her words.

Rowena quickly undid the front of his trousers and slid her hand inside. His cock leapt against her palm, stiffly eager.

"Lady Fairchild, I—" Inspector Maxwell drew in a hard, deep

breath.

"How lovely." She licked her lips. "So thick. So hard. And so very, very long." She wrapped her hand around his cock and slowly stroked it. "And don't you think we've moved beyond your addressing me as Lady Fairchild."

"Yes, I believe we have." He pressed the back of his head against the wall, his throat working as she ardently stroked his cock.

"Rowena, Rowena," he murmured. "Yes, yes, oh, yes, my sweet Delilah."

Her eyes widened. "What did you say?"

He looked down at her and smiled. "You are a beguiling temptress. And consequently you have made me your slave."

She slid her hand up and down the hard velvety length of him. "As I am yours, William."

"You should know—"

He stopped, breath hissing between his teeth. Rowena's palm now encircled the bulbous head of his cock. He groaned and closed his eyes.

"You should know that although I believe you are innocent of murdering your husband I still hold you culpable for his death."

"Really?" Rowena rubbed his cock harder.

He opened his eyes and looked at her. "Therefore, you will be punished for it. Daily."

Rowena stopped stroking his cock. "Daily?"

He nodded, his mouth hard but his eyes soft.

She smiled. "Good. Keep thinking that."

Then she quickly lowered her head and took him into her mouth.

The Accidental Spanker

by Sean Meriwether

After eight years of marriage, when our relationship, and especially our sex life, had become expected and routine, I found myself masturbating to fantasies decidedly more exotic than our plain-Jane coupling. I had always been fairly conservative in the bedroom, but when my hand slipped between my legs and my eyes closed, my mind flashed over images of myself tossed over the knees of a hairy man, one who would pink my ass with repeated, heavy slaps. I'd come violently, perplexed by the darker flavor of this recent obsession, feeling as guilty as I was aroused.

I was afraid to mention these desires to my husband, uncertain of his judgment, but occasionally, when I was on top, I'd move his hand into position and silently will him to spank me; instead, he would pet my ass like a prized kitten. I'd roll off of him after he heaved himself into climax, frustrated and worried that he would never give me the opportunity to bring these desires out in the open.

What made it worse was working with a predominantly male staff, dozens of junior brokers who had this locker-room familiarity, often spanking one another after a big sale or huge commission was earned. I would watch them with envy, wondering which one of them would best deliver my spanking. While I sat in board meetings, listening to them ramble about market fluctuations, my thoughts would drift to being physically restrained, hands and feet bound, and having one of these cocky traders paddle me, teasing my ass with those thick, pampered hands, building into a crescendo of slaps that raised the temperature of my skin. That all of these men reported directly to me only added to the allure of this very inappropriate fantasy. I was not only afraid of becoming entangled with a colleague, but also that I was drifting into adultery. I loved my husband, but I feared he would not be able to fulfill this one demanding desire.

One night, I woke from a dream in which a faceless man lifted my plaid Catholic-schoolgirl's skirt and spanked me relentlessly, his huge hands covering every square inch of my petite ass. I awoke panting and soaking wet, wondering if this was what teenage boys experienced as wet dreams. I looked over at my sleeping husband and knew I had to make him understand what my body and brain were demanding, and have him administer it before it was too late.

To sweeten the offer, I staged a romantic evening by shipping the kids off to my mother's and cooking his favorite meal. When he got home and noticed that not only were we alone, but that there was wine on the table, butternut squash soup on the stove, and a chicken in the oven, his playful smile made his expectations blissfully transparent. If he only knew what I had in mind!

Our dinner conversation was lighthearted and flirty, reminiscent of when we were dating in college, before we had high-pressure jobs, a mortgage, and two kids. I felt an adventurous spirit return and a heat burn inside of me that I had almost forgotten. I was no longer the conservative mom and investment banker, but a naughty girl eager to be reprimanded. Our conversation quickly detoured into sex as we dallied over the chocolate mousse.

After sharing a bottle of wine, having spent weeks planning this moment, the words rushed out of my mouth; I couldn't restrain myself any longer. "Were you ever disciplined by your parents?"

"Huh?" His eyes responded to the erotic undertone of my question, but he was a little confused by the question.

"Were you ever *spanked*?" There, the word was out. My heart caught in my throat, fearful that Ben wouldn't share my interest.

"You mean Mike and Carol Brady? Tina, you know they would sooner vote republican than hit their children." He laughed, but stared deeply into my eyes, curious about where I was going with this conversation. He smiled mysteriously. "What about you?"

I felt my face flush, hopeful that he knew exactly what was on my mind. I slipped a spoonful of mousse into my mouth, swirled the velvety chocolate over my tongue. "Nothing. Not even a tiny little spank on my bottom." The smile, pure naughty girl. "Not even when I deserved it."

I listened to his breath deepen, could almost hear the gears spinning in his head. He looked at me with a gleam in his eye that announced we were both on the same page.

"*Real-ly?*" The word split into two syllables—excited yet incredulous. He beckoned me to his side of the table.

I stood up, letting his eyes run over my body, feeling like he was looking at me the way he did when we were younger. I traced my hand down the curve of my breast, cupped it, offered it to him. He stared at me, playfully dumbstruck, but obviously interested. I sauntered over to him, wiggling my ass, feeling as if another woman had stepped into my skin and was performing for the man in the chair. Benjamin swallowed hard as I approached.

I wanted to say what a bad girl I was, but even in my head that sounded staged, even pornographic. In my fantasies there were no words, only that heavy hand on my bottom, the steady drumbeat of his meaty palm warming my flesh. Words were unnecessary when the body was given what it craved.

"Would you like to..." I led.

"What?" His throat sounded dry, his eyes bright and wet.

"Spank me?"

I stepped between his open thighs and pressed my body against him, feeling taller and in charge. His hand tentatively brushed my naked left leg, ran deliberately north to cross beneath the barrier of my short skirt, and cupped my ass. I shivered against him, sensing the spanking that would follow. His fingers were warm and tender, but uncertain.

"I don't want to hurt you," he sighed.

"You won't," I told him.

He squeezed my ass, and then delivered a light tap, which only mocked my fantasy.

"I *want* you to spank me, baby," I cooed in his ear, but I felt him stiffening, and not in the right way. This scene was not appealing to him. I backpedaled and shifted gears. "Or maybe you would like me to spank you?"

I felt his erection press against my thigh. I smiled against his face, perplexed. Was being spanked a fantasy we both shared but never discussed? "Have you been a bad boy?" I immediately tossed out my objection to porn dialogue; I somehow knew he would eat it up with a spoon.

"Yes," he whispered, barely audible.

"What's that, bad boy? I didn't hear you."

"Yes." More certain, less timid.

"Yes, what?" I pressed myself against him, his face buried in my breasts, and I pressed hard against the tent in his pants.

"Yes, ma'am. I've been bad. Very bad." He rocked his head, his hair tickling my chest. I smacked the side of his face lightly. He looked up at me with a mixture of surprise and excitement in his bright brown eyes; I wondered when was the last time we had looked at each other with that same level of intensity.

"You should be punished."

Then my husband of eight years—the man whom I had spent the bulk of my adult life with, the father of my children—nodded like a petulant boy. I felt completely empowered; I enjoyed the texture of the moment, of my man submitting to me.

"Get up." He complied too readily, jarring the table and sending the dishes clattering. "Kneel." I wanted him to be the size of the naughty boy he claimed to be, one half my size. He knelt on the carpet, first on one knee as if proposing, then on both. His erection was visibly straining his khakis; a dark pearl-sized stain of pre-cum indicated his interest in the scene I was directing. His eager submission threw me off-balance, and I wasn't sure what to do with him, other than make him wait. I counted off the seconds, listening to his breath grow more rapid and impatient.

"Over there," I ordered and pointed to the sofa. He crept on his knees to the side of the sofa, then leaned his face into the pillows and presented me with the blank canvas of his khaki-covered ass—mine for the spanking.

I knelt behind him, cupped both sides of that handsome butt, explored the strong muscles that his daily runs had developed. I sent a light tap against him, testing my strength and his tolerance—he barely flinched. A second slap with more weight behind it caused him to moan, but it was the third volley, one with the full force of my hand, that made him grunt. I felt something liquid stir inside of me, eager to explore my new role as dominatrix.

I believed his pants and underwear were deadening the sensation, so I ordered him to lower them. My authoritarian voice, one used when enforcing the rules with the traders and children, dropped an octave lower than my normal tone. Ben fumbled with his belt, the jangle of his buckle an auditory aphrodisiac. He slipped his pants and boxers down his thighs to expose the curved muscle of his ass. I pushed his shirt up over his lower back, excited by the expanse of flesh I had seldom paid attention to—the march of vertebrae, the wispy patch of hair at the small of his back, the dark cleft of his ass exposed to me with the trust of a lover. I sent another hard slap to his backside; my hand stung, but there was an excitement in the sting, my fingers tingling from the connection, the warm imprint of my hand glowing on Ben's ass.

Another ringing smack against his bare skin, and a red oval blushed across the white meat of his ass, a rising sun the size of my hand. I ran my fingertips over the spot, testing its heat, confirming that my own actions had caused it. Another one and he groaned into the pillows and inched his ass up to offer easier access. I sampled different speeds and hefts, interchanging spanking with massaging his skin, aroused and alarmed at the pattern of red spots that flushed his nether cheeks like a fiery sunset. Ben's face was lost in the pillows, emitting a series of grunts and groans I'd *never* heard from him before.

But this was not my fantasy. I was supposed to be draped over his knees, the peach of my ass bared to his open hand, being smacked with the same passion I was delivering. How had my fantasy been inverted, where I was the disciplinarian instead of the *disciplinee*? And why was it becoming more erotic than my original fantasies?

"Strip," I ordered, my voice deep and commanding. He rose up on his knees, staring straight ahead at the sofa, and awkwardly removed the rest of his clothing without getting off his knees or sitting down. I slipped my panties off, aware of how wet I was, but left my short skirt on. "Turn around."

Ben swiveled around, his face level with my crotch, and instinctively leaned forward, his tongue racing ahead. I pushed his head back and wagged my finger at him. "Not yet, bad boy."

His face puckered with impatience, but I could tell he was enjoying this. His cock was almost painfully erect, a spider web of pre-cum drizzling to the carpet; I knew he wouldn't be able to hold out much longer.

I pushed past him and sat in the middle of the sofa. "Lay across my lap." He arranged himself across me, the heat of his cock pressed hard against my thigh.

I caressed his ass, feeling like a conqueror, excited that my husband shared my own desire to be spanked. I wanted him to feel the full weight of his punishment, like the one the faceless man in my dream had given me. I smacked him hard—one, two, three, four—marking time by smacking first the left cheek, then the right, until both glowed.

"The belt," he suggested, his face buried in the sofa's cushions, his cock on fire against my thigh. He reached down and pulled the leather snake from the pile of his khakis and handed it to me. I looked at it with alarm; what was I supposed to do with *this*? And why was he so eager, so compliant, so...rehearsed? My thoughts started to spin off in the wrong direction, fearing that he'd been keeping his spanking secret from me, seeing another woman to administer his punishment.

I folded the belt in half and smacked him.

"Harder."

I didn't like him hijacking my fantasy. Not only was I the one who was supposed to be draped across his lap, but he was obviously already experienced in this arena, a secret he had not shared with me. He wanted harder? I gave it to him. I spanked him with the belt, the raw energy of my emotion fueling the impact, the belt smacking against him with a metronomic precision. Each slap came with a question. Who is *she*? Who is *she*? Who is *she*?

He groaned heavily, his body tensed with each belt-snap, his butt painted with angry stripes of white and maroon. I stopped, my arm aching, and stared down at the belt; it slipped from my grasp and slid to the floor. I felt Ben shift uncomfortably as he turned his head back to face me. "Are you all right?"

I looked down at his back, the red marks on his butt, then at his eyes, brimming with concern.

"I'm sorry, my arm hurts."

"I never would have thought you would do that. I've thought about it forever."

"Thought about it?"

"I didn't think you would want to...I mean...I didn't think you would like it and...I don't know. I've always wanted you to spank me."

"Me?"

"Of course. Who else would I let do *that*?"

"You've never...?"

"Never." He sank back across my lap, his sweaty erection hard against my leg, his pre-cum making him as wet as I was.

"Why did you know how to...?" My mind buzzed with millions of questions, but there was only one I wanted answered.

He rolled off my lap and kneeled on the carpet next to me. He took my hand, the one that had delivered his punishment, and caressed it. I winced; it was sore.

"Call it instinct. I've fantasized about this for a long time."

"Me too. You must be a natural."

"I could say the same for you," he said with a laugh.

"I thought that our roles would have been reversed."

A smile burned across his face and he moved quickly. He slipped onto the sofa beside me and had me over his lap, my skirt flipped up over my back, and my pale ass exposed to his fingers in seconds.

The first smack was light, tentative, testing, but the tingle illuminated my flesh. I was surprised at how different, how immediate, the feeling was compared to my daydreams. He followed with a few light slaps, building momentum, bringing the blood to the surface, playing me like a fleshy bongo drum. "If it gets too hard, you have to let me know," he warned before cutting loose.

The sting of the first real spank radiated out from my butt through the small of my back, and then raced through my body like an earthquake. My clit and nipples tensed from aftershocks. I grunted louder than he had. Another heavy smack had me quivering over his lap.

"You have such a beautiful ass," Ben said, running his warm hand over it. I didn't have time to respond before he sent another series of quakes through me. Again his hand came down, hard, harder, still harder, until my entire backside radiated with racing blood; a million tender nerves were very much alive. I was edging not toward pain, as one would have expected, nor exactly pleasure, as I'd fantasized, but instead into a hyper-awareness of my physical body. Every time Ben's firm palm connected with my skin, I felt it radiate out to every inch of my body.

His thick fingers slid down the back of my ass, over my perineum, and toyed with me from below. He never quite entered, just danced on the surface, soaking his fingers. "Had enough?"

I shook my head, unable to speak, biting down on my wrist to keep myself from coming. Every nerve in my body was on high frequency, every point of contact with him blissful torture. I wanted him to roll me off his lap and fuck me hard, but I knew that was not going to happen; tonight was about exploring a new way to enjoy one another.

He removed his fingers and spanked my butt again, each slap issuing a fresh wave of intensity in my body, becoming more sensitive as he progressed. I could feel the heat of my butt radiating against his palm, the warmth of his hand as Ben rubbed me between spanks. My body felt like an orchestra, each instrument singing its own part of the score. Then everything played together in a chaotic symphony, crashing into a breathless, mind-shattering orgasm. I tensed and exploded, collapsing across his damp lap, unable to move.

Ben caressed my tender back with the understanding only found in a long-term lover. "You okay, baby?"

I nodded into the cushions, exhausted and elated, light-headed from panting. Everything was tingling, inside and out; my body was smiling from his attentions. I sat up awkwardly, the telltale smear of white announcing that he'd come. I'd been so wrapped up in my own orgasm that I'd failed to even register his.

"Wow," he sighed at last. He cradled me against him, spooning me into our normal pre-sleep posture. "Wow, Tina." Our entwined bodies were several degrees above body temperature and dreamily pressed together.

"Why didn't we do that before?" I asked, my head still clouded, my body still reeling from orgasm.

"I don't know." He shrugged, kissed the back of my neck, and hugged me closer. "Are you all right?" he asked, his voice heavy with imminent sleep.

I nodded, distracted, wanting to remain in the moment, my butt sore from being punished by his hand, but the raw sensations were fading into a joyful memory, like the wet dream. In some odd way, I felt like I knew this man better now that we had shared this unspoken fantasy, our mutual desire for spanking.

"That was amazing," he sighed, the z in the final word long and lazy, signaling his crossover into sleep. "Let's go to bed."

"Yes." He took my hand and led me into our darkened bedroom, my mind still trying to grasp how everything had changed, but remained the same. We lay together beneath the sheets, two newly intimate strangers. I listened to his breath slow and deepen. I felt his furry body cradle mine, his softening cock nestled against my sore but grateful ass, and wondered if we might reenact this evening, or if it was a one-shot deal. I drifted between sleep and wakefulness, crafting our next erotic adventure. I wondered if Ben might also like to be restrained with rope and then spanked. I smiled into the dark, picturing it.

Necessary Roughness

By Beth Wylde

"Hurry up, babe. You're gonna be late."

I threw on my jacket and dashed downstairs to find my wife waiting for me by the door with a thermos full of coffee in one hand and my car keys in the other. She handed me both items and then leaned in for a kiss that set my mouth on fire.

"Mmmm, good morning to you too. Where'd that come from?"

She smiled and shrugged. "Not sure. I saw you all dressed up and I suddenly needed to show you my appreciation." She ran one hand down my chest, pausing to caress my breasts through my dress shirt. "You look fantastic. What's the special occasion?"

"We've got a big meeting this morning about the new merger. We find out who gets to keep their job and who gets the ax."

Lynette's eyes widened with concern, but I hastened to assure her.

"No worries, hun. I've been there for eight years. My place is secure. Besides, I'm a shoo-in for the empty VP spot. I'll call you later and we can make plans to celebrate."

She smoothed down the lapel of my blazer, the worried look

still in place on her face. "Oh Trish. I don't mean to be such a worry wart, but I can't help it. It's one of the reasons why I can't commit myself to play with you. I trust you completely, but I can't give anyone permission to hurt me."

I sighed as Lynette once again dredged up the subject of my domme alter ego. She was right though. I missed the thrill of playing something fierce, but at the time, it seemed like a small price to pay to be with the woman I loved. I'd also been sure that I could change Lynette's mind by easing her into some light scenes. So far, almost fourteen months later, she was still steadfastly refusing my offers.

I pushed the depressing thought out of my mind and smiled. "No time for ugly thoughts. It's going to be a great day. Now pucker up and lay another one on me, hot stuff. I need something to tide me over until I can get home and get my hands on your smokin' little body."

She snuggled in, coming up on tiptoe so that her chest rubbed against mine. "You're the only person that calls me little. I like it." Then her tongue was in my mouth and mine was in hers. It was a glorious way to greet the day.

Things went all to hell shortly afterwards.

By the time I walked into the corporate office an hour later, I felt like shit and looked even worse. Halfway to work, I hit a pothole and spilled scalding hot coffee in my lap. Then my tire went flat and I had to change it, spotting my hands and my new suit with grease. After fighting bumper-to-bumper rush-hour traffic, I ended up having to park a million miles away.

I dashed into the conference room like the very fires of Hell were licking at my heels and, in a way, they were. Being late to this board meeting could make or break my career. Judging by the pissed-off look on my boss's face when I arrived, it was already broken.

Just as I settled into a seat, everyone else got up, clapping one another on the back and shaking hands in congratulations. It looked like they'd reached an agreement after all. I sighed and walked out, pausing in the hall to rub my throbbing temples.

"Miss Price!" I jumped halfway to the ceiling as Mr. Leftwich snuck up on me. "I expected a better showing from you today." He looked me over from head to toe, blatant disdain evident on his face. "I thought you were serious about the vice presidency. Obviously not. You're late, your clothes are filthy, and you're still dressing like a man. I thought for sure you'd get over your image concerns and put on a nice dress for a meeting as important as this. In my office in five."

I could feel the heat building up under my skin as a deep blush spread across my face. The embarrassment just served to piss me off further. He had no right to address me in such a way in front of the entire board of directors. At that moment, I would have given up everything I had for some strong rope, a paddle, and some time alone with my boss. I was pretty sure I was about to get the boot, but if I was on the way out, I was going to let Mr. Leftwich know personally what I thought of him and his homophobia first.

"Fucking asshole." I slammed the boss's door behind me so hard it rattled in its frame, and then headed straight to my office, wanting desperately to be left alone. I looked over my shoulder at the two guys in uniforms following me. No such luck.

I did my best to ignore them, tossing my personal belongings in the box I'd been given as I headed for the exit. All the while, two overly large security guards stayed close by, one on each side. Apparently Mr. Leftwich hadn't enjoyed being called a pompous, self-righteous, homophobic prick. I'd enjoyed it just fine. In fact it had been one of the highlights of my day, coming in just shy of my sweetheart's early morning make-out session.

The thought of my wife made me pause. Lynette was going to freak out when she discovered I'd lost my job. My severance check would hold us for a while, but not permanently, and I couldn't ask her to drop out of school. Not after getting accepted into the master's program. It would break her heart. There had to be another way.

I tossed the box in the backseat of my car and got in, giving the duo a single-finger salute as I drove away. My muscles were tight and my head felt like it was going to explode. I desperately needed to work out some stress, but the thing immediately guaranteed to clear my head and get me back in the game was the one activity I couldn't indulge in. It looked like Lynette and I were going to be discussing more than our financial situation and my unemployment options when I got home. I couldn't go on suppressing such a huge part of myself because my wife wasn't comfortable with it. Eventually I'd crack. I wondered if there was a padded room reserved specifically for wayward dommes. Maybe Lynette could be my nurse.

I finally decided to give my partner a heads-up that I was on the way home. Truthfully, I just needed to hear her voice.

She picked up on the fourth ring, sounding breathless. "Hello?"

"Hey, it's me."

"Hi, baby. I was just thinking about you."

"Really?"

"Yes, really." She paused. "What's wrong? You sound funny?"

I pulled over in front of the liquor store, debating whether to make a purchase or not. Getting drunk probably wasn't the best idea, but at the moment, it seemed like a decent option. I would have preferred putting Lynette across my lap and spanking her ass until she screamed, but my lover couldn't fathom the idea that a whipping could be arousing. I had so many people to introduce her to that would back up my statement. I cranked the car back up and moved on. "Nothing. Just a lot on my mind right now."

"How did the meeting go?"

I groaned. I just couldn't drop such life-shattering news to her over the phone. "Not as good as I expected it to."

"Aw, Trisha, I'm so sorry. I know how much you wanted to be the first female VP for the southeast division."

"That's okay. I think Mr. Leftwich would cut off his own balls before he'd let that happen."

Lynette's voice deepened with the first hint of anger. "What's that supposed to mean? If he's been giving you shit again about the way you dress, I'm going to sue his ass. That's discrimination. Forget the VP slot, you're going to own the fucking company."

Her protectiveness melted my heart and I smiled despite my own rage. Lynette only cursed when she was well and truly mad, and nothing made her angrier than prejudice. As a full-figured, bi-racial lesbian she'd endured enough bigotry while growing up. It was one of the things I admired so much about her—and the reason her refusal to even watch a scene confused me.

"I think it goes a little deeper than my clothing preferences. Apparently Mr. Leftwich is intensely homophobic. He stood as far across his office as he could get from me as he called me every derogatory name in the book. Then he fired me."

"He what? That motherfucking flea bag. I'll bend his skinny ass in half and feed him his dick."

I realized what I'd let slip, but it was too late to take it back. Oh God, it was going to get bad. I pushed down harder on the gas. "Shit. Honey, I didn't mean to say that. I wasn't going to tell you until I got home. You shouldn't have had to hear that over the phone. I wanted to tell you face to face."

Lynette didn't say a word, but I knew she was still there. I could hear her heavy breathing over the line. "Lynette? Honey, talk to me." Her lack of speech was completely uncharacteristic. "Lynette?" I sped up even more.

"How long until you get home?"

Her voice was way too calm for my liking. "I'm almost there. Maybe ten minutes."

"Okay, I'll see you soon."

I was left with a dial tone in my ear and a bad feeling in my gut.

I parked the car and hit the sidewalk running, dropping the keys twice in my haste to get in the door. "Lynette? Lynette Margaret Mitchell, answer me!"

"Is that a request or a command?"

I whipped sideways to find my sweetheart staring back at me, still wrapped in the robe she'd had on earlier. "What did you say?"

She sauntered towards me slowly, her hips swaying provocatively from side to side. There wasn't a trace of anger or irritation on her face. She looked completely calm, almost cocky in fact. I wasn't sure what had changed, but whatever it was, it was a real turn on. I'd never seen her look so confident and sexy.

"I asked if that was a request or a command." She dropped to her knees at my feet. "I realized something today."

I jerked my tie open in an effort to get more oxygen into my lungs. Surely she wasn't about to offer what I thought she was?

Though she was definitely in the perfect starting position for it.

"I've done something stupid." She opened her robe just the tiniest bit and I moaned, unable to catch my breath. She was wearing something shiny and silver. The brightness really highlighted her light brown skin. Where had all the fucking air gone? Before I could ask, she shrugged out of the robe completely, revealing a silver bodysuit with cutouts for her breasts and at the apex of her thighs.

"Holy shit!" I rubbed my eyes to make sure I wasn't hallucinating. "What the...? Did you? Um...when?" I couldn't even form a coherent sentence. The sight before me had me completely tongue-tied.

She smiled serenely. "I told you I'd been stupid. I've done the very thing to you that I despise. There is no room in our relationship for prejudice. Our conversation on the phone made me realize that. I'm no better than that piece of shit you used to work for if I'm not willing to at least try to understand your ways. I'm your wife. I should want to do the things that please you too. A little pain is nothing compared to your happiness."

I'm not sure what part of my body was more excited over her speech. My heart thumped, my pussy throbbed, and my nipples hardened. I knew we were going to have to start off with something simple. A gentle scene, but the fact that she wanted to try at all spoke volumes. I wanted to wrap her in my arms and show her that BDSM wasn't about pain, at least not all of it.

"You do know what you're consenting to, right?"

She nodded. "I've done my research."

My eyes widened. "Have you?"

"Yes. I joined a few BDSM chat groups. Not those phony dating site things, but some real forums where interested people can ask questions and get honest answers. I also bought a couple books on the subject and talked to a few lifestyle dommes, one-on-one, on IM." She tilted her head inquisitively. "Did you know Donna and Amy are into the scene?"

I laughed. "Yeah, I did. You're looking at Amy's trainer. She was my sub before she met Donna."

Lynette frowned. "I didn't know you and Amy..."

I stroked one finger down her cheek. "We never were a couple. It was strictly a club partnership."

"Okay that makes me feel better. It would be odd to think of you boinking one of our best friends."

I laughed. "No boinking involved." I took a deep breath and tossed my jacket and tie over the back of the couch. "Are you sure about this?"

"Yes."

I unbuttoned my cuffs and rolled up my sleeves. "What's your safe word?"

"Bigot."

I smiled; it seemed oddly appropriate based on the day's events. "That works for me." I sat down on the couch and patted my lap. "Come on over here sexy and let's get this show on the road.

She crawled to me on her hands and knees and I almost fainted. I'd never seen anything so hot in my life.

She paused for just a moment before lying face down across my thighs, presenting me with a view of her backside. The outfit was completely crotchless.

"Holy hell! Where in the world did you buy this? If it's a local store, we have to go there again—soon." I ran my hand down the back of the bodysuit, letting my fingers linger to caress her ass. "I've dreamed of you like this."

She looked at me over her shoulder. "You have?"

"Oh yes. Now be a good little girl and be quiet while I have my way with you."

"Yes, ma'am."

I smiled at her use of a formal title. "Very nice." I patted one cheek gently and then the other. "Now we should start off easy. Just a little introduction." I patted her left cheek a bit firmer. "It doesn't have to hurt. The point is to get you to a place where everything is amplified. To make what would normally cause pain feel good. A good domme knows what turns her partner on and uses that until she can't tell where the pain stops and the pleasure begins. It's a delicate balance." I smacked her rump for emphasis. "I'm going to enjoy walking that fine line with you."

I drew back and laid the first slap down with the palm of my hand, still taking it easy. I went on that like for a few minutes, alternating sides and the strength of my blows until Lynette was squirming against me. The feel of my hand on her ass and her breasts rubbing against my legs was sheer heaven. Blushing the prettiest pink against her naturally tan color, her ass started to lift into my thrusts. Her skin grew warmer against my hand with each extra whack, and though I'd gotten a bit rougher than I'd intended, she didn't seem to be feeling any pain. If anything, she was actually enjoying our session.

She slid one leg out a bit, giving me a glimpse between her thighs as she tried to ride my leg. I gave her a serious spanking this time for her disobedience. She just moaned and thrust against me harder. I laid down a series of spankings that had her ass turning a gorgeous cherry color. "You'll come when I say you can come."

"Please."

"Are you wet?" I slid my hand between her legs so I could feel the results for myself. I could already see how slick she was, but I wanted to touch it too.

"Trisha!"

Smack. My hand came down again. "What did you call me?"

"Ma'am. I meant ma'am. Please, ma'am, please let me come."

There was no way I could refuse when she begged like that. Without warning, I slid two fingers deep inside her cunt, thrusting in and out as my other hand smacked her rear once more.

She squealed and arched her back. "Harder."

"The spanking or the fucking?"

"Both. Harder for both!"

She was panting now, every muscle in her body wound tight as a bow ready to snap. I did two things at once. I delivered a heavy-handed blow to her ass, spreading out my fingers to cover as much area as possible. At the same time, I reached down with my thumb and gave her clit a sturdy tap. It was a move guaranteed to work, and it did.

"Fuuuuccckkk! Trissssshaaaaaa!"

She gripped my knees with a crushing force as she exploded into orgasm. I ground my bottom against the couch, searching in vain for some much needed stimulation on my needy clit. She was still spasming around my fingers when she reached her hand between us and pressed against my inseam, her hand expertly finding the right spot. I shot off into orbit with her, shaking and grunting as I found my own release. We collapsed side by side on the couch, eventually tumbling off onto the floor, where we had more room. Neither of us minded, though. We'd just had the most mind-blowing encounter—and both of us with our clothes on, though my sweetheart was showing quite a bit more skin than I was.

I finally recovered enough to prop my head up on one hand. "Did you enjoy that?"

Lynette rolled over and stared at me with eyes still slightly unfocused. "Oh, yes, ma'am."

I chuckled at the dreamy look on her face. "You can call me

Trish again."

She blinked and, as I watched, some of the focus came back into her gaze. "Is it always like that?"

I shrugged. "Sometimes. And sometimes it's even better."

She gasped. "I'm not sure I'd live through it if it were any better. That was amazing."

"Would you be willing to do it again?"

She nodded and cuddled up against me. "Oh yes. If playing with you is like this, then you can get rough with me anytime you feel it's necessary."

I smiled and wrapped one arm around her waist, pulling the blanket off the back of the couch as she shivered slightly. "That's a job I'll do happily." I fell asleep next to my wife with dreams of future spankings dancing happily through my subconscious.

The Good Soldier

By Sacchi Green

Gunther squirmed in the grip of the familiar dream. *Fräulein* Ludmilla, in the old schoolroom, raised her wooden ruler to bring it down on his knuckles. When the boy hid his hands behind his back, she bent him harshly across the desktop, yanked down his woolen drawers, and proceeded to inscribe a lesson onto his tender buttocks. The red streaks imprinted by her hands were the introduction; the ruler added the main argument in lines of purple welts.

Punishment, yes, surely he deserved every blow. But could justice be done if it gave him such twisted pleasure?

Her grunts of exertion beat in harsh counterpoint to his sobbing cries. The punishment went on and on, exciting him more and more, bringing him to the brink of...of...

A hail of bullets against a Panzer's armored turret drowned out every other thought. In a jolt of panic sharp as lightning, the dream shattered.

Battle-honed reflexes kept him low, struggling to shelter his head—but his arms could not move! Something held him immobile, face-down! Paralysis? Had he been hit? No, he was able to twist his torso with an effort, but his wrists and ankles were restrained by strong bonds. Oddly soft bonds, yielding a scant fraction of a centimeter before holding fast. When he fought them harder, one ankle sent a stab of pain up along his leg. So he *had* been wounded!

"Take it easy, Gunther. It's only a storm." The voice was weary, stern, and unmistakably female. "You're safe enough. Looks like you'll be stuck being my prisoner for a while, though."

It *was* still a dream, then, and taking such strange new turns! But a sharp flash and the bone-shaking rumble of distant artillery set him to struggling again.

"Cut it *out*, Gunther! It's only...only *donder*. And, uh, *blitzen*. Thunder and lightning, and some damned impressive hail on this tin roof."

Memory began to trickle back. The escape from the British prison camp at Halmuir Farm...the endless, bramble-thatched Scottish moors. His companions had been recaptured while he crouched in a thicket hoping to snare a rabbit for their dinner. And then, after two days of wandering, he'd sighted the sheepherder's hut through pelting rain. There his memory hit impossibility. The rest could not have been real, not here! A fighter plane roaring down upon him so close that he'd thrown himself flat onto the cold, wet grass? The sands of El Alamein would have made more sense. But then the world had vanished in a burst of pain, thrusting him suddenly into darkness and silence. He could remember nothing more.

Now Gunther opened his eyes to a stormy dawn. He turned his head. The dimness of the morning was dimmer still inside the little stone hut, its one window covered by a leather flap, but the rattle of hail on the roof was diminishing. The narrow wooden door stood open to let in some light. And there the woman, silhouetted against the grayness, lounged against a doorpost.

She straightened and came to stand above him. Not a woman from any of his favorite dreams. Nothing like *Fräulein* Ludmilla, nor movie goddess Marlene, so naughty in *The Blue Angel*, so sultry in top hat and tails in *Morocco*, so deliciously cruel with an imagined riding crop in her elegant hands.

This woman was tall, dark-haired, self-assured—and in military uniform. He could not have imagined such a vision even in dreams! She wore dark blue trousers, a belted tunic with a "USA" insignia on one sleeve, and silver wings pinned above one high, firm breast. And such boots! Heavy leather boots, so much like...

No. He must not think of Field Marshal Rommel's boots. The Führer, for all Gunther cared, could rot in hell; it was the Desert Fox he had fought for, escaped for, should have died for. And must never soil with his dreams.

To be taken prisoner by a woman was no greater humiliation than he deserved. He stole another glance. Yes, strong, attractive in a handsome sort of way, and, at this moment, looking quite severe. Possibly she was more than he deserved, after all. His buttocks prickled as he felt her gaze move over him.

"C'mon, Gunther, it's just about morning." The voice was edged with irritation. The inflection, the tone, the shape of the words—English, yes, which he understood well enough after nine months in British POW camps, but different. Like in a movie. Not one with Marlene, though, nor Garbo. An American movie. With cowboys.

"Wake up, and convince me to let you move around a little. No bedpans in this place, and I'm sure as hell not going to clean up after you." In one quick motion, she yanked away a ragged woolen blanket reeking of sheep.

Chilly air washed over him. Gunther made one final attempt to believe he was dreaming, or still serving with the field marshal, but it was useless. However fiercely he squeezed his eyes shut, no Panzer's steel plates enclosed him. The *Afrikakorps* no longer battled in Egypt. The Desert Fox had withdrawn across the Mediterranean to France, and Sergeant Gunther Bernhardt would never serve at his side again.

He tested the bonds on wrists and ankles once more. They seemed to be tied to the crude frame of a narrow wooden bed with no mattress and only interwoven leather strips for springs. He gave up, and looked back toward his captor.

"Last chance, or I'll just leave you here," the woman said. "My landing gear may have knocked you out, but that lump on your head doesn't amount to all that much. Didn't even break the skin."

Gunther hadn't noticed the ache before, but now it startled a groan out of him.

"Too late for that," she said callously. "And I know you can talk. You're lucky I didn't gag you last night to shut you up. Seemed like you had nightmares there for a while, muttering in German and English, but just now, whatever was going on in your head, you were having *way* too much fun for an escaped POW."

Gunther struggled to make sense of the situation. What should he say? Did she hold a genuine military rank? How much authority did she have over him—aside from the undeniable fact that he was tied down and completely at her mercy? His vulnerable backside tingled at the thought.

"Suit yourself, then." She shrugged and seemed about to step out into the light rain.

"*Fräulein*, wait!" he blurted out. "What...who are you?"

"Make that 'lieutenant,'" she barked. "Commissioned

temporarily in the Air Transport Auxiliary of the RAF. And *I'm* the one who gets to ask for name, rank, and serial number, Sergeant Bernhardt!"

"*Ja!*" Gunther's bound right hand strained in vain to snap a salute. "Yes, Lieutenant! But...already you know my name and rank. How is that?"

She slid a hand into the pocket of her blue trousers and drew out an envelope. He recognized a letter from his sister that had most recently been in his own pocket.

"I didn't read anything beyond name and address, and that last part is already stamped on your underwear. 'Halmuir Farm POW Camp, Dumfries, Lockerbie.' Which is good to know, since I was supposed to be flying that brand new Spitfire fighter to the RAF airfield at Lockerbie. If you got here on foot, it can't be too far. Shouldn't take them long to locate us."

This woman had peered into his underwear? The limp, dirty garment he'd been wearing during five days of stumbling across boggy moorland? Gunther wriggled just slightly in embarrassment. Then, imagining her hands on his nether garments, perhaps even brushing his flesh, he struggled to hold himself rigidly immobile. Every movement of his body against the leather strips beneath him made his cock lurch and stiffen, and the pressure of his full bladder only amplified the discomfort.

He was not, he realized, wearing the rough gray trousers issued at the POW camp. He was not wearing any trousers at all, not even the thin underdrawers she'd mentioned. Nothing but the equally rough gray shirt, disarranged now so that its tail did nothing to shield his buttocks.

The woman must have seen his grimace of humiliation.

"Sorry," she said brusquely. "I'm not sure the Geneva Convention covers anything like this, but I reckon they'd take a dim view of it. You can have your pants back if you give me your word that you'll submit to being my prisoner, and won't try to escape."

"Yes, Lieutenant, ma'am," Gunther said wearily. Her frown made him wonder whether he should have said "sir," but his mind was more occupied with wondering how much submission she expected. Turning his head with an effort, he looked up into eyes as gray as the cloudy sky. "I submit myself. I will not try to escape."

"Okay then. If you haven't managed to get anywhere beyond the moors yet, chances are you wouldn't have any better luck even if you did run." She moved to the head of the bed and bent to release his wrists.

With her body so close to his face—a woman's body, inside an officer's uniform!— arousal became even harder to suppress. When he saw that he had been tied down with a pair of ladies' nylon stockings, and caught a faint whiff of woman-scent as one brushed his face, he very nearly groaned.

In Germany no one had such luxuries. Even in Paris only the highest-priced whores wore nylons. Or so he'd heard. This woman—this lieutenant and pilot—had nothing of the whore or the flirt about her. He could tell by the fit of her trousers that her legs were as elegantly long and slim as even Dietrich's, but to think of her pulling the stockings languorously up over calves and knees and thighs seemed wrong somehow. And profoundly, erotically disturbing.

She straightened, and he could swear that she lowered her face very briefly into the filmy stockings to inhale their scent before tucking them inside her tunic. For a moment, an expression that might have been pain crossed her face. Then she moved briskly to the foot of the bed to tend to his remaining bonds.

"Hey, this ankle doesn't look so good. There was a bit of swelling last night, but it's worse now, and purplish. Ought to be bound up."

Might he feel those nylon stockings, delicate, strong, and sensuous, tight against his skin once again?

"I think there was twisting when I fell." It occurred to Gunther that she bore the responsibility for his injuries. "When you flew your airplane at me."

"Tough luck. You were right where I had to make an emergency landing in the storm. Could've been a lot worse; I saw you in time to pull up a little. If it's any satisfaction, that sent me off-kilter enough that one of His Majesty's brand new Spitfires is now stuck out in the middle of nowhere with its landing gear too bent to take off. "

She laid his underdrawers and trousers across his backside. The garments were still damp from the rain, and he could see from the creases that they had been used to tie his ankles to the bed frame. Then she tore a strip from the tattered blanket and tossed it onto his clothing.

"Get with it," she said impatiently. "Tie up your ankle with that, and dress yourself. I'll be just outside. If you have trouble walking, there's a broken piece of a shepherd's staff in the corner." She left the hut while Gunther was still trying to sit up.

It was all he could do to make it to the entrance, nearly tripping over a rustic three-legged stool, the hut's only furnishing besides the bed and a tiny iron stove. She was waiting outdoors just to his right. He clutched at the doorframe, his bladder demanding relief, but his ankle refused to bear his weight. "*Fräulein*...Lieutenant..."

She caught the desperation in his voice. "Just aim to the left. The grass could hardly get any wetter."

Embarrassment fought with urgency. Gunther fumbled with

his trousers. "Please, I cannot, not while you watch."

The woman raised an eyebrow, turned away, and took a few steps. Enough, Gunther realized, that he could not have reached out quickly to strike her with the staff while her back was turned. Not that he would have done such a thing. Then he could think of nothing but the hot, hissing stream he could release at last, sending up waves of mist as it hit the cold grass.

Finally, with a sigh of relief and a lingering flush of humiliation, he rearranged his clothing and turned. She was gazing off into the gray sky as though watching for a search plane. Little clouds of denser mist rose around her. At first he thought perhaps—but surely not! Women could not piss while standing!—and then the scent of tobacco smoke hit his nostrils.

She swung around to face him. "All set? Smoke?"

Gunther stared at what she held out. American cigarettes! For those, he was sure, one could buy a reasonably clean whore even in Paris. His hand trembled as he slid one smooth white cylinder from the proffered pack, but when she tossed him a battered steel lighter he caught it adroitly enough.

"*Danke*, Lieutenant." The smoke was euphoria in his lungs, though it made him cough a time or two. "I have not smoked for a very long time." The pleasure was mixed with an odd sense of disappointment. He had begun to hunger for something far less kind from her.

"Neither have I." She stared off into space again, but this time he could see that her gaze was inward, not outward, and profoundly sad. Suddenly, she straightened as though standing at attention, glared at him with challenge in her storm-dark eyes, and said flatly, "She didn't like to taste it on me when we kissed." Then she strode off through the light fog toward the fighter plane just visible a hundred meters away.

Gunther's mouth would have hung open if he hadn't been

gripping the precious cigarette between his lips. He had a notion that the challenge had been for herself, not for him. She couldn't give a damn for his opinion, which made it easier to let out a truth she must surely have had to repress to keep her military career.

When the last pleasure had been wrung from the cigarette, he went back inside the hut and stretched out again on the wretched bed. The lieutenant's revelation, if such it had been, explained the underlying sorrow he had sensed, as well as the nylon stockings imbued with what he was now certain was another woman's scent.

The thought only intensified his arousal. Two women together! The strong hands that had tied him, caressing another's smooth female flesh, perhaps even leaving a red imprint on full, round buttocks...

When she returned to the hut, he had to turn quickly onto his stomach to conceal the state his fantasies had brought him to. If only she had waited a few more minutes!

"No radio contact yet. Nothing but static."

It took him a moment to realize that she had been trying to contact the air base from the plane. "Perhaps the weather..." he mumbled, trying not to wriggle against the bed.

"Maybe I should try hiking to the base instead of waiting, and leave you here. You couldn't get far on that ankle even if you decided to break your word."

"You could tie me up again, to make certain." He held his breath, not quite daring to hope.

She hadn't been looking in his direction, but now she came to stare down at him on the bed. "I guess I could do that. Now that you mention it so helpfully."

"You could...you could try to force me to tell you the way to the prison camp."

"I'm sure I could beat it out of you," she said sternly, but when he stole a look at her face, he caught a hint of a smile, the first slight lifting of her mood.

"What's eating you, Gunther?" she asked, almost companionably. "I don't need your information—you can't grow up on a Montana ranch and then become a pilot without developing a good sense of direction—but why the angling for punishment? Who'd *you* leave behind?" Her voice turned bitter with the last sentence.

Now hope seemed more permissible. He looked at her slantwise, gauging her expression, and took a chance. In an exaggerated drone he began, "I tell you nothing. Only name, rank, and..."

Before he could get to "serial number," she grabbed his shirt by the collar, hauled him over onto his back, and dragged his body entirely off the bed. From flat on the floor, he saw her knowing glance at the bulge in the crotch of his trousers, and felt it surge even higher.

"On your knees, Sergeant Bernhardt," she snapped. "Arms across the bed, ass in the air."

Gunther scrambled to obey, hindered only a little by his bound ankle.

"Drop your pants."

The dingy fabric was bunched around his ankles in moments, effectively hobbling him. He heard her move away, dared a look, and saw her drawing leather gloves from the pocket of a flight suit hanging on a peg beside the door. He shivered in anticipation, until she drew the scented nylons carefully from inside her tunic and tucked them into that same pocket. Startled, he blurted out, "Will you not tie me, *Fräulein*?"

She let the form of address pass. "Nope. This is your party, buddy. Just hang onto the bed frame and pretend." In two steps she was right there, swinging the pair of gloves, whipping them across his buttocks in a series of blows so fierce that he did have to grip the wooden frame to keep from flinching away.

"Now," she ordered, pausing and pulling up the stool so she could sit, "tell me your sins! Who have you left behind?"

Gunther had to let it out. "*Mein...mein General! Feldmarschall Rommel!*" Just speaking that name in German brought him close to tears.

She slapped his backside again. "Rommel? A fine soldier in a rotten cause. And you deserted him?" The contempt in her voice hurt more than the blow that came after, harder than any yet. The gloves had dropped to the floor, and now she was using her bare hand. Gunther visualized how it must look against his reddening skin, and came so close to ejaculation (Not yet! Not yet! She might stop!) that telling his story was a necessary distraction.

"Not deserted, no, never! We were his personal troops, the very best, sent to hold off the enemy at El Alamein while the main forces retreated." The chaos, the despair, the exhaustion, came back to him in waves.

"And you failed?" More blows now, from an open hand, varying the angle and the sharp, cracking sounds striking new territory, down to his thighs, and then returning full force to flesh already sore and beginning to throb. Then she paused again.

"No!" Gunther was half-sobbing, as much from memory as from pain. "We held as long as possible, as long as was needed, as long as enough were left alive..." He had to stop for breath.

She struck him again, but not as hard. "And then?"

"And then we were captured."

"That's *it*? That's all?"

"*I* should have died, as well." The hot tears rose behind his eyes. It all seemed so real again, yet so indistinct, the sand, the choking clouds of artillery smoke, the berserker's fury that had possessed him until it crashed at last into helplessness. "I swore that I would return to him, or die."

"And *that's* what you call a sin?" The lieutenant leaned back. Gunther could sense her beginning to retreat into her own sense of guilt.

"Please!" he gasped, lifting his hips toward her. "Please!" At any moment his arousal would turn to unsated pain. She *must* push him that last lap, raise him to the final, highest pitch. "Ma'am, Lieutenant, *Fräulein, bitte, mehr!*"

So she gave him more, spanking his sore buttocks in an unrelenting rhythm that varied but never faltered, switching hands from time to time, driving his body into the bed's leather straps until his cock felt so savagely huge and hard that he thought it would surely burst through them. What an arm she had, and such hands! At any instant now the impact of her blows would surge right through his flesh and set him off, soon, soon...but what was that sound? Artillery again?

"Now!" the lieutenant barked. "That's an order!" Suddenly her hand was no longer striking his buttocks, but squeezing them, digging into the flaming soreness, making his hips move so that his cock thumped into the straps in rhythmic thrusts that drove him to a peak beyond retreat. Then a knuckle pressed hard at the base of his balls. "Now!"

And Gunther obeyed, all guilt submerged by the power of her authority, all pleasure embraced in its full, searing glory. The long flood of release brought also a storm of cries and groans and possibly words, but if he called out any name, he could never afterward recall whether it had been that of the field marshal, or of the American woman he knew only as Lieutenant, or Ma'am. And in any case, soon enough he was crouching beside the stool with his head in her lap, face against the wool of her uniform trousers, sobbing incoherently as she stroked his hair.

"Time to pull yourself together," she said firmly after a minute or two. "That was an army jeep you heard laboring up the hill, and now it's here. We've been found."

Gunther scrambled up, forgetting that his trousers hobbled him, and nearly fell. "Please, ma'am, don't let them see!" To this woman officer, he had revealed all of himself, but he could not bear for other soldiers to know of it.

She stood, steadying him. "I'll head them off for a few minutes. Get dressed, and clean up all that." She gestured toward the bed, where the pooled proof of his great ejaculation had begun to drip between the leather straps.

Then she headed for the door, paused for a moment, and looked back over her shoulder. "You're a fine soldier, Sergeant Bernhardt, worthy of your field marshal. May you stand beside him again someday." Her expression retreated just for a moment into private sorrow before she became again the strong, confident RAF officer, and stepped out into the lifting mist.

The House on Oxford Street

By J.Z. Sharpe

Charlie, my first husband, was a gentle man. I am quite sure that's what drew me to him at first: his mild nature, the assumption that he would never hurt me, never raise a hand to me.

So, in the later years of our marriage, why did I find such fascination in those classifieds, the personal ads that filled the back pages of the freebie papers? You've seen them around: a new issue every Wednesday, fresh copies in those colorful metal boxes, lined up along the sidewalk on the way to the train station. Most people read them for the movie reviews, the listings of live music and community events, even the horoscopes. But I always turned to the personals first, and not the ones seeking mere romance and companionship:

> *Intrigued by the thought of discipline? Over the lap, bent over a chair, or on the bed? I'm experienced with the safe and sane use of spanking. All I want to do is to leave you with a little blush on your naughty bottom, no severe or permanent*

marks. But we can incorporate other kinks if you desire, such as dirty talk or teasing. This can be non-sexual, but if you become aroused by a spanking, we could discuss solutions to that too. Whatever you need, I can provide.

What magical words, how they lifted me out of the dull gray world of my marriage, my too-small-for-the-money apartment, my job. Six days a week, I went to an office where I spent long hours looking busy, working in an industrial advertising agency which catered to advertising the most unglamorous items imaginable: specialized vehicles for exterminators, massive machines for kneading dough and baking bread, computerized paint mixing systems. I worked for the agency's founder, Mr. Bean, who expected me to put in five full days during the week and half a day on Saturday. I sat at a gray metal desk and answered the phone, typed letters, and filed, filed, filed–and when I had nothing to do, I learned how to look busy, spreading papers across my desk and shuffling them every so often. It bought me time to fantasize.

Could I answer one of these ads? Did I dare?

As a matter of fact, I answered the very ad I quoted here. I crafted my reply on a Saturday morning, while Mr. Bean wrote copy for a gasket manufacturer. Every so often, he would come flying out of his office, demanding coffee or sharpened pencils, and I would quickly shove my own project under a copy of Confectionary Supplier Monthly. Mr. Bean has been known to rifle through any idle pile of papers, and I hoped he wouldn't choose my desk as this morning's target. Fortunately, my luck held out, and I was typing up an envelope to Box B345-5 at The City Gazette when Mr. Bean announced that he'd had enough for one week and would graciously allow me to leave at 12:30, half an hour earlier than usual. I slipped my envelope into the mailbox on the corner and made my train home in plenty of time.

Three weeks passed and I heard nothing. I'd given Box B345-5 my work phone number, because any strange phone calls at home would raise Charlie's suspicions, of course. Not that he really cared, but he had a tendency to latch on to the strangest things and turn tiny teapots into terrible tempests. At the office, I had to watch out for Mr. Bean, but fortunately he had no interest in my personal life. As long as I typed correspondence without a flaw and kept paper in the copy machine, my boss was happy.

Imagine my surprise then, one Tuesday, when a stranger slipped in behind the mailman, his presence impossible to ignore as he looked around the agency's tiny waiting room. I assumed he was a colleague of Mr. Bean's, perhaps the lunch appointment with a prospective client, which graced my boss's calendar for today. But no, this was not Allan Dwight from Metropolitan Optical Supply, nor was he yet another cold caller from yet another office supply dealer.

"I'm looking for Ana," he said in a soft voice that sounded just a little too calm.

"Um...that's me," I replied, peering through the little pass-through window into the reception area.

"Well, I hope you will forgive me for not calling you. My name is Rolf Warren—I believe you know me as Box B345-5."

All at once, I felt thrilled, afraid—and a little bit pissed. "How—how did you find me? I gave you my phone number, but nothing more than that."

He laughed, showing off a set of even white teeth. "My dear, information in this day and age is free. Free and easy." He held out his hand, over the narrow ledge of the window, and I stood up to shake it. "Besides, I wanted to meet you first. Very important, as I'm sure you will agree."

I could only nod.

Rolf Warren was a tall man, slender, with dark hair slicked back from a high forehead. A mustache framed his moist lips; below them grew a "soul patch" shaped like a tiny heart. He wore a long black leather trench coat and boots to match. His dark glasses were soon swept from his long nose so he could glance around the cramped reception area. "What is this, anyway?" he asked, nodding toward a framed advertisement for the Mountain Lion Professional Backhoe. "A construction firm?"

"An ad agency. Industrial accounts only, business to business. Mountain Lion is one of our biggest clients."

He nodded. "So you wouldn't take on, let's say, ice cream bars. Or a company that makes paper towels."

"Unless they were specialized paper towels. We did a whole campaign for a company that does cleaning supplies for super-clean laboratories."

"Sounds interesting."

"Not half as interesting as you might think." I looked over my shoulder, fully expecting Mr. Bean to come down the hall in search of an eraser or a handful of paper clips. "Listen, this isn't the best place to talk. I'm here until six. I don't even get a lunch hour, I'm afraid."

"That's all right," he said, sliding a cream-colored business card toward me. "I've seen all I need to see, for now. Meet me at the address on the card, as soon as you are free."

"I–I don't know if I—"

"You can. You will. I have what you are looking for, if you have the courage to receive it." He flashed a wicked smile. "I have a feeling you are the sort of girl who is never late."

Then he turned on his heel, swung the door open, and disappeared down the hall. I wanted to watch him go, but just as I got up from my seat, Mr. Bean called for me, demanding coffee. I had the afternoon to decide my fate.

I found Rolf Warren's townhouse easily enough; it was on Oxford Street, only five blocks from the agency, tucked down a narrow alley where the downtown skyline blocked the afternoon sun. Yet I had to walk around the block twice before I could face the brief journey up the marble steps to his door. I took the first circuit with my head down, storming along the sidewalk as fast as my feet would carry me. This tired me out, and the second go-round took a lot more time than the first. Still, I needed to burn off the nervous energy, and I would have done a third trip if his earlier words hadn't stopped me: "I have a feeling you are the sort of girl who is never late." No, for this, I didn't dare.

He had no doorbell, just a huge lion's head knocker that could have used some polish. Its hard sound echoed down the tiny alleyway. I waited, shifting from one foot to the other as I listened for signs of life on the other side of the door. I was about to knock again when the door swung open and I found myself face to face with a somber-faced young black man, dressed in a carefully tailored gray suit.

"You are Ana," he said in a Caribbean accent. "Mr. Warren expects you. Your punctuality will be rewarded." He waved me into the foyer and let the door fall shut behind me. "I am Creed, Mr. Warren's personal assistant. Allow me to take your coat."

I followed Creed down a narrow hallway that served as a gallery for a number of enormous oil paintings, dark and highly detailed. Each one seemed to feature a naked woman, somewhere, viewed from behind; some of them appeared to have a rosy derriere that seemed to glow amid all those deep tones. I stopped to study one in particular, with a sweet-faced blond peering over her shoulder at someone unseen. Perhaps I stopped too long, as indicated by Creed's discreet cough. "In here, please," he said, swinging open a tall oak door.

I wish I could describe my first sight of that study, but that fleeting initial impression was overshadowed by Rolf Warren himself, his hands folded, a quizzical half-smile on his face. "Thank you, Creed," he said, his eyes never leaving my face. "Lock the door behind you, will you, please?"

And then, there I was. Alone, in a room, with this man who, I suddenly realized, was about to change my life.

He stood up and walked around me, scratching his chin. "Stay right where you are," he said when I turned to follow his path. "I want to look at you. All of you." He paused behind me. "So, Ana, tell me a little about yourself."

"What would you like to know?"

"You are married, I see," he said, touching my left wrist. "For how long?"

"Eight years."

"Does he spank you?"

Well, now, nothing like getting right to the point! "No, he never has."

"Pity." He came around to face me. "You have a lovely ass, my dear. It was made to be soundly thrashed, I think." Then his face grew somber. "Do you want to be here? Answer me honestly."

I swallowed. "Yes, I–I do. I think so, anyway."

"Have you ever been spanked before? As an adult, that is?"

"No, I never have." Right away, I regretted my answer. Admitting my inexperience would not work in my favor. "But I think about it all the time. It's one of my favorite fantasies."

"Fantasy and reality are not at all the same, my dear Ana."

"I know that."

"And your husband wouldn't do this? Not even if you asked him?"

I couldn't imagine Charlie even pinching my ass, let alone toasting it with a bare palm. Hell, for the longest time, even a French kiss was more than my poor husband could handle. The time had come for something more.

"Mr. Warren, I want this," I said in a strong voice that I hardly recognized as my own. "It's something I want to experience. If I want more—well, that's for me to decide. But I want this, I can't explain why."

"Very good." From the tone of his voice, I appeared to have passed some kind of a test. He lowered himself into a nearby leather armchair and took a sip of something, probably whiskey, from a crystal glass. "Since this is your first time, I will be considerate. Not gentle, but considerate. Is that fair?"

"Quite fair."

"I must insist that we agree upon a safe word. So, if I do something you cannot bear, say 'red' and I will stop immediately. Do you understand?"

I nodded. "Okay."

"I promise you that much, at least."

"Okay."

"Well, then, now that we are in agreement, we might as well begin, yes? Go to that table, over there, on the other side of the room, and stand with your back to me. Slip off your shoes and leave them here."

I did as he asked. For the longest time, he sat silently; the only sounds were the rattle of ice in his glass and the faraway sounds of traffic in the street below. Was this all he intended to do, I wondered? What the hell, anyway! I'd come here to be spanked, to see if reality was anywhere near as good as the fantasy! I was beginning to think that I'd been had by some downtown pervert who would probably help himself to my wallet before he let me go.

But my wondering was short lived, as it turned out. I jumped as I felt his breath against the back of my neck. "Lift up your skirt," he hissed. "What do you have under there? Panty hose?" I nodded. "Argh! Miserable things!" I heard a snipping and felt cold metal against my thighs. What's this? He was cutting away my tights!

"Please don't–"

"Please don't what?" He ran the tip of the scissors along the back of my neck. "If I am doing something you don't want, use your safe word."

But I did want it, and if the price was the loss of some cheap hosiery, I was willing to pay. I held onto the edge of the table and let him chop away the rest, until my ass was exposed to the cool air of the room. He stepped back, presumably to admire his handiwork.

Then, silence. For what seemed like forever. Had he left the room? I turned my head, ever so slightly, to see if I could catch my host in the corner of my eye. Perhaps he had left the room?

Oh, no, not at all.

The first blow sliced through the air and landed on my left butt cheek, hard enough to throw me against the table and make me cry out. "What?" he said. "Isn't this what you came here for?"

"Yes, it is," I replied, my skin still burning.

He leaned closer. "Is it what you imagined?"

I nodded. It was indeed what I had imagined, what I had wished for–but not quite the same. I thought back to all the nights I had spanked myself, hidden under my blankets, while Charlie watched the eleven o'clock news downstairs. At least then I knew when the blows were coming. Here, I could predict nothing; I could only wait for that slight breeze as his hand moved toward me–

Slap! And again! The sting stayed behind, building every time he touched me. I could cry out, I could use the safe word he'd taught me, yet something held me back, something that changed as the blows rained down, switching from cheek to cheek. First the right, then the left, then perhaps two on the right, just to change things up. They still hurt now, but in a different way. I felt a blush across my face, warmth on my forehead, a quickening of the breath. He found a rhythm and I leaned into it, eager for more. I could have gone on forever.

And then–he stopped. I whimpered.

"What's wrong?" he said, laughing.

"Why? Why did you stop?"

I felt his fingers trace the curves, where my ass met my thigh. "You're getting a little too red. I can't send you away with marks. Your husband will notice." Then he slipped two fingers between my legs where my lips were already moist. He spread those lips and let his fingers take the plunge. "I see that I've made an impression."

"Yes..." I sighed, pressing myself into his hand. "More... more..."

"No, that's enough."

He took his hand away. I reached out for it, trying to find it and bring it back to me, but it was gone. Didn't he know how ready I was, how much I wanted to come? It wasn't fair!

"That's enough for the first time. Pull down your skirt. Here are your shoes."

I took the shoes from him, but didn't put them on right away. Some part of me couldn't believe that this was all I was going to get. In the meantime, my host had gone on to other tasks: raising the window shades, opening the door, and calling down the hall for Creed, who appeared almost immediately with my coat.

I followed Mr. Warren to the foyer (I don't know why, but even now I can't bring myself to think of him on a first-name basis). He opened the door himself, Creed having disappeared as quickly as he had appeared. "This is enough for a first time," he said again. "More than enough. Trust my experience, please." Then he smiled and touched my face. "You need time to consider if you want more."

"But, I do!"

"No, now is not the time to decide. Give yourself a day or two. When you are ready, you may come back. Anytime." He stepped closer to me, giving me no choice but to go through the door, out to the front step. "Anytime, my dear Ana," he said. "You were delightful." Then the door closed behind me.

I didn't realize how late it was until I got to the train station and discovered that if I didn't run like hell, I would miss the last train of the day. Miraculously, I made it and, except for a group of college students at the other end of the train coming back from a concert, I had the car to myself. This gave me time to think and to feel every bump in the tracks on my well-tanned hide. What had I done? How would I explain my late arrival home to Charlie? And more importantly, when and how could I return? An uncontrollable lust fell over me like an imaginary silk sheet. When the train pulled into my home station, I ran, once again, until I was pulling open the door to my tiny apartment. From the darkness, I knew Charlie had gone to bed already, which is just where I hoped he would be.

I stripped and pulled down the covers, climbing on top of my slumbering husband, swinging my breasts against his face until he sputtered awake.

"Huh? Ana? Izzat you?"

"Come on, honey, I want you."

"I'm sleeping..." He pressed his nose into the pillows.

"No, come on, sweetheart." I straddled his thigh so he could feel the wetness oozing from between my legs. "Let's fuck."

"Huh?" He sat up, suddenly awake. "Ana, what's wrong with you? Where have you been? Are you drunk?"

"No, I'm not drunk." I touched his hand and tried to coax it to my pussy. "Have you ever wanted to spank me?"

"God, no, Ana. That's crazy! That's sick."

"Then, let's fuck, at least. Let's fool around a little."

He reached out and gently pushed me away. "I'm tired. I'm not in the mood."

"But, Charlie, please?"

"Maybe tomorrow," he muttered, hiding under the blankets again. "But not now. I had a long day. G'night."

I sighed. Snatching a comforter from the bedroom armchair, I went out to the living room, where I spent the balance of the sleepless night with my dreams always returning to Rolf Warren and to his study, only five blocks from where I worked.

He said I could return, anytime, and I was determined to do so. I suffered through Sunday, visiting Charlie's parents in the suburbs, enduring a turkey dinner and an afternoon of boring conversation, where my mind simply could not stay in the room. How could I go back? When? I'd been given my first taste and it was not enough. I needed more.

I hatched a plan for the following day: I could tell Mr. Bean that I had a dentist's appointment in the late afternoon, which would give me a way to slip out of the office and find my way to the townhouse. I'd considered arriving first thing in the morning, but that seemed somewhat presumptuous and besides, it would mean spending the rest of the day at work on my stinging derrière. Which would be delicious, in its own way...However it happened, regardless of the time of day, I had to return as soon as possible. I had to have more.

Remarkably, Mr. Bean accepted my excuse, didn't even bother to give me the usual lecture about his preference for healthcare professionals who saw patients in the evening. I found myself headed for Rolf Warren's house, turning down his tiny street and looking for the door with the lion's head knocker—only when I came to where I thought the house was, I saw no knocker of any kind. This door was flat metal, gray, industrial, with a row of doorbells to the left, hand-written labels with company names: Spanish Scientific Transport LLC, Astrosys Inc., Application Service Unlimited. But wasn't the house here barely a few days ago? I walked around the block, and went up to the next block, just in case. No oak door, no lion's head anywhere.

Perhaps they had remodeled? Yet from the rust along its edges, this door looked like it had been there for a while. Confused, I rang one of the doorbells at random, and a disembodied voice greeted me through a tiny speaker. "Application Service, how can we help you?"

"I'm looking for Mr. Warren? Mr. Rolf Warren?"

"Sorry, nobody here by that name."

"Are you sure? I had an appointment with him here last week, in this building."

"We know everyone here. Nobody here by that name."

"Are you sure?"

My pleading was met with a click, then silence. I rang the other two doorbells, but got no reply. Baffled, I had no desire to go home or back to the office. Instead, I walked back toward the train station, and found a Starbucks, cramped and busy. I ordered a latte and took it to a corner table, where I lowered my head and began to cry.

I returned to that same block, several times, going there almost daily for several weeks after the incident. I still go back from time to time. But I never found the house; never saw Mr. Warren again.

The free papers have now been replaced by the internet, and sometimes I do browse the ads on *Craigslist*. Sometimes, I must confess, I am intrigued, especially since Charlie and I have divorced, for reasons only marginally related to my secret desires. Would I seek someone else, answer another ad? I don't know.

But every day, I still go to work at Mr. Bean's ad agency, I still type correspondence and sort through trade journals, even though Mr. Bean is nearing retirement and I know I could do something else that would pay much, much more. Yet, if I leave, how will Rolf Warren find me? Every day, as the mailman arrives and slaps another pile of envelopes and magazines on the counter, I expect to see someone else behind him. I expect to see the man to whom I would give up everything, just for his touch. I expect to see him—because I believe that yes, someday I will.

Finally

By Jessica Lennox

Saturday night again...*and not likely to be different from every other Saturday night*, my inner sarcasm chimed in. It had a point—each Saturday night was starting to look like every other one. Most people look forward to Saturday night—no work that day or the next, party as late as you want, sleep in as late as you want. I used to look forward to that too, but Saturdays had started to become routine, boring even. But I couldn't change things up. I kept holding out hope that I was going to find that one person to rock my world, and since there was only one leather club within a fifty-mile radius, that was going to have to be the place where my knight in shining leather would appear.

Every Saturday night for the past six months, I would arrive at the club early, hoping to get first dibs on anyone I might feel a connection with. The problem wasn't so much that I didn't get first dibs—I'd had plenty of offers. The problem was that I never seemed to feel a connection with anyone. I watched endless streams of people pass through the entryway, dressed in an array of fashion, from jeans to leather to latex, but not one of them sparked that tightening sensation in me that would eventually lead me to sexual abandon.

Like every Saturday night, I arrived at the club early and chose a spot in an alcove that had a perfect view of the entryway. I ordered a drink and sipped it slowly, watching and hoping for *him* to show up. After forty-five minutes of watching and sipping, I realized it truly was going to be like every other Saturday night–Mr. Wonderful was a no-show again. I finished the rest of my drink in one gulp and made my way to the bar.

As I waited for the bartender to take my order, I glanced sideways and watched a couple engaged in a boot-worshipping scene. They were close enough that I could see the submissive's tongue tracing the seams of her Master's boots, her lips kissing the leather with reverence. I felt a sudden pang of envy and quickly turned back toward the bar just in time for the bartender to appear. He prepared my drink in no time and I gave a quick glance once again toward the couple as I made my way back to my table.

As I approached the alcove, I noticed my seat was no longer unoccupied. I looked toward whomever I was now annoyed with, and stopped dead in my tracks as my eyes met the powerful stare of the person occupying my former seat. My stomach dropped and I actually felt my knees go weak for a moment before I forced myself to continue walking forward. It was *him*, and since he was only a few feet away, I had mere seconds to decide how I was going to engage him. I decided to go the easy route. I walked right up to the table, cast my eyes downward, and asked, "May I get you anything, sir?"

He didn't answer right away. He waited a few moments before responding, "Are you a waitress?"

I quickly stole a glance at his face and saw the amused smile there. "No, sir," I answered softly. "I only wish to serve you."

"Ah. Very well then..."

"Melissa, sir," I offered.

"Very well then, Melissa," he said, gently taking my hand and pulling me closer to him. "Melissa. That's a very pretty name." His hand was now caressing my arm, giving me goose bumps, causing a stirring in my pussy. He pulled me down so that I was kneeling in front of him and leaned forward, whispering in my ear. "Melissa, I would like to spank you. Would that be agreeable to you?" he asked, still caressing my arm.

His voice was like liquid pleasure, and I shivered not only from the words he spoke, but from the sensation of his breath on my skin. "Ohhh, yes, sir," I answered, squeezing my legs together to maximize the pressure on my swelling clit.

"Over my lap then," he said, patting his hand to his knee.

I gracefully arranged myself face down over his lap, suddenly full with the realization that this was going to happen, that I had finally found someone who made me feel sexy and alive and willing.

I shivered again as he lifted my skirt, pushing the fabric up over my hips. I was wearing silky black panties, and he caressed my skin through the fabric, making me wet and excited. Then he started massaging my buttocks, sometimes hard, pinching, and other times soft and sensual. I was extremely turned on and wondered when the first slap would come.

I felt his hand travel between my legs, with two quick swipes, forward then back, again through the fabric. I was certain he could feel my wetness. I wanted more of that, but he had other things in mind.

He pulled the fabric of my panties inward, anchoring it in the cleft of my ass and my pussy, the fabric pressing unmercifully against my swollen clit. I let out a moan, unable to help myself, and then I felt nothing for what seemed like an eternity. My mind started racing, wondering what he was doing. Was he looking at me? Was he watching someone else? Was he merely doing this to torment me?

My next thought was interrupted by his hand coming down on my right cheek with a stinging slap. I gasped, more from the suddenness than anything else. A few more seconds and another slap, in the perfect spot. I moaned and tried to rub myself against his legs, hoping to create some friction, but I wasn't in the proper position for it. I did, however, become aware of his hardening cock pushing into my hip. That excited me even further and I whimpered with the thought of it. Then came a barrage of slaps, some harder than others, but always in the perfect spot, alternating from left to right. I knew I would have bruises after it was all said and done, but I didn't care–it felt delicious and I didn't want it to stop. I was getting wetter with each slap and I was sure I was leaving a wet spot on his jeans.

I started feeling that familiar tingling sensation that signals the beginning of an orgasm, and I secretly prayed he wouldn't stop until I reached my peak. I tried to squeeze my legs together, but he must have felt it because he said, "No, no...not yet," and nudged them apart with his boot. I whimpered in frustration, but obeyed his implied command and forced myself to be still.

He alternated between caresses and slaps until I was on the verge of begging him to make me come, but I didn't have to. He slowly slid one hand between my legs, massaging my pussy, squeezing the lips and applying pressure to my clit while his other hand continued to alternately slap and caress my ass. That was the perfect combination and I knew he would soon push me over the edge into orgasmic bliss. Before I lost control, I had the good sense to gasp, "Sir, please, may I come for you?"

"Oh, that feels good, does it?" he asked, knowing full well that it did.

"Yessssss," I answered through gritted teeth.

"Yes, what?" he corrected.

"Yes, sir," I panted.

"Good girl. I know this feels good because I can feel how wet your pussy is. You're dripping all over my leg and making my cock hard. I wish I could fuck you right here and now, but I think I'll settle for you coming while I spank your pretty ass and fondle your pussy. You'd like that, wouldn't you? To come all over my hand?"

"Yessss, sir...*please!*" I begged.

"Mmmm. Good girl. Come for me. Now."

His voice was so commanding I would have done anything he asked, and I couldn't have been more grateful at that moment that he was allowing me to come for him. I concentrated on his hand massaging my pussy, his hand stinging my skin, and then I took a deep breath and let out a moan so loud I felt it vibrate throughout my entire body. As I twitched and bucked, he squeezed my pussy, clamping the lips together, forcing my juices out and over his hand.

When I was completely spent, I lay there like a limp rag doll as he caressed my thighs and buttocks with his fingertips. "I take it you're satisfied?" he asked, the amusement apparent in his voice.

I was in such a state of bliss, it took every ounce of remaining energy just to mumble, "Yes, sir. Thank you."

"My pleasure. Come here," he said softly, pulling me up so that I was sitting on his lap. I relaxed and leaned into him as he held me with one arm and stroked my hair with the other. I felt his breath against my skin as his mouth traveled its way up my neck and settled against my ear. "I'd like to take you home with me, Melissa. There are things I want to do to you that can't be done here."

I thought I knew what he was implying, but then I was certain when he took my hand and slowly moved it downward, forcing it between us where my hip met his lap. I felt the hardness there and silently thanked my lucky stars for finding him—finally.

Fit to be Tied, Bound to be Gagged

By Allison Wonderland

"When I say bend over, you say how far."

It wasn't a command.

It wasn't a demand.

It wasn't even a reprimand.

It was a wisecrack, plain and simple, a riposte delivered in response to a mildly witty comment I'd made about my fiancée's promotion to station manager. But her remark had sparked my curiosity, let loose a slew of what-ifs. *What if she means it?* I wondered, sensing the beginnings of a smile. And then my pessimistic side kicked in–*what if she doesn't?*–and the smile began to shrivel.

I spent the remainder of the day alternating between two of the seven deadly sins: lust and envy. I imagined myself reclining on our bed, a riding crop pinched like a rose between my teeth, waiting for Charlene to whale on my tail end. I thought of the imprints and handprints she would stamp on my flesh. I'd be seeing red, bold red, like the stripes in the American flag. And what could be more patriotic than a good old-fashioned spanking? The more I fantasized, the more I yearned for a promotion of my own. Or was it a demotion?

People were always talking about rising to the top. But what about rising to the bottom?

Charlene had awakened in me a dormant desire to be dominated. That woman never fails to amaze me—we hadn't even explored the fantasy yet and already she'd proven herself a power player in power playing.

By week's end, I'd become flat-out fanatical about my fantasy. Everything became something we could use to enact it. I'd glimpse the clipboard in Charlene's hands and wonder how big of a bang it would make if it struck my backside. I'd get together with a college buddy and bemoan the fact that the school had no lending library for fraternity paddles. Even the Bible had paddling potential, I realized—Charlene could beat the word of God into me, giving the term Bible-thumper a whole new meaning.

I created entire narratives in my head. In my favorite scenario, I waltz into a sex toy store and inquire about one of the whips on display. *How much is that flogger in the window? I'll take it. She'll love it.* I purchase the paddle for Charlene's birthday, which we won't be celebrating for another seven months, and request that the clerk gift-whap the present. When the big day rolls around, Charlene opens the box and starts salivating. *I take it you love it*, I say. *Spanks for thinking of me*, she says. Then we hug and kiss and I make one of my mildly witty comments: *I thought we'd try something a little different this year—instead of getting your birthday whacks, you'll be giving them.*

I wondered what started it all. Was it really just the power of suggestion? No, I think I've always been partial to pain, ever since high school at least. You know how guys all across America like to go around whupping each other's butts in the locker room? You come out of the shower and there's a guy there, lurking, smirking, just waiting to smack your bare behind with a crisp white towel? Well, I liked being his victim. I always looked forward to gym class.

Now that I was older, wiser, hornier, the fantasy didn't stop with spanking. I began considering the chains of command. I'd step over cords and wires strewn throughout the studio and wonder how they'd feel coiled like rope around my wrists. I'd pass a cop car and yearn to hear the cold clink of handcuffs as the lock clicked into place, binding my wrists behind my back. Or perhaps the cuffs could be fastened in front, the shackles resting against my thighs, the chain of the manacles curving against my erection. I even thought about applying to the police academy, but decided it was too late in the game for a career change.

Ambitions aside, I continued to think kink, to nurture the fantasy, to keep it alive and throbbing. I knew it was a selfish fantasy, that it completely went against the whole it's-better-to-give-than-to-receive philosophy. But I would have given anything to be on the receiving end of a knick-knack paddle whack.

I made the mistake of divulging my desires to our male coworkers, some of whom had cited rage and resentment, among other things, as proper reactions to the news of my fiancée's promotion. Being happy for her, they'd insisted, was not only inappropriate, it was also not an option. I'd tried to assure them that I didn't feel threatened, that I was more than comfortable working for a woman—and one whom I was in a relationship with besides—but I didn't get very far.

So I should have known better than to confide in them about my fantasies of being dominated. They were hardly understanding, much less encouraging. After the initial shock wore off, after they got the guffaws out of their system, they proceeded to issue warnings. I won't regurgitate the nonsense they spewed about emasculation, but one snippet of the conversation is worth repeating:

"I'd say you're plenty whipped as it is," a veteran cameraman informed me.

"On the contrary," I lamented, "I'm not whipped nearly enough."

Undaunted by my coworkers' words of discouragement, I mustered the mettle to talk to Charlene.

Two months later.

It wasn't that I expected her to be a hard sell. But I couldn't just assume she'd be up for it. We'd hit bottom before–she'd walk past me, smug in a snug pair of jeans, and I'd give her posterior a pat; I'd walk past her, smug in a snug pair of briefs, and she'd give my posterior a pat. But those were love taps–not amorous but frivolous, spontaneous.

Just like our sex life. We never had a game plan, didn't strategize. We only discussed it after the act, when we'd sit and recap the highlights like sports commentators.

So I couldn't just spring this on her. That would mean risking assent with apprehension, or worse, dissent with disgust. This had to be consensual, mutual, because even though I would be the one feeling pain, Charlene would be the one dealing pain, and she had to be okay with that.

"Are you okay with that?" I asked, my casual inflection no match for my tattered nerves as I sat in front of Charlene's desk while she stood behind it.

Charlene seemed to glory in my distress. "What exactly are you suggesting?" she queried, hoisting her hands onto her hips.

I tried hard not to revert to my squeaky pubescent voice as I said, "I'm suggesting that we take our work home with us."

I took in Charlene's expression–the tiny twinkle in her eyes, the giddy grin on her lips.

I could tell that she was up for it.

More than up for it.

Into it.

Like she'd been thinking about it too.

As much as I had.

As long as I had.

How about that? I worried for nothing.

"It does seem logical, doesn't it?" Charlene replied, rubbing the rounded edges of her clipboard. "I'm already your superior at work. Why not also be your superior at play?"

"What are we going to feed these people?" Charlene ponders, sifting through a pile of catering menus.

"The wedding guests? I don't know. Let them eat cake."

Charlene's attention strays from the menus to me. "You're fixated on that package over there, aren't you?" she says, referring to the nondescript cardboard box presently sitting on top of her bureau. "You and your wandering eyes," she scolds, wagging her finger at me.

"There's something in there."

Charlene chuckles. "You're about as sharp as a feather," she quips, and whacks me in the arm with her pillow. "It's no wonder the marketing department still hasn't given you a raise. You, my love, are a hack-of-all-trades."

My cock quivers. When Charlene belittles me like this, when she subjects me to this kind of degradation and humiliation, I feel like a million fucks. I like to think of this debasement as an aural aphrodisiac, a preamble to our power play.

Charlene sets the menus on the nightstand, indicating that, for the moment at least, she no longer cares about the sustenance we are obligated to provide for our wedding guests. She climbs off the bed and shuffles across the room. When she returns, she is holding the coveted parcel. I watch as she peels away the tape, folds back the flaps, and reaches into the confines of the box. When her hand emerges, it is accompanied by a paddle.

My cock shivers. I scrutinize the implement. The flapper is fashioned from sturdy plastic and enveloped in red velvet. Near the top there is a large aperture designed to resemble a valentine heart.

Charlene's lips curve into a shimmering moon of mischief. "I really love the symbolism it conveys," she shares, and flicks her wrist, treating the flapper like a ping-pong paddle. "You know— you always hurt the one you love?"

Were I not too busy wondering what sound the paddle will make when it connects with my rear end, I would say something in response.

"Proposal position," Charlene instructs. Her words are sharp and emphatic, and I feel as though I've just been jolted out of a sound sleep. "And if you need to get down on both knees for this," she continues, as I scramble out of bed, "I have no objections."

I drop to my knees. I can feel my smile expanding, stretching until it fills my entire face. Contrary to my coworkers' caveats, I've never felt more masculine than when I'm submitting to Charlene. As I await further instruction, I take a moment to admire my fiancée. Charlene doesn't go for the traditional dominatrix getup–she has no interest whatsoever in leather or latex or lace-up boots. Instead, she prefers to do her dominating decked out in flannel *I Love Lucy* pajamas and a pair of rubber-soled slippers.

Charlene shoves her pants and panties off her hips and

toward her ankles. I watch as she slips her hand between her legs, dips her digits between her thighs, splaying the lips of her cunt and unveiling her clit. "Let the cunnilingus commence," she commands, and I am all too happy to acquiesce.

Charlene orchestrates my every move, telling me how and where and when to touch her.

"In," she says, and I begin at the slit, my tongue venturing inside, streaking the sleek interior. I soak in her wetness, letting her flavor fill my mouth, her aroma spur my arousal.

"Out," she says, and my tongue quickly emerges. I traverse the length of her labia, navigating the folds of her pussy, seeking every curve, every crinkle, as though I am tracing the configuration of lines on a roadmap.

"Fuck," she says as I caress her clit. Her hands grip my hair, her fingers scraping my scalp. I manage to tilt my head back slightly so I can admire her climax–the avid rocking of her hips, the fervid rippling of her belly.

"Stand erect," she instructs, still panting, now pulling her pants and panties back into place. I am on my feet in an instant. Charlene takes a gander at my groin. My cock resembles a flagpole. "You're such a good listener." She points to the door. "Powder room," she dictates, and I trail her like Mary's little lamb. En route to the bathroom, she makes a brief stop at the bureau and collects a trio of silk scarves.

Charlene will use these scarves as manacles. She will wind them around my wrists and swaddle me to the stainless steel shower rod mounted above the bathtub. Self-proclaimed progressives, Charlene and I consider the bondage-and-bedposts custom a little outmoded, though it would hardly matter if we felt differently, as our bed has no posts to which she can tie me. Recently, Charlene began wearing the scarves to work. It is her way of reminding me of my pleasure.

And, more significantly, my place.

We move at a leisurely pace, she facing me, me facing her, the floorboards groaning beneath our feet as we navigate the hallway, in pursuit of our destination.

"You're going to look adorable with little hearts all over your heinie," Charlene coos, tracing the outline of the valentine with her fingertips.

I huff, my eyes spinning in their sockets. "Gag me."

"Only if you ask nicely," she returns, and advances toward me, the scarves clenched in her fists.

I gasp and gulp and grimace. The whole Cowardly Lion routine.

"Cut the histrionics," Charlene demands.

I disobey, whimpering in anticipation. "Please," I plead.

Charlene smirks. "Try to restrain yourself."

I eye the scarves in her hand. "I like it better when you do it."

"Lazy bones," Charlene scoffs as she grasps my wrists, propelling my arms above my head. Then swiftly, because practice has made perfect, she affixes the restraints, leaving absolutely no wiggle room. Finally, with a single yank, she divests me of my boxer shorts, baring her bottom's bottom.

"Bend over," she commands, pinching the flesh of my ass between her fingers.

I twist my neck to look at her. She is all smiles and her eyebrow is cocked, much like my phallus. "How far?" The second the question leaves my lips, Charlene stuffs the scarf between them, filling my mouth with the taste and texture of silk.

She seizes the paddle with both hands, wielding the implement like a baseball bat. "Arch your back," she instructs, and I thrust my rear end toward her. "Good. Stop there." I do as I am told, my spine curved just enough for her comfort.

But not for mine.

Charlene takes a swing at me. The paddle cracks against my flesh, causing my ass to sting, and the pleasure to zing through my body.

Batter up. Another swing, another hit. I close my eyes. This helps me focus. I don't want to block out the pain–I want to lock it in, wallow in it.

As the paddling progresses, Charlene's whacks become rough and rapid and rapturous. "I heart you," she says, and giggles. She takes such pleasure in my pain.

She swings again, scores a home run. My entire body cheers, ecstasy clenching every muscle, squeezing every nerve.

My wrists ache. I strain but don't struggle. My backside pulsates, mimicking the thrusting motions of fucking. It's erotic, hypnotic. There is power in submission, the power of having complete trust in another human being.

Charlene pummels my posterior until my cock is rigid and turgid, as stiff as the paddle clutched between her fingers. She releases me from the restraints. "Take care of business," she dictates, and I obey. I wouldn't dream of asking her to defile her own hands.

She peers over my shoulder while I work–supervising, I should note, not observing. She ensures that my fingers are folded securely around my cock, checks the speed of my fist as it travels along the shaft. "It looks like you're shaking a bottle of champagne," she quips, just before the cork pops and the ejaculate, thick and slick, splashes against the tiles.

Charlene squeezes my shoulders, kisses my neck. "You really took a beating," she says, removing the gag from my mouth. She takes my hand and guides me to the mirror.

I turn around, crick my neck, and inspect the bruises. My flesh flares. I'm seeing red. Charlene rubs the rounded edges of one of the hearts, then ventures inside its outline. Her nails scrape the sentiment *Be mine*.

The spanking's over, but I'm still under her spell. "With pleasure."

"And pain," she adds, squishing my sore cheeks between her palms.

I groan, grinning, head spinning.

Being a bottom is the tops.

Thin-Skinned

By Jean Roberta

"You're sweet, baby," she laughed, running a warm hand up my neck as she pulled me close for a kiss. "Always ready."

The bouquet of orange prairie lilies Carrie had just given me lay on my kitchen table like a collection of toy trumpets, perfuming the air. She often gave me flowers, like a chivalrous suitor courting a lady in a Hollywood romance set in imaginary Times of Old.

"Just for you," I corrected her. "You're the one I want."

"Mm." I could feel the strength in her arms as she wrapped them around my ribs. She squeezed me, reminding me how small and slim I was by her sturdier standards. Everything is relative.

Carrie felt solid, not fat or self-indulgent. Her flesh felt reliable. "I can smell you," I told her. Her breath, her scalp, her neck, her armpits, her cleavage, her sensitive belly, her hot crotch—I loved the different aromas that came from each distinct location to blend into a unique symphony of smells.

Her eyes held a question. Beneath her assertive dyke bravado, she was terribly afraid of being told that some essential part of her was sour, offensive, redolent. I knew that much about her.

Carrie's smell could probably bring me out of a coma. Words couldn't describe how much I loved it, but I had to try.

"I love your smell," I explained. "I don't want you to wash it away." I wondered why she couldn't read my mind and recognize a compliment when she heard it. Then I realized that she wasn't an egotist, someone who expects compliments. Everyone was like a bouquet to her, and I wanted to give her enough to let her know her own worth. Enough to bind her to me.

She kissed me in her usual way, pressing my lips as gently as though I were sleeping and she didn't want to wake me up. As I responded, she pressed harder, parting my lips. Her tongue slid inside to touch mine. Her arms held me possessively, urging me closer until my breasts were mashed hotly against hers.

As her tongue explored my mouth, her hands rose as if of their own accord to the back of my head and slid up beneath my sweaty hair. Oh, this was almost the best part of the seduction. The palms of her hands were electric with her energy, and they sent tingles all through my scalp.

I moaned. She chuckled, not smugly, but with delight in the magic that always brought me into the well, as I thought of it: a bottomless place of wanting, of getting, of dissolving together.

"Baby." It sounded more intimate than my name, Joanne, which anyone could use. "I want your skin."

I reached down to my chest and undid the top three buttons of my sweater. Carrie took over, steadily working her way down to the bottom and pulling the two sides of the clingy garment apart, revealing my shiny beige bra. It was almost the color of my skin, but was lightly padded and made of a fabric that drew attention to my breasts. The construction of the cups created a suggestive shadow between them. I wanted to look as sexy as possible, for her.

Please admire me, I thought. I remembered that to her, and to all the other butches I had known, pillowy breasts of one's own were a nuisance, unwanted headlights over a muscular chest and deep lungs, something to be stuffed into no-nonsense sports bras and tight T-shirts, the firmer the better.

She unhooked my bra as though opening a surprise package to find a treasure within. My little breasts reacted to the cool air of my apartment and her hot gaze by shivering. My nipples puckered and hardened.

I hoped she loved my tits just as they were. She had told me she did, and I wanted to believe her.

She cupped them, squeezed them, and ran her thumbs roughly across my nipples. She was pushing for a reaction. "Jo," she asked me, "d'you think you'll ever have milk in these?"

I wished I knew how to turn myself into a fountain—spontaneously, just for Carrie. I imagined my breasts as sources of nourishment, nectar for a god or goddess. The imagined pull of her hot lips sucking milk out of me sent chills up my spine.

I remembered why all female mammals can produce milk. "If I have a baby. Sure, I'll breast-feed when–if, if the time comes."

Did she want to find a sperm donor to get me pregnant? Did she really want to co-parent a child? That would be the most serious commitment she could make. How well would that fit in with her plans for a scholarly career?

"Mm. You'd be a sexy mama." This was obviously her fantasy of the moment, not a serious proposal. I needed to stay present, not run on ahead to a domestic future that only looked cozy from a distance.

She bent her head to suck on each of my hard nipples in turn. The wet heat of her mouth on my flesh mixed with the sight of the short, thick, wood-brown hair on the top of her head and the smell of her shampoo and her scalp-sweat rising to my nose. I had thought of my hair as being the same color as hers until I had seen us together in a mirror that showed my hair as several shades lighter, almost honey-blonde. Everything is relative.

I could imagine Carrie as a fur-bearing animal suckling its mate, preparing to mount her.

What animal would do that? Well, a shapeshifter, then. A werewolf or some other magical human who grows fur and fangs under a full moon.

I moaned, softly at first, then louder to let her know how much I liked her attention. She nibbled my left nipple like a playful but well-trained dog, and swirled her strong tongue around it. She kneaded my right breast to keep it alert until she switched sides. She was leaning on her elbows but letting me feel the pressure of her body on mine.

I felt heat in my face, and knew I must be flushed. She eased me down from a sitting to a reclining position on my sofa. So this was where she planned to take me, as though we were both too impatient to walk a few feet to my bedroom. *Was sofa-sex more casual or more passionate than bed-sex? Or did it depend on the situation?* I couldn't think.

She held my right nipple tightly between her lips and gently pulled away, stretching my flesh. When she let go, she smiled into my eyes, assuring me that she would never really hurt me. Or at least, this was how I interpreted her look. I looked down and saw how long my nipple was before it eased back into a rounder shape. *I'm the shapeshifter*, I thought. *You can mold me any way you like. Almost.*

She stretched my left nipple as she had the right one, and left them both bigger and redder than they were before. They both shone with her saliva.

My thighs spread apart as though they had a will of their

own. I wanted to invite her in.

"You're so beautiful. You're not crying, are you?"

I felt as if she had poured cold water on my head. Were my eyes filling up, and could she see the pool of need and disappointment just waiting to spill over? "No," I insisted. I didn't want to be the kind of woman who weeps for no good reason. Or who weeps for any reason. Tears had always seemed to me to be visible proof of feminine helplessness and lack of control. I would not cry.

"Okay," she soothed me. "I just thought your eyes were wet, but I bet you're wetter somewhere else."

Okay. It was okay for my cunt to cry with need, to leak pungent moisture into my panties or leave a puddle on my furniture because I wanted to be filled down there, stroked and teased and fucked raw. It was okay for her to feel a feral joy running through her veins when I showed my hunger for her. Now that the Feminist Sex Wars were over, it was okay for her to bring her inner predator and our favorite toys out to play when I was ready and begging. But neither of us thought it was okay for me to cry.

I would have to think about the politics of body fluid when I was less distracted.

"Do you want a spanking?" Her mouth was so close to my ear that she seemed to be thinking aloud, inside my mind. "Maybe it's what you need, baby. You could let go."

We were both far from being veterans of the local leatherdyke community, and neither of us trusted the ones we knew of well enough to play with them. In the dim light of the dyke bar, they looked as hard-eyed as reptiles, and they gave off a smell of amused condescension toward us peasants, the ones without titles who didn't go to the bar in black leather from head to foot and who weren't in their loop.

Or maybe Carrie and I were both too afraid of rejection.

We did well enough on our own. Carrie, the dyke in my life ("girlfriend" seemed too casual a term, and "lover" sounded like a role in a Victorian scandal), and I tried out our fantasies in private. We had each spanked each other's asses until they were as red as ripe tomatoes, and we were secretly proud of how far we had come.

I suspected that our switchable natures were as *politically incorrect* to the in-crowd now as sex toys were to the anti-porn feminists of a quarter-century ago, but we didn't care. I knew I could hit her sassy bottom until my palm stung like crazy, and she would let me. That gave me permission to lie squirming and wailing under her hand until she had given me enough. Or until my submission had gone to her head like champagne.

I pulled her face to mine and kissed her, slowly and deeply. Reluctantly, I pulled away to catch my breath. "Yes," I confessed. "I need a spanking."

She grinned. *Oh yes, she wanted to dish it out.* "Is Jo a bad girl? You need some correction, don't you?"

"Not now," I told her. I hoped she understood me, despite the clumsiness of my words. "Please don't punish me tonight. I'm not a brat. I just want to be—at your mercy. Life is unfair, that's the thing." I couldn't be sure this made any sense to her, but bless her, she smiled knowingly. Even if she wasn't exactly on my wavelength, she could fake it.

Carrie backed off me and sat upright on the sofa, looking at me like a theatre-goer watching the stage. I stood up and lowered the zipper of my jeans. Trying to strip for her as gracefully as possible, I shimmied as I pulled the waistband down over my hips, my thighs, and down to my ankles, where I stepped out of each denim pant leg.

I stood still for a moment, letting her grin at my red silk

panties, my little indulgence. Then I slid them down, bending my knees so I wouldn't have to bend over from the waist. When my panties were around my ankles, I quickly pulled off my socks so I could remove everything together and toss it all aside as though I never planned to wear clothes again.

She patted her lap. I could smell my own crotch as well as a gust of perfume from the lilies in the kitchen. They needed to be placed in a vase with water and the powdered preservative that always came with a bouquet from a florist shop. Lilies seemed like the divas of the plant world—"thin-skinned" as my mother would put it, though she only applied that term to human beings, usually to me. My mother didn't understand my relationships with women, and accused me of being "thin-skinned" when I reacted to her advice on how I could find a good man before it was too late.

I spread myself over Carrie's lap. Here was where I belonged.

I felt her hesitate for a second, trying to decide what tone would go with a thrilling but unfair spanking. I pictured myself as the victim of a kidnapper or a corrupt cop who had arrested me on a trumped-up charge. "You can't get away from me now," she growled, though she wasn't holding me in place. I was bracing myself with my hands on the floor. "Your sexy bum is just too tempting."

The first slap was harder than I expected. I heard it before I felt it, and then the shock spread outward from the center of my right ass-cheek like the vibrations of an earthquake. I wriggled, and she responded by laying her non-spanking arm across my lower back and curling her finger around my ribs.

She left me in suspense just long enough for my left cheek to twitch, knowing what was coming. I felt her thighs move under me as she settled into a comfortable position.

Whap! Somehow it took me by surprise, and then she picked

up the beat, hitting me on alternate cheeks. The repeated stings transformed into heat that spread beyond the point of impact.

Whap! "D'you give in?"

Her question surprised me, since I didn't know my surrender was her goal. After all, she was holding me down and spanking me. I had given my consent before she started.

Two thoughts flashed into my mind: *I've already given in, so don't ask me to say it.* And: *I'll never give in. Or give you up. I'd rather die.*

I couldn't think clearly, but I could squeak out an answer. "No."

Her rhythm faltered. She ran a light, comforting palm over both my burning ass-cheeks as if to show me her good intentions. "Stubborn little thing, aren't you?" I knew this was not a rhetorical question. She really wanted to know.

"Yep." I didn't know what else to say.

Whap! This time it really hurt, and I couldn't hold back the tears.

Her rhythm picked up, as though she were responding to a dare. "You want me to stop, baby? You have to say it." We hadn't agreed on safe-words. When we started out, we thought we could communicate perfectly well in plain English.

"Owwoo, that's enough! Stop!" I felt wet and raw all over.

"Baby, it's okay." She was helping me to scramble up and off her. I couldn't bear to sit down, so I straddled her lap, kneeling on the sofa and hanging onto the back of it. She pulled my arms around her neck and wiped my face, shushing me. "Honey, good girl, sweet thing, baby," she called me, the endearments pouring out like a lotion to soothe the pain. "Do you know how much I love you, Joanne?"

How could I? No one really knows what someone else feels, but at the moment, I was willing to take her word for it. The heat in my sore ass had ignited my cunt. My clit was on full alert.

She was kissing me, running her sweaty hands up and down my back. "Are you my hot bitch?" The answer seemed obvious.

I rubbed my hard nipples against her fuller breasts, moving up and down in my semi-seated position. I still didn't want to rest my behind on anything, even the inviting surface of her thighs.

I wanted to inhabit a role that would make me feel less exposed. "You pig," I told her, smiling to show that I didn't mean it. "I bet you always rape your prisoners."

"Especially when they're sassy young women," she agreed. She slid one finger easily up into me and used it to scope out the territory. "You're so wet," she sneered. "You're asking for a good fucking."

I groaned as another of her fingers slid in beside the first. She used them to stroke my wet folds, carefully avoiding my sensitive clit. She probed certain spots and gently scratched my inner walls, making sure that no part of my center remained untouched. "You can't resist me," she dared.

Trying not to respond brought me closer to coming. I felt a strange dull ache deep inside my cunt, and guessed she was rubbing my cervix. For some reason, the feeling made my heart ache too.

"I'm just getting started," she bragged. "Sluts like you can never hold out." That almost brought me over the edge, but not quite.

She readjusted her position in order to bring her other hand to her crotch as she held me impaled on three fingers. She found my clit and squeezed it in rhythm, almost in time with my heartbeat. I closed my eyes, afraid of what must be showing on my face. "Ohhh!" I moaned as she fucked me harder, mercilessly rubbing my clit.

I came hard, over and over, releasing a whole kaleidoscope of feelings. I could imagine them bursting out between my legs in splashes of red, orange, yellow, all the colors of the rainbow.

Carrie raised her pungent hands to my head and buried them in my hair, mixing the smell of my innermost depths with the scent of hair products and natural hair-smell. She guided my face to hers and kissed me. Her tongue slid into my mouth in imitation of her fingers in my cunt, and I welcomed it.

She pulled her mouth away to tell me her plan. "I hope you're not tired yet, baby. There's more coming." I was tired, but I didn't want the sex to end. I had never felt so closely connected to her, and I knew what was coming after this night: her departure to the city.

"Go find Roger," she said. "Bring him to me." Roger was our dildo, the one she liked to use on me, and that I liked her to use on me, as distinct from the one I used on her, which we kept at her place. Roger was named for an old word meaning "to fuck." As a history major, Carrie had been seduced by the exotic charms of the past, like those of a foreign country. I liked the sense of secret rebellion that clung to archaic words for sex.

I walked to my bedroom, feeling her eyes on my sensitive ass. Roger was a sparkly silicone device, not like the temperamental cock of a real man. He was more like a magic wand from Fairyland, and he had already brought me so much pleasure that just the sight of him could make me damp and tingly.

I opened the bottom drawer of my bureau, and pulled out the patchwork square (originally a quilt for a doll) that I kept Roger wrapped in. The harness was under the short red nightgown with white fake fur that Carrie had given me for Christmas.

I walked back into my front room, fitting Roger into the harness that would go around Carrie's hips.

"I'll do that," she told me. She was glowing, and I guessed that she was offering to take control of the ravishment scene.

"Yes, ma'am."

"On your hands and knees, girl. Keep them spread apart."

I planted my knees and my palms on the carpet, noticing the fine grit that needed to be vacuumed out of it. The smell of dust added to the realism of the captive-humiliation scene.

I heard the rasp of Velcro as Carrie adjusted the harness that held Roger at her crotch. Not being able to see her behind me added to the suspense.

Then I could feel the heat of her body near my ass as her fingers slid down my crack and into me. The floorboards creaked as she planted her knees behind me. She held one of my hips with one hand, and the pressure of her fingers made me jerk.

The smooth head of Roger nosed my opening, guided by Carrie. I tilted my hips and spread my knees farther apart as he was pushed all the way into me.

"Take it," she advised. Carrie moved tentatively at first, then settled into a steady rhythm of push and pull. "Good girl," she told me.

I moved as well as I could in my position, loving the fullness inside me. The heat and friction of Carrie moving against my behind felt distracting until I stopped trying to focus either on being rubbed or being fucked. The fucking felt like such a logical sequel to the spanking that the twinges in the stretched skin of my ass-cheeks blended with the deeper twinges inside me in a kind of symphony of feeling.

As if from a distance, I heard sounds coming out of my mouth. My clit was teased as Roger was pushed in and withdrawn, rubbing the outer lips of my cunt. I felt overwhelmed, but I didn't know yet if I could come.

Then Carrie pressed herself up against the touchy skin of my ass-cheeks. "Good girl," she repeated. "Let go." And I did, squeezing Roger inside me in a series of spasms. I wailed as I came, letting out lungfuls of air and breathing them in.

After a few more thrusts, as if to squeeze out the last drops of my ecstasy, Carrie carefully pulled Roger out and held him possessively. I turned my head and caught a glimpse of the dildo covered with my juice.

"Honey," she said, "lie here with me. On the floor."

I sprawled on my stomach at first, then rolled onto my side. An image of myself vacuuming in the nude flashed through my mind before I decided to think about housekeeping later, at a more convenient time. I heard the sounds of Carrie removing the harness with Roger in it, and carelessly tossing the whole contraption onto the sofa.

She spooned me from behind, pressing her whole body against me. My ass-cheeks responded to her presence. I imagined them saying "Eep!" and "Uh!" and "Ahh!"

She pushed one arm under my ribs so she could hold my two tits in her two hands. I knew that the weight of my body would force her to change position soon, but in the meanwhile, I felt weightless in her arms.

"Joanne," she said against my neck. "You know I'm not leaving you behind."

I knew she didn't intend her move to the city to be a coward's way of dumping me. I trusted her good intentions. But I also knew that the university would be full of other smart women, including other Ph.D. candidates. Somewhere between a heated discussion of the true political significance of the Magna Carta and one about the role of women in modern revolutionary movements, Carrie might recognize an unexpected soul mate.

"We'll visit," she told me. "You can come see me there, and

I'll come home here on holidays."

"I know." I felt very small.

"If I spent all my time with other historians, I'd go berserk." *Ah yes, the ecstatic battle-rage of Scandinavian warriors.* I could picture her in berserk mode, but more from the lust I knew than from lust for the blood of enemies. I could feel her breathing.

"Mm," she said, "turn around. My arm will fall asleep if I don't move it." Obediently, I rolled over to face her. She wrapped one arm around my neck and the other around my hips.

Beyond the musky smell of our bodies and the smell of my carpet, the perfume of the lilies wafted into my consciousness, reminding me that they were also alive and needed attention to keep them perky for as long as possible.

"Joanne," she persisted, "you know I need to do this if I'm going to have a teaching career to pay the bills and write books. Eventually."

"I know." I really didn't want to hold her back. I just didn't want to be left behind.

An image of ivy-covered stone buildings arose in my mind's eye. I could see her entering one of them, looking nervous but eager, another aspiring scholar who would memorize the campus map as she adjusted to her new role in the temple of knowledge. I could sense that part of her was already there.

"Baby, would you consider giving up your job here and moving to the city? It would be cheaper if we shared an apartment."

I stared into her brown eyes, and saw her anxiety. *She* was asking *me* to join her, and she couldn't be sure how I would respond.

That was why she hadn't asked me before. I could hardly

believe my luck. Then I could hardly believe I hadn't guessed what was going through her mind.

"I'd have to give two-weeks notice," I reminded her. She already knew this.

"There are community-based arts organizations in the city. More of them, actually. You would be in demand as a coordinator."

I almost laughed aloud. "So you think I'd be hard to replace?"

She made some growling sounds in her throat, recognizing a double-bind when she heard it.

"Do you *want* me, honey? Right now?" I gathered one of her generous breasts in one of my hands, enjoying its heat and pliability.

Carrie groaned. "Yeah. I don't want to spend a whole year without you. I want you with me."

"Okay," I told her, rolling her onto her back as I raised myself up on my elbows. I smiled into her eyes. "Okay. You asked for it." I had never thought of her as a delicate plant before, but now I felt her trembling with need, vibrating in a frequency that was very clear to me.

As I kissed her lips, I wanted to taste her somewhere else. I wanted to swallow her uncertainty, her fear of not measuring up, and feed her the taste of her own natural goodness.

I wanted to spank her without mercy for making me worry so much about losing her. I didn't care whether my need for payback was fair. I suspected I could satisfy us both by first getting her to confess her feeling of guilt. Then I could dish out the cure. That scene might not be logical, but I knew it would work.

A roomful of bare bottoms, in all shapes, sizes, and colors, sprang into my mind. Oh yes, there were asses willing to be spanked, and hands willing to land on bare flesh or wield the implements that could leave interesting marks as well as memories.

I knew there must be spankers as well as spankees in the big, wicked port city where both of us were going to make a fresh start. If Carrie and I found a group of kindred spirits, their company might strengthen our relationship by expanding our options.

The thought of other people watching our spankings, and letting us watch theirs, made me squirm. But it no longer freaked me out.

Sliding down Carrie's body to her dewy bush, I caught a whiff of something rich and salty that could have been the smell of her or of a phantom breeze from the ocean beyond the city.

"Just wait," I promised. She seemed to know what I meant.

Slippering

By Lee Ash

"She needs a good slippering."

"Excuse me?" Duncan was not sure if he had heard the words correctly. He frowned as he leant closer.

"I said, she needs taking in hand. She needs a good slippering."

It had been a typical Friday night at Jake and Veronica's, but this comment was far from typical and completely unexpected. After dining, they had retired to Jake's study to indulge in port and cigars as though they were in a Victorian gentlemen's club. The walls were lined with care-worn books and, whilst the furniture was all old, it helped to maintain the comfortable atmosphere. The air was rank with the stench of spent Havanas and the port had already created a warm glow in the pit of Duncan's satiated stomach.

Leaning forward in his batwing chair, Duncan said, "Slippering?"

Jake laughed. "You make it sound as though the idea hadn't occurred to you. You've just spent the last ten minutes telling me about your ailing finances, and your wife spent forty minutes over dinner telling me about the three new frocks that she's bought and the pearl necklace she's *needing* from the jewelers. Trust me, Duncan, I know what I'm talking about. Debbie needs a good slippering."

Duncan smiled uncertainly. He wondered if this was a joke that he was too muddleheaded to catch. "Slippering with a slipper?"

Jake drew on his cigar. When he spoke, the words were made solid by smoke. "One of you needs to show a little discipline and the other one needs to respond to it. It might as well be you wielding the rod. It would sort out your financial problems, and it might just save your marriage."

Duncan shook his head. He waved the suggestion away with the hand that held his cigar. "I can't beat my wife. That's not a solution and I'm damned sure Debbie wouldn't stand for it either."

"I'm not suggesting you beat your wife. I'm simply suggesting that the pair of you come to an arrangement. How many of those ports have you had?"

Duncan checked his glass, and then realized he was being jibed for his lack of comprehension. "I've not had so many that I've started thinking my marriage will benefit from my becoming a wife-beater."

Jake rolled his eyes with good-humoured exasperation. "May I show you something?"

"If it gets us away from your ridiculous ideas of how to better my finances and sustain a happy, healthy marriage, then yes, you may show me anything."

Jake made a rude noise. He went to the study door and called for his wife.

Veronica appeared a moment later, holding a pot and a dish cloth. Debbie was behind her wearing a pair of vulgar pink rubber gloves to protect her manicure. Veronica smiled warmly at her husband. "Darling?"

"Of course." Jake slapped his hand against his head with a gesture reminiscent of amateur dramatics. "I forgot. You've had a couple of drinks already. I was going to ask if you could pop out and get us another bottle of port."

Veronica frowned. "But I thought there was plenty of port left?"

"Not enough for me to be a truly hospitable host," Jake assured her.

"I could go," Debbie piped up. "I'm driving tonight, so I haven't been drinking. I could go."

Jake smiled. "Would you?"

Duncan watched, uncomfortable with Jake's theatrics and not overly happy that his wife was being dismissed by such an obvious ruse. Before he could think of a way to protest, a brand had been named and Debbie was disappearing from the house in search of a bottle of port.

"Darling?"

Veronica turned to face her husband, clearly aware that the three of them had been left alone for a reason.

"Fetch my slippers," Jake said. "Duncan and I will wait for you here."

Duncan saw the curious sparkle in her eye and knew she was trying to fix her husband with a quizzical expression, but Jake had already turned his back. Veronica left the study before Duncan could question her and he realized that his only recourse was to wait with his host.

"What are you planning, Jake?"

"I'm planning a demonstration," Jake replied. "I'm planning to show you how much you could benefit from exerting a little control over your wife."

"I don't particularly want to see that," Duncan told him.

Jake laughed. "No. You don't want to see it. You *need* to see it."

Before the conversation could progress into an argument, Veronica appeared in the study. In one hand she held a pair of slippers.

She was a stunning woman, Duncan thought. Although she was edging towards the end of her thirties, she had managed to maintain the complexion and figure of a twenty-year-old. Her long dress concealed the shapeliness of those curves that he had noticed when they dined together previously, but that air of mystery somehow added to her allure.

"Your slippers," she said quietly.

Jake ignored the offered footwear. He drew on his cigar and drained his glass of port. "You took Debbie shopping today and you encouraged her to buy all those things that she couldn't afford."

Veronica flushed and shook her head. "It wasn't like that, darling," she began. "We just..."

"Don't make excuses," Jake warned her. "Your actions have made me unhappy and we both know how I deal with that."

"But, Jake," Veronica pressed. Her voice was a nervous whisper. She cast a sideways glance at Duncan and said, "We still have a guest."

Jake took the slippers from her. He kept one himself and handed the other to Duncan. "I'm perfectly aware that we still have a guest," he said sharply. "But for the moment, that's immaterial. Your actions need to be addressed."

Veronica cast a final, unhappy glance in Duncan's direction, and then meekly nodded her assent.

Duncan cleared his throat, about to tell Jake that he didn't want to be involved in this. A silencing glare from Jake stopped him. Still holding the slipper, Duncan took a step back to watch the couple.

"Bend over," Jake whispered. "Then raise your dress."

"This is so embarrassing," Veronica whispered. Her cheeks had turned to the same dull purple Duncan had seen in his port glass. "I'm sure that Duncan doesn't want to see this."

"You've earned yourself two more strokes for talking back," Jake told her. "Bend over and raise your dress."

She did as she was told. Her cheeks were still the furious crimson they had been before, but now Duncan realized he wasn't looking at Veronica's face. As she doubled herself, his gaze was drawn to the hidden flesh she was exposing. He had noticed the shapeliness of her legs on countless previous occasions, but he had never seen so much of them. Veronica raised the hem of her skirt high, until the white panty-covered cheeks of her backside were exposed. She placed a hand on each knee, holding herself in readiness for whatever punishment Jake had in mind.

Duncan swallowed and contemplated making an excuse that might extricate him from the room. A part of his mind still insisted that he did not want to witness this. And, although that inner voice was growing smaller, he felt sure he should be listening to it.

Jake slapped a cheery palm against one cheek.

His wife flinched beneath the blow.

"Doesn't she have a gorgeous backside?"

Duncan could not have argued with the sentiment even if he had wanted to. The peach-like mounds of Veronica's backside were an intoxicating vision and he was suddenly embarrassed by the stiffness of arousal. "Very lovely," he said thickly.

Seeming to notice Duncan's predicament, Jake grinned and said, "She affects me like that as well. But this is what I wanted to show you." He stroked his hand over Veronica's exposed backside, tracing his fingers along the edge of her white panties. It was a loving caress and Duncan saw that Veronica trembled ever-so-slightly beneath his touch. Speaking to his wife, Jake said, "It was wrong of you to take Debbie on a spending spree that she couldn't afford, wasn't it?"

"Yes, darling." Veronica's words were a sultry whisper. "I'm sorry. Please forgive me."

He shook his head. "Punishment first, forgiveness afterwards. Isn't that the best way?"

"Yes, darling," she repeated.

Jake turned to Duncan. "For modesty's sake, I could slipper her like this, but I always think that the fabric of her knickers might cushion some of the blow."

Not knowing what to say, Duncan shrugged and tried to look as though he sympathised with Jake's dilemma.

"Of course," Jake went on, "I could always pull the panties tighter..." He hooked his finger beneath the waistband of the underwear and pulled the back panel upwards. The crotch of her knickers pressed firmly against the mound of Veronica's sex. Her arse was split into twin orbs by the brilliant white fabric of her knickers.

With his attention rapt, Duncan couldn't help himself from staring at the gusset of her panties. Wiry tendrils of dark brown hair, as luscious and lustrous as those at Veronica's head, peered from the sides of the elastic. But it was the centre of the panties where his gaze lingered. The shape of her labia was clearly visible through the taut fabric. A dark spot of fresh wetness told him that Veronica was enjoying this humiliation.

"Doing this makes her arse cheeks free for me to slipper them," Jake explained. He tugged the underwear firmly upwards. "It also helps Veronica to retain a little of the modesty that she's so desperate to retain." He rolled his fingers against the exposed buttock, running the tips close to the crease of her sex. "But after her behaviour today, I don't think I should trouble myself with her modesty. I think she should suffer a little embarrassment, as well as the slippering."

Veronica gasped as Jake tugged the panties down.

Duncan barely heard the sound. His attention was riveted on the sight of her exposed cleft. The wiry tendrils he had noticed came from a profuse thatch of dark brown curls. The hairs edged the tops of her legs but parted to reveal the dark pink split of her sex. The flesh was glossy with fresh wetness. Her anus was a tight, puckered ring that seemed to quiver nervously in anticipation of the punishment.

Duncan licked his lips as he studied Veronica's exposed behind. "You're not going to hurt her, are you?"

"I'm giving her a short, sharp lesson in the error of her ways," Jake explained. "Of course I'm going to hurt her." Speaking to his wife, he said, "I want you to count them. Six for the shopping spree, and two for talking back to me." Without another word, he raised the slipper high in the air and brought it smartly against her backside.

She drew a shocked breath.

Duncan wondered if he had made a similar sound.

"One," Veronica whispered. The word sounded as though it was spat from between clenched teeth.

Jake brought the slipper back down again, harder and swifter this time. The slap of the leather sole against her bare arse echoed from the dusty books that lined the walls.

Veronica gasped. On a heavy sigh she murmured, "Two."

As Jake continued to redden her bottom, Duncan watched with growing arousal. Veronica delivered the count with breathless words. Her pain and humiliation clearly increased with each escalating number. She remained beneath her husband's hand with such devout obedience Duncan was stung by a pang of jealousy. More than that, he could feel his arousal growing like a heavy weight in his pants. Her glowing backside had taken the pallor of a virgin's blush and Duncan was touched by the urge to caress the cheeks of her arse and see if they were as painfully warm as they looked.

"Seven," Veronica growled. Her breathing had deepened to a husky drawl.

Duncan longed to know if that tone was caused by discomfort or excitement. He could see that the lips of her pussy had parted. The dark entrance to her sex glistened slickly.

Jake raised the slipper for a final time and drew it down harder than before.

Before muttering the number eight, Veronica winced. The mounds of her backside were a flaming crimson. Her entire body trembled.

"I've forgiven you now," Jake said piously. "And we'll speak no more about this in future." His hand caressed the glowing cheeks as he made this assurance.

Veronica shivered.

"I'm going to submit you to one final indignity," Jake decided. "And then we can consider the matter closed."

Duncan heard something in Jake's tone and turned to frown at him. His host wore a broad grin. He nodded at the slipper in Duncan's hand.

"Your turn," Jake said simply.

"Jake! Please! No!" Veronica gasped.

Duncan wanted to echo the sentiment. The weight of the slipper in his hand suddenly felt monumental.

"Stay silent, darling," Jake instructed. "Duncan's only going to slipper you once right now. He will do more if I tell him."

Duncan stared at her raised backside, wishing he had

listened to the warning voice that told him to rush from the study. He knew that the time for escape was long since past, but it didn't stop him wishing for a world that might have been. Now he was unable to leave the room, and not just because it would cause embarrassment to his friends. Now, he needed to stay because he desperately wanted to smack the slipper against Veronica's blushing backside.

"In your own time," Jake encouraged.

Duncan swallowed and stepped forward. It suddenly felt so right to be wielding the slipper that he wondered why he had never tried it before. With an almost unconscious gesture, he reached forward and stroked his fingers over the shape of Veronica's backside. As he had expected, her buttocks were warm where they glowed. She shivered beneath his exploratory caress.

"Just one?" Duncan asked. It was difficult to conceal his disappointment.

Jake nodded. "There's little point punishing her for punishment's sake."

With a slightly saddened smile, Duncan raised the slipper. He brought it down with a resounding slap.

Veronica gasped. The exposed lips of her sex quivered. And Duncan thought they looked slightly wetter than they had before.

Two hours later, after they'd left Jake and Veronica's, Duncan was still trying to come to terms with the potential possibilities. His thoughts were a chaotic whirl that swept from the beauty of Veronica's reddened backside, to the mortified flush of her cheeks, to the resounding echo of the slipper striking her arse. The knowledge that such pleasure could be his was enormously tempting. The only thing standing between him and a world of sexual domination was the unknown quantity of Debbie's response.

"What's on your mind?" she asked.

He hadn't even realized he'd been ignoring her. Turning his inward eye back to the study with Jake and Veronica, Duncan had lost track of the time as he revisited every delicious detail of the punishment again and again.

"You're not worrying about money again, are you?" Debbie persisted. "Because if that's—"

"It did have a little to do with money," he broke in quickly. Shaking his head, he added, "But we'll be talking at cross-purposes if we begin like this."

She shrugged and encouraged him to continue.

"Finances are tight," he started solemnly. "And it's because you've been overspending again. We've discussed it before, and you've said you'd try to stop yourself, but it hasn't worked. The overspending is worse than ever."

"You're right," Debbie agreed. "I haven't learnt to do recessions yet. What are you thinking?"

It was Duncan's turn to shrug. "Jake thinks I should take a slipper to your bare backside."

She snorted. "I hope you told him that we don't have that sort of relationship."

"I'm thinking of acting on his advice," Duncan replied. He watched her as he said the words, eager to see how she would respond.

"You aren't serious, are you?" she spluttered.

Duncan raised his eyebrows, turning the question back on her. "Do you think it would benefit us?"

"You want to use a slipper on my bare backside?" she breathed the words in a husky whisper that sparked his stiffening arousal. "You might hurt me."

"That would be the intention," he agreed. "It doesn't worry you, does it?"

Her eyes were open wide now. "You're serious, aren't you?"

He stood up and fixed her with a stern expression. Swallowing his growing fears, he prepared to say the most daring words he had ever spoken in his marriage. "Go upstairs, fetch my slippers, and prepare to be punished."

She drew a startled breath and Duncan wondered if he had gone too far. He opened his mouth, ready to try and retract his demand and pretend it was an over-ambitious joke that had gone wrong. Before he could say a word, Debbie had flounced out of her chair and he could hear her storming up the stairs.

He stared at the empty door she had walked through and wondered how long her anger would last. She was a passionate lover but equally passionate with the other extreme of her emotions. He had insulted her and could imagine a month of silence in return for his badly chosen words—thirty days of loveless nights and no end to her overspending.

He glanced up from his depressing thoughts when he saw her appear in the doorway. In one hand she held his carpet slippers.

He stared at her, momentarily dumbstruck. The urge to grin was almost overwhelming, but he knew that would destroy the moment's austerity.

She blushed as she held the slippers out for him. Her eyes shone with the excited sparkle that usually precipitated their lovemaking. "Your slippers, sir."

He reached for them, but she held them out of his reach.

"We can try this," she assured him. "But I'm not saying it will curb my overspending."

Duncan nodded. He reached again for the slippers, but Debbie continued to hold them out of his reach.

"Truth be told," she added, "I know about Jake and Veronica's arrangement, but I also know that Veronica will sometimes do things deliberately, just so Jake will slipper her arse." Lowering her voice to a pantomime whisper, she added, "Veronica likes it."

Duncan smiled. The revelation did not surprise him. He reached again for the slippers and, again, Debbie held them out of his reach.

"Are you prepared for that potential outcome?" she asked softly. "What if I enjoy this punishment? What if I start doing things to upset you, just so you'll take a slipper to my bare backside?"

Firmly, he reached for the slippers, took them from her fingers, and motioned for Debbie to bend over. "If that happens," he said, raising the slipper, "I suppose we can both learn to live with the situation."

A Well-Red Bottom

By Maggie Morton

The book that was to blame for everything had a very suggestive cover. But, then, it was a very suggestive book. On its front, a bare-bottomed woman lay over a man's lap. His hand was raised, and a look of shock was on her face. Above that intriguing image were the words, "Bare Bottoms and Raised Hands: Tales for the Spanking Enthusiast."

Jenna didn't know if she could be considered a spanking enthusiast, exactly, but she'd gotten bored with the type of sex you could find in more typical books, romance novels and the like. She was sick of women being "ravished" with "throbbing members" by "rugged" men. She wanted women who were convinced with mere threats to bow before their masters. No "masters" had been in her life up until then, only a milquetoast boyfriend who had always worn his socks during sex and always made annoying grunting noises while he was inside her. She'd tried to work a little excitement into their sex life, but it had been hopeless, and now she didn't know if she'd ever get laid again. Her first foray into having a sex life had been so disappointing she didn't even know if she *wanted* to get laid again. Were all men that dull and unimaginative? She certainly hoped not. The men in the books she'd taken to reading were not boring in the least. When she read their lovely threats, she became wet, and when they followed through on them, her arousal only grew.

It was close to closing when her boss entered the room and, quick as she could, Jenna shoved the spanking book beneath some papers by the register. She couldn't have him knowing that not only did she read while it was slow in the bookstore but, more often than not, what she read contained words like "cock" and "pain slut" and "submissive."

The book hidden from view, Jenna smiled at Mr. Franks, hoping that a flush wasn't rising to her face, although she almost certainly was starting to blush. It didn't help that she was very attracted to him. Not only did she have an age-difference fetish, she had a *boss* fetish as well. If that weren't enough, Mr. Franks always wore a three-piece suit, which would have made her weak in the knees on principle. She doubted he felt the same way about her, and she didn't even know his first name—he was still "Mr. Franks" to her, even though she'd worked for him well over a month. She didn't even know if he thought about *anyone* sexually. He just seemed too proper and professional for things of that nature. But his propriety, of course, only added to his appeal.

She watched as Mr. Franks approached. "Jenna, this may be a bookstore, but your job here does not include reading the merchandise." He was pissed, and now she was definitely blushing. "Close up, and then meet me in my office."

"But it's half an hour 'til closing, and I'm sorry, I didn't mean to..." Jenna trailed off.

"'You didn't mean to be caught,' is what I suppose you meant to say. Bring that book you were reading with you. We certainly can't put it back on the shelf with the spine bent to hell." Mr.

Franks turned and strode away towards his office, and to Jenna's slight relief, he didn't slam the door, like she'd half expected.

Jenna was worried. She couldn't have imagined Mr. Franks angry before now, and she certainly never would have imagined he swore. She hoped she wasn't about to lose her job; rent was due in two weeks and she was depending on her next paycheck to cover most of it. She couldn't help that there had been no customers all afternoon, although she could have at least chosen more tasteful reading material. It was exciting to worry about getting caught reading erotica, but not to actually get caught, she was quickly learning.

All alone, she set about getting the store ready to close. Mr. Franks had sent the rest of the staff home based on how slow business had been that afternoon. She flipped the sign in the window to show that they were closed, and then she grabbed the book—the stupid, fucking book that was probably going to get her fired—and headed straight to Mr. Franks's office, not looking forward to what might happen behind the closed, black door.

Jenna knocked twice and while she waited for the door to open, she tried to figure out if she could cover her rent without her next paycheck. Was she really about to lose her job? She prayed to the benevolent god of bibliophiles that she wasn't. She chewed on her lip as the door swung open, her nerves getting the better of her.

"Come in," Mr. Franks said. Jenna entered the office, and Mr. Franks shut the door behind her. The thud of it closing was anything but reassuring.

The room was relatively empty, containing only a desk and a chair behind it, with the only light coming from a tasteful, glass lamp sitting on the desk. Two framed posters were on the wall—

one was from a noir movie festival in the 50's and the other Jenna recognized as a Man Ray photograph. It was a nude, something she had certainly not expected to see in her quiet, mild-mannered boss's office.

"Well, now that you've spent enough time reviewing my taste in art, it's time for me to review yours. Hand me the book." Mr. Franks held out his hand, and Jenna placed the offending article in it, her hand shaking almost imperceptibly, but shaking nonetheless. "Hmm," he said, a look of surprise on his face as he examined the cover. "So that's what you young women are reading these days. Well, well, well." He began to flip through the book, stopping every now and then to scan whatever page he was on. Although she'd previously been worried about losing her job, now she was starting to worry that she would die of embarrassment before he even got around to firing her. Could one spontaneously combust if they got embarrassed enough?

"Have you ever tried anything like this before?" Mr. Franks asked, taking off his glasses and placing them on the edge of his desk.

"No. No, I haven't, Mr. Franks."

"Call me Jonathan, Jenna." He was smiling now, of all things.

"No, I haven't. Jonathan." Was this how he usually fired people? Begin by asking them incredibly embarrassing questions, and then *wham!* drop it on them like a truckload of remaindered books? "Are you...are you going to fire me?"

"I'm not sure I've decided yet. Were there any stories in here that you especially liked? Any that, well, caught your eye?"

"I...I've only read three so far." Jenna wondered what was going on. Was he coming on to her?

"Then let's start with the fourth one. I'd like to hear you read it out loud, because it's been ages since someone has read aloud to me. Go over to my desk, and feel free to lean on it, but don't sit down."

Was this really happening? Jenna was shocked, but maybe a little delighted too. She'd been attracted to Mr. Franks since he hired her. She'd been fired before, but the firing had never been, well, enjoyable the other times. Maybe she'd get a little fun out of it before she was gone for good.

"OK," Jenna said, and walked over to his desk, a slight smirk on her face. She leaned over it, placed both of her elbows near its middle, and opened the book to the fourth story. It was called "A Reddened Bottom."

"Good, good. Now, don't mind me, just go ahead and read as well as you're able to, although I won't be surprised if you get a little distracted while you read."

Jenna heard him walk up behind her, then felt his hands on her thighs—he was pushing up her skirt! Soon it was above her hips, only her black cotton underwear stopping him from seeing her bare ass. Huh, so *this* was what he had in mind. Nothing wrong with that—Jenna had even fantasized once about a scene not unlike this, Mr. Franks included. He'd been topless and in leather pants, though, and there had been a shiny, black strap involved. She'd never thought, even for a second, that her fantasies about him would leap all the way into reality.

"Go ahead and start reading," Jonathan said, and she felt his hand cup her left ass-cheek, and then he squeezed it—one quick, firm pulse—making Jenna squirm against the desk.

Jenna began to read:

> *Paradise had worked in the strip club for two months before he started coming in. He told her to call him "John," and she told him that all the*

customers seemed to be named "John." He'd tell her stories, stories about how he'd fucked this woman or that woman, and she'd slither across his lap in the dimly-lit room, her full ass shoved up in his face, her shaved pussy shoved against his—

Jenna jumped, and stopped reading instantly. Mr. Franks—Jonathan—had just smacked her, hard, across the ass.

"Keep reading Jenna, we're only just getting started," Jonathan growled, the sound of his lowered voice sending vibrations to all the right places. Jenna bit her lip, stuck her ass out a little more, a little higher, and began reading again.

—her shaved pussy shoved against his bulge, one that would have left most men ashamed of their own meager offerings.

Jenna continued, barely pausing this time as Jonathan's hand came down again.

H-he especially loved it when she was facing away from him, and he commented many times on how lovely that firm, full ass of hers was. Oh, she'd certainly heard this before, but none of the other men sounded quite as reverent when they told her—

Another smack, this one jolted her against the desk just a bit. Jenna was only mildly surprised to start feeling a bit of heat flowing into her crotch, only mildly surprised to feel her underwear start to get moist. So, she liked being spanked, after all; what a wonderful thing to know. As Jonathan's hand came down once more, and her pussy became slicker and warmer still, she changed her mind. She didn't *like* being spanked, she *loved* it!

Jenna continued to read, and Jonathan continued to spank her, stopping to massage her ass and squeeze it now and then. Each firm smack across her behind made her more and more aroused, and she found herself losing her concentration every time his hand came down. As she neared the end of the story, Jonathan pushed himself up against her, his hard cock only separated from her by a few pieces of fabric. God, how she wished he were inside her right then. Instead of fulfilling her silent wish, though, Jonathan grabbed her breast, sliding his other hand into her underwear. Seconds later, his finger found her swollen clit, and she started having a lot more trouble reading.

> *Paradise's ass be-became warmer and warmer, and...John commented on the lovely flush it had taken on.*

Jenna paused, moaning. "Oh, *fuck.*"

"Continue reading, my lovely little slut, or I'll stop," Jonathan said softly, his breath hot against her cheek. There was a note of warning in his voice, and she felt his fingers slow. Jenna quickly picked up where she'd let off.

> *"Oooh, baby," John said, "you sure have a mighty spankable ass. And look at the way you squirm around when I spank you with a little more oomph."*

Jenna soon noticed that Jonathan stopped rubbing her clit every time she messed up on a word, even every time she paused, and so she took the deepest breath she could and continued to read, trying to be a little more careful with her enunciation and her elocution. Jonathan's fingers came to her nipple, and a quick pinch made her mess up for the last time, because with that pinch came a glorious, overpowering orgasm. Luckily for Jenna, Jonathan didn't feel the need to stop this time, and he managed to make her come not once, but twice, something she'd never experienced. Jenna's whole body quaked with the power of each orgasm, and she jolted against Jonathan's crotch as each one crashed through her. When her second orgasm finally stopped, she collapsed against the desk, and Jonathan slowly removed his hands from her underwear and shirt.

"So, Jenna," Jonathan said, walking around his desk and sitting down, "I think you've learned your lesson. No more reading during work. Also, I've decided that I want to make sure what you read in your free time is up to my standards. That story was passable at best. Maybe some Anaïs Nin next time, or perhaps the classics of the Marquis de Sade. That man was certainly full of intriguing ideas."

Jenna smiled, and began to pull her clothing back into place. "Do we have either of them in stock right now?"

"No, I don't think we do," Jonathan said, a most mischievous grin on his face. "But I think you should order one or two copies when you come in tomorrow. Maybe you can stay after work and help me choose which, in particular, might be best?"

"I think I could manage that," Jenna said, still grinning. "I don't have any plans after work tomorrow. Does this...does this mean I'm not fired?"

"All good bookstores need staff who love to read so much

that they read even when they aren't supposed to. That doesn't mean I want to see you reading during your time on the floor again, though, Jenna. Am I understood?"

"Yes, sir."

Just as she reached the door, Jonathan spoke. "One last thing—I've decided to let you keep this book. You can pick it up after work tomorrow. After all, like I said before, we certainly can't sell it with the spine bent to hell."

Jenna laughed.

When she got up the next morning, there were dark marks on each side of her behind, lovely purple reminders that she hoped would last for quite a while. Or at least until Jonathan caught her reading erotica again—had he really thought the spanking would serve as a deterrent? Now, who was this Marquis de Sade he'd been talking about?

Just Rewards

By Tara S. Nichols

Quarter to six, with rush hour traffic well behind him, Geoff had made excellent time. With a resounding click, the key turned in the lock. He turned the knob and put his shoulder to the door, the same as he had five days a week for the past twenty years. Only this time, it felt different. A heavy weight bore down upon him, years of disregarded weariness settled on his shoulders, found a place within his muscles, and threatened to drag him down. His familiar schedule was about to change, about to come to a grinding halt. Retirement, at the age of fifty-five, was something most people dreamed of, yet he felt an inexplicable tension when he thought about the potential and opportunities ahead of him.

He'd always known there would be an adjustment period, but after a life of nothing but work, it was hard to think about settling down, to consider a slower paced future, a life without deadlines. He owed it to Kate, his wife, though. He owed it to himself.

All those long days at the office had taken their toll. He was tired all the time, worn out, lost in thought, and usually asleep by nine, but now they had all the time in the world, just for them, to catch up.

If only he could muster up enough energy, he thought. Before he left the house that morning, Kate had mentioned they would celebrate starting with dinner out that evening. He'd far rather eat something easy, snuggle up on the couch, and watch murder mystery reruns on TV.

He felt bad. She'd put up with so much—long, lonely evenings waiting for him to get home from the office. She deserved to be treated specially.

When he opened the door, a pile of shoes bunched under the woodwork, halting his entrance with an abrupt jerk. Frowning, he stepped inside and studied the shelf they had been sitting on, wondering if, somehow, he'd missed news of a small earthquake. Nothing had been mentioned about it on the news and he supposed they could have tumbled if the door had slammed shut.

Dismissing them, he stepped over the shoe avalanche and closed the door behind him only to discover a bright red lipstick outline marring the beveled glass. He stared at the bright red stain as though he didn't even recognize his own wife's lip print. How could that have gotten there? He cocked his head, and pictured his wife bent over and struggling to get into a particularly tight shoe when the wind caught the door and struck her in the mouth. Even in his fuddled mind the thought seemed implausible.

Feeling puzzled, he set his briefcase down on the floor by his feet and then noticed a row of boots that had been placed upside down. He studied the tidy line of footwear, his eyes squinting at the patterns on the soles as he tried to make sense of their rigid order. Perhaps Kate was sorting through their shoes, no doubt fussing over the details of their evening, he decided after a moment. Whatever the case, she'd been busy.

Sliding his arms out of his suit-coat, he grabbed for an empty hanger, and stopped short when he noticed all the other coats hanging in the closet were one button notch off.

A slow smile spread across his lips then. This wasn't evidence of an earthquake, an overzealous door-slammer, or the work of mischievous pixies. Oh, no. Each act of chaos had been meticulously executed with such care that it could only be the devious actions of his playful, and rather ambitious, wife.

Clearly, Kate couldn't contain her excitement that he was finally retiring either, only she'd chosen to show it in a way that he'd least expected. It had been a long time, but he could recognize the signs from a game they used to play, a game that promised to wake him from his dull mood and thrust him headlong into a night of wild sexual decadence.

His weariness melted off of him, fell away in waves, just thinking about what awaited him, somewhere within the walls of the house. His heart pumped hard, filling veins long abandoned, and he dragged in a long hearty breath, stretching his lungs with renewed vigor.

Instantly feeling rejuvenated and refreshed, he looked around wondering where Kate was. Most often, she'd hear him enter and, unless she was working late as well, meet him by the door. Seeing that her briefcase already graced the bottom of the closet, he knew he would find her home, but in what room?

Collecting his briefcase, he carried it along with him as he passed a lopsided oval mirror, a rug that had been bunched in a heap, a bookshelf with all of its contents facing spine in, and the seventeenth century portrait that hung upside down. The trail of organized destruction led him straight to the bedroom, but he bided his time getting to her, righting things as he went.

With his cock already hard, he hesitated once he reached their bedroom door. It wasn't the fact that the doorknob had been unscrewed, and now lay on the bench to his left, that made him pause and take inventory, but more the fact that he wanted to draw out their fun, prolong their pleasure, and of course, make her yearn for the punishment she sought just a little longer.

With his libido barely under his control, he entered the dark, spacious room, and found her exactly where he imagined her, laying on her stomach, a pillow propped under hips, and her plump bottom thrust high in the air. A black, lacey bodice with matching panties stretched taut across her lissome figure, while a set of satin garters held a pair of black nylons in place. He groaned inwardly but otherwise didn't make a sound.

He approached the bed slowly and she peered over her shoulder, greeting him with a mischievous smile. His heart swelled at the sight. After thirty years of marriage, they had both thickened out, but he believed his wife had never looked more beautiful.

Moving with slow, deliberate actions, he set his briefcase down by the bed and, taking his time, rolled up each sleeve. He came to stand behind her, just out of her range of vision. A pang of loneliness and desire washed over him as he realized how much he'd missed her through the intensity of their working years.

"I don't suppose you know anything about the mess out there, do you?" It was a struggle to keep his tone firm, and he managed only because he knew it was required of him.

His wife shook her head and then raised her bottom higher.

"And we're undoubtedly going to miss our dinner reservation because of these shenanigans. You do realize that, don't you?"

This time she nodded.

A broad smile spread across his face, and he wondered if she'd even bothered to make them.

"You know, you don't have to go to so much trouble, love," he said after a moment.

"Oh?" Her husky voice rose and fell. "Exactly how much trouble am I in?"

Pretending to mull it over, he finally said, "I'd say at least three spankings' worth."

"Three!" Her brow knitted and she rose up higher on her elbows. Then, spying his pillow, she thrust one arm out and tossed it to the floor. "How about now?"

He shook his head and tried to hide his grin.

Lowering his body down beside her, he knelt on one knee and brought his lips close to her ear. "Well, now you're in for at least ten."

"Mm, that's more like it." She purred, her body responding to the close proximity of his. A galaxy of goose bumps rose up across her shoulders and her hips instinctively swerved closer to his groin. Their eyes met, and looking into her daring gaze, he couldn't remember the last time they'd had playful sex.

"Now we're talking." Her voice came out as a growl.

"How right you are," he said, spearing her with a mischievous look of his own. "Talking, that is." He held out his hand and she placed hers in his, then allowed him to pull her to her feet.

Moving to a sitting position on the edge of the bed, he brought her to stand in front of him. Her breasts hovered inches above his nose and he pressed his face between them, nuzzling her a moment. He inhaled deeply, marveling at her intoxicating scent. Sliding his palms over the smooth fabric covering her buttocks, he gave her bottom a firm squeeze, and she cooed with contentment. He couldn't remember when he'd last taken the time to savor their time together.

"Perhaps there is something in my briefcase that can take

care of that." Moving with the deft agility of a horny eighteen year old, Geoff reached for his briefcase and brought it up onto the bed. "In fact, I'm certain there are a few items in my bag of tricks that might serve a dual purpose." With that, he held up one of his unsharpened wooden pencils. Knowing she wouldn't object, he brought it to her mouth and smiled as her teeth closed down upon it. Her eyes beamed with sinful delight and he could see she was ready for anything.

"Well, that takes care of that, but, let me see..." He made a show of searching the contents of his work supplies, occasionally pulling out one obscure item after another. His wife watched his every move with eager curiosity, the pencil still wedged firmly between her teeth.

Only when the entire contents of the case had been emptied and left in a pile on the bed beside her did he turn his attention back on her. "I think that should about do it," he finished, closing the case with a click. "But I'm going to have to think of something to do with all these extra supplies." He held up two large paperclips as an example.

To his delight she glanced down at her breasts.

Homemade nipple clamps? Did they dare?

As though to persuade him, she moved her shoulders quickly side to side, jiggling her breasts.

It was certainly worth a try, he thought, reaching up. He teased the lacey trim of her teddy down over her breasts until her prominent nipples came into view. Bending the thin wire so it would fit but not pinch too sharply, he sized up the shape he desired and then slid one over a bright cherry-red bud. A small gasp escaped her as the wire bore down, but she said nothing on the subject of removing it.

Encouraged, he quickly fastened a paperclip to the other, then pulled back to admire his handiwork. Kate cupped each breast, lifting them slightly, and his cock surged at the sight.

He wanted nothing more than to push her back onto the bed and plunge his cock into her over and over again, but he knew how hard she had worked to set the mood and he couldn't risk disappointing her.

"It's been a long time since you unraveled the house, my dear." His hand closed down upon one silk-wrapped leg. "Too long, I'd say." Pulling back on the elastic garter, he let it snap and smiled at her mild protest. "It must have taken you hours to adjust the buttons on all of those shirts." He stole a glance at her face to read her expression. Her eyes darted between his face and the pile of office supplies on the bed. "You have unfathomable patience, but I can see you are growing antsy." His hand moved higher, finally dipping beneath the narrow bridge of cloth between her thighs. Using two fingers, he caressed the fine hair covering her mound until they worked their way into the slick groove of her sex.

With little effort, he located her swollen clitoris and passed one finger on either side of it, trapping it momentarily time and again. She began to rock her hips in a vain attempt to control the pressure and speed and, for a short while, he just watched her. It was the most aroused he'd seen her in a long time, but he had no intentions of letting her come just yet. He still had to give her what she really wanted, what they both wanted. He could almost feel his palm tingling just thinking about it.

"Oh Kate, you are very, very naughty," he said, pulling his fingers away.

"Naughty enough for a spanking?"

He chuckled at the eagerness in her voice. He pulled her across his lap and sucked in a breath when she brushed against his cock. He struggled to ward off an explosive orgasm, believing any amount of friction threatened to push him over the top.

Taking a calming breath, he lowered his hand onto her bottom. His fingers splayed across the soft fabric and made a feather-light sweep across her skin. Kate responded with a moan and raised her hands to remove her panties.

"Oh no you don't," he said, catching her wrists. Holding her still, he tugged on his tie and managed to unravel it until it came away in his hand. With Kate's help he looped the tie around her wrists, keeping the knots loose enough that she could break free if she chose to.

With fingers trembling from anticipation, he fumbled to pull her panties down, tearing stitches in the process. Kate giggled good-naturedly, but Geoff was lost in the glory of the moment. Something about the way she lay, her wrists bound, her panties down, he almost gave in to his craving and let his climax come.

He thought of all those long years of hard work, of dreaming about the day he would retire and all the rewards he would reap; well, he was about to indulge in one of them.

Without any warning, he let his hand connect against her bare ass with a loud crack. Kate jerked and the pencil creaked as her teeth sank in deep. She growled and lifted her feet off the floor.

He paused, reading her expression, waiting for word whether he should continue. When she wriggled her hips, he knew she wanted more. His hand swung through the air and his open palm caught her just under her left globe. A groan, more from ecstasy than pain, gurgled forth. Another slap evened out the other side, only to be followed by three more, in quick succession. A deep pink bloom had begun to color her cheeks, but she leaned into each measured stroke as though it was his cock hammering into her and she couldn't get enough.

"You've wanted something like this for a long time, haven't

you?" he asked quickly following the question with a well-placed swat. "I'll bet you imagined exactly how this was going to go down as you went about reorganizing the house this afternoon, didn't you?" An open-handed slap caught her across her pussy and she arched her hips higher and grunted her approval. "And I don't suppose you have any idea how stiff you've made me, how ready my cock is to ride your sweet cunt, do you?"

He smiled when his wife managed to nod. *She did, she always did.*

He paused to caress the warm flesh, rubbing the sensitive spots in a way that he knew would equal a spanking, and still feel good. His fingers slid along the crease of her buttock, dipping into her hot center, where he found her slick and ready. He longed to penetrate her, lose himself in her in a flurry of thrusts, but forced himself to breathe, to go slow, to be patient and savor every moment.

"Oh darling, I have missed you," he confessed with a soft laugh. "I've missed your playfulness; the tender moments waking up slowly; your bold, kinky nature that once shocked and mystified me. As of today, I plan on indulging in all of your fantasies. I'm all yours, Kate. If you want me to spank you every night, or first thing every morning, I'll do it, but honey, I have to admit, right now, all I want is to sink my cock deep and lose myself in you."

Pulling the knot that bound her wrists, he raised her up just enough to roll her onto the bed. She landed with a gentle bounce, sending her paperclip bound breasts bouncing along with her, and the pencil up and out of her mouth. Driven by desire, he pulled her panties off where they still hindered her movement, then parted her legs so he could have a better look at her. His eyes made a hungry sweep across all of her vulnerable points as he tore off his own clothes.

The moment his briefs hit the floor, he threw himself at her, his arms wrapping around her shoulder and waist, his lips locking with hers, and his cock sliding along her groove until the head found her entrance. With one mighty thrust, he buried his shaft in her wet cunt. Wrapping her legs around him, she raised her bottom up off the bed, her hips making tiny jerking movements as her desire took control. He seized the opportunity to grasp both buttocks and squeeze. Just as he expected, she gasped and loosened her hold. Now free to move once again, he began to slam into her, his fingers never leaving off her reddened bottom. Thrusting deeper into her, he quickened his pace, his orgasm sneaking up on him. Thoughts of the sex he trusted would be in his very near future quickened his response. With Kate's tender flesh tight in his grip, he felt his sac begin to tingle and the telltale pulse creeping up his shaft.

Praising each thrust, Kate matched his pace, coming hard. Crying out, she dug her fingers into the meaty flesh of his hips, sending him toppling over the edge.

He collapsed, laughing and giddy on top of her, his cock pulsing inside of her.

He felt thoroughly spent, but it was a different kind of weariness—physical rather than mental. For the first time in years, he felt alive, energized and, amazingly, almost ready to go again.

"About that reservation..." Kate started.

He curled up around her, his hand lightly stroking her bottom. Her thoughts trailed off and he knew he'd successfully distracted her.

"Why don't we just stay in and celebrate all over again?"

Kate's warm laugh filled him and the heavy weight he had

felt upon first coming home, lifted. Perhaps he had just retired from the labor force, but he began to see a whole other kind of labor in his future. He smiled. He'd like nothing better.

Sugar

By Sommer Marsden

I suck the chocolate off my finger, feeling something akin to a state of arousal. I'm locked in a traffic jam of bodies as everyone crowds and drinks and jostles to find the birthday boy. I sip my vodka and tonic and sigh as if I've just had a good, good orgasm.

"What's that on your breath, babe? Thought we were off the sugar," Jake says against the back of my neck. His lips press to the small spot of skin to the right of my nape.

I freeze, heart pounding as if I've been caught mid-pillage or plunder or rape. All I've really done is eat a piece of chocolate fudge. One that was roughly the size of a dime. That was all. One little nibble and now...now I'm fucked.

"We are," I sigh and take a big swig of my drink. No dainty sip this time. I have a feeling I will need the liquid courage soon.

"Is that your impression of abstaining?" He's still pressed to the back of me, but his hand comes into view. Large, powerful, freckled at the knuckles. He turns my hand over, palm up, and traces the lines on my skin. Then he points, matter-of-factly, at a smudge of fudge on the tip of one finger. "That's a pretty sad rendition of refrain."

My stomach is turning, turning, turning nervously. An invisible Ferris wheel of emotion, lit with small colored lights of anticipation. It turns inside of me and I try to hear the party din over my heart beating in my ears. "It was just a tiny piece," I say.

Someone bangs into Jack, thusly banging him into me. I feel his cock, hard and eager, press into the back of my short denim skirt. My panties grow wet in the space of two breaths once I feel that. Now I am certain. I am definitely in trouble and I am in that kind of trouble.

His one visible arm wraps my waist in a possessive snaking grasp and he laughs softly in my ear. My nipples respond, my pulse jacks up, I try to swallow and my throat feels stuffed with cotton or tissues. I am a mess, but when someone waves to me calling, "Sheila!," I grin and nod as if I am totally in control. The taste of fudge is still on the tip of my tongue. Just a tiny sugar resonation, but it seems to be all I can taste.

My thigh muscles still ache up the inside from my morning run. The length of my thigh is firmer. My ass is a work of art and my abdominals are even responding, though I shun ab work like the plague. I have done a fine job with the program that Jake and I have set up. Healthier, more efficient, cleaner-living us. We cook fabulous meals together, run around the lake, walk the dog, and eat seasonal fruit till the cows come home. My only weakness seems to be...well, sugar. And I have promised to keep away from it. Promised and failed.

Speaking of my inner thighs, his hand runs up, under my skirt for a split second, caresses the slightly looser black leggings I wear underneath for just an instant, and his thumb grazes the front seam. Beneath it, my clit thumps with new and intense arousal. I am in so much trouble and yet, him touching my body has overridden my fear.

"It always starts with a tiny piece with you, love." He laughs again and his fingers stroke over the denim that covers my skin. My body goes haywire and, for all intents and purposes, I might as well be naked in the middle of this crush of people. "And if I don't reign you in, Sheila, what happens?"

"I get out of control," I admit. I hang my head and my hair falls forward, a nut-brown curtain for me to hide behind. Jake's lips come down again on that small bundle of nerves at my nape and I shiver like I have the flu. My stomach takes another bright, amusement ride turn and my pussy is wetter than ever. He's so aggressive and he's about to remind me just how strong he is.

"Exactly, you get out of control. Now I was just out on the balcony there. I'd like you to see it. Would you like to see it?"

It sounds like a suggestion. It isn't.

I nod and his hands come down on my shoulders, the same way they do when I'm on my knees for him. Taking his cock deep into my mouth, relaxing my throat, sucking him so that he says all the things I need him to say and then usually, if I am good, he comes at me, takes me, fucks me. Makes me say all the things that he in turn needs to hear from me.

He steers me toward the double French doors with their quaint sectional windows and brass knobs. Guides me to the balcony that is nearly abandoned since no one seems to smoke anymore. Pushes me toward the sharp bite of February wind and the festively strung ornamental trees that give the small balcony a magical white glow.

"Isn't this nice?" Jake asks, smiling. We have the whole small spot to ourselves. To the left of the door, tucked back a bit, is what my grandmother used to call a fainting bench.

"It is nice," I manage. My throat is still too small, my

heartbeat too big.

"As nice as sugar?" he asks, tracing a line from my belly button to between my breasts. I shake a little under his touch and when the wind kicks up, I shake a lot.

"Nicer," I laugh. It's a real laugh, but it's laced with anticipation and anxiety.

"Good girl."

Jake takes a seat like he's king of the world, pats his lap like he's offering me a quick seat in a crowded situation. But I know the drill and I drop to drape my belly over his denim-clad legs. He smoothes his big powerful hand over my ass cheeks and I bite my lip, hold my breath, say a short prayer.

"Please—" I start, but I stop. Shake my head.

"Please, what, baby?" he asks, sounding amused. "I haven't even started yet."

I had been about to ask him to keep it short. But I know Jake too well. The request for brevity will lengthen my punishment. A request for secrecy will almost guarantee that we get caught, or damn near close enough to stop my staggering heart in my chest. I shake my head.

"Tell me or I'll pull it all down and do you bare-assed right here."

I blink, the cold air stinging my eyes. Even though his words are harsh, his hand is still taking a lulling, soft tour of my curves. "Please be kind," I stutter for lack of a better answer.

"I don't know about kind, Sheila, but I'll be fair. How's that?" He bends and kisses my temple, an oddly comforting and sweet gesture. A this-is-going-to-hurt-me-more-than-it-hurts-you gesture.

"That's good," I say.

"What's fair for sneaking sugar?"

I shake my head.

"Tell me?"

I shake my head. He gives me one warning swat. Hard enough to drive me forward into his bulk just a touch.

"Give me a number or we'll start with fifty. And by fifty, you know damn well one of those partygoers, who isn't supposed to smoke any more but secretly does, will be sneaking out here for a few puffs."

"Thirteen!" I blurt. Because thirteen is my lucky number and it is the first thing that popped into my head. Damn. Why couldn't my lucky number be three like Jake's?

"Good choice," Jake says and he runs his wide, warm hand over my now cold ass cheek again. I let my eyes drift closed, knowing it's coming but not when. My husband is a master of redirection. "Was it good?"

I raise my head, the wind kisses me full on the face and my lips tingle. "What?"

"The fudge," he says and then they land. Fast and hard, one, two, three. So fast they steal my breath. And before I can fully register the cracks of pain, he's rubbing my bottom again.

"Yes. Not good enough for this, though," I say. I'm lying. Or part of me is. I am, as usual when it comes to a punishment from Jake, torn between craving it as surely as I crave that sugar and fearing it.

"Too bad," he says. He sounds truly remorseful and I start to smile, but the blows start again and this time it is four. The pattern is hard, soft, hard, soft. My right cheek throbs while my left can't quite keep up. I gnaw my lip and tears prick my eyes for a moment. How many was that? My brain scrambles, rewired by the shocks of pain and spurts of endorphins.

"It was seven," he says, reading my mind. "Now ask me for more."

Someone opens the door, but then shuts it. The wind has

licked at the doorframe and I wonder, as my knees start to knock, if they thought better of their craving for nicotine and cold air. "May I have the rest of my punishment, Jake?"

He pinches the back of my thigh, just hard enough to make me gasp, and I remember my manners. "Please!"

His hand snakes down the back of my thin leggings, under my taupe-colored panties, and he flicks the tip of his digit to my wet slit. There is no hiding this from him. "Look at you, you little slut. Sugar slut, pain slut, my slut." His voice is a tidy mix of malice and love.

I nod. Wiggling a little. Wiggling to get him to touch me more or to hide my arousal? I haven't a clue.

"Was it dark or light?"

I blink, trying to focus as his finger dives into my soaking pussy and flexes one single time. Like he's pressing a button. My G-spot sparks to life and I hold my breath. But then his hand is gone and I stutter again. "Wh-wha-what?"

One, two searing hard blows and he whispers, "Chocolate."

"Dark!" I cry and I am doing some combo dance of clamoring on his lap and humping him. I am ashamed, I am cold, my ass stings, and more than anything in the whole world, I am wet and willing and I want him to fuck me. Hard and fast and right here.

"Our favorite."

"God, yes," I say as tears wet my cheeks and then the February wind does its best to freeze them to my burning skin.

Four to go and before I can inhale he does it. This time favoring the right cheek with the fiercest blows. Below the waist, my body responds to my heartbeat. My pulse echoes in my ass, but I do not move to stand. I know that would be bad. I wait. Jake's hands roam my ass, soothing and plucking at my leggings. They wander low on the backs of my thighs and my cunt grows wetter still. I would give up sugar for the rest of my life to have him fuck me now.

"I'm not going to fuck you," he says. He's in my head again. "And how many did we say for your breach?"

"Thirteen," I whisper.

"You promised no sugar, right?"

"Right."

"You lied," he clarifies. His voice holds disappointment and promise and something secretive.

"I lied too." He snatches my leggings from under my skirt and tugs them down. My panties surrender willingly and slide down too. His hot hand comes down in a rain of blows on my bare skin. Too fast and sharp to count and now the tears trail freely down my face.

My bottom burns, my pussy lets loose a warm and shameful slick of excitement, and he pushes his fingers into me again. "Jesus, Sheila. Look at you. Look at this." He holds his fingers under my nose and in the fairy lights that dot the ornamental trees, I see it. The wet evidence of how easy I am. I feel like the stars in the midnight velvet sky are watching us.

"Do you see it?" he asks.

"Yes."

"I think it's sweet. Like sugar. Taste it," he says and raises his fingers. I lick them clean. It is sweet. Not so much like sugar, but like fruit.

His cock is hard under my belly and I stay there, nervous as hell but obedient with my bare ass to the wind. My body trembles, but there's nothing I can do about that. Finally, Jake sighs. A long beleaguered sigh of a man used to dealing with a difficult mate. "I lied again," he confesses and a sharp bright sliver of hope flares in the pit of my belly. "Stand up, Sheila."

I stand so fast I stumble. Leggings still around my thighs,

panties too. He grabs me to keep me from falling and hustles me to the far back corner to the left of the French doors. He pushes my hands into the sparkly lit tree and says, "Hold on to that and don't you let go. And tomorrow–" I hear his zipper and practically weep with joy. "Tomorrow, there will be a price to pay for making me lose my control."

He pushes the head of his cock to my entrance and I grip the thin tree trunk tight, pushing back to greet him, meet him, open my body for him. He's in me and moving and it is the most delicious feeling in the world despite my throbbing ass cheeks, despite the cold that nibbles and nips at my skin, despite the amazing dessert spread in that room over there. It all falls away and he is fucking me hard, fast, and eager in the sparkly mystical lights. I bury my face in the back-lit leaves as his fingers find my clit and he rubs me to the point of no return. Nudging my G-spot with his cock, my clit with his fingertips until I'm sobbing into the leaves and coming around him, a slippery wet orgasm that steals my breath.

He comes with a grunt and a sigh, his lips on the back of my neck, fingers biting into my hips. Then he's putting me back together. Tugging up panties and leggings, pulling down my skirt. He kisses my temple and pats my bottom saying, "How's that ass feeling?"

"Sore."

"Don't forget about tomorrow."

"I won't." I've never been more honest in my life. At home, there are paddles and switches and crops. My scalp tingles at the thought.

The door whisks open and my heart skips at how close it was. How close we came to being stumbled upon and seen. "Sheila! Jake! There you are! Rumor was you were here."

"Here we are," Jake chuckles.

Ericka steps back to let us in because I am shivering. "Your cheeks are so red!" she says to me and Jake chuckles again. I try not to smile when his hand skitters across my bottom where those cheeks are red too.

I lean in and kiss my friend on the cheek and she says, "And oh, my god, I brought the best cheesecake. You still like cheesecake? How's your sweet tooth, Sheila? Can it handle another nibble of dessert?" She grins.

"Yeah, Sheila, how's your sweet tooth?" Jake asks from behind me. I can hear the Big Bad Wolf quality of his smile.

"Actually, it's satisfied," I say. "For now."

The Trumpet of Destiny

By Roxy Katt

It was a very large, very modern house just outside the city, set well back from the road and surrounded with gorgeous landscaping.

I hardly felt worthy to ring the bell.

She opened the door.

A skinny blonde—and totally gorgeous. I thought so. That would be just the type to steal my husband, wouldn't it? I had phoned her in advance on the pretence I was a collector and interested in looking at some of the expensive avant-garde art she sold. I couldn't very well tell her who I really was, could I? I likely wouldn't have even gotten my foot in the door. Besides, I wasn't sure I really did want to talk to her, tell her I had found out about her and Hank. I wasn't sure what I would say even if I did spill the beans—maybe just beg for my husband back.

This wasn't the first time he had done such a thing.

Her hair was shoulder length and cut in a kind of spiky, enticingly witchy fashion. She had big green eyes, a strong, sharp chin, and looked French—which she was. She was wearing a thick, close-fitting, copper-colored woolen sweater with a cowl neck that almost slipped off one shoulder.

"You must be Augustine."

"Yes. Adrienne?"

"Very pleased to meet you. Won't you come in?"

She turned and I followed her sashaying ass (*very* tightly bound in a knee-length skirt of thick, dark green leather) over the hardwood floors of the high-ceilinged, immaculate palace she owned.

I asked myself now for the thousandth time why I should come here. I knew I had a right to feel outraged. I knew it should be she rather than I who was intimidated, but I had walked through that door feeling I was already defeated. I was just here to survey the battlefield, meet the general who had outdone me and, hopefully, not add to my humiliation. Why the hell had I come? Maybe to put a human face on the victor, so I would not be tormented by dark imaginings of an almost mythical Other Woman. Well, if that was it, it wasn't working. She was magnificent.

Take her ass, for example.

Still walking behind her, I noticed her magnificent skirt-stretching derriere was actually a little large for the rest of her skinny frame. Her backside was not fat, but wide, well-rounded, and very firm. This was not surprising, given that Hank, I knew, could never go for a woman not built to receive a thorough spanking.

It had been a long time since he had given one to me. Yes, doubtless this leather-lapped backside before me was the one that had been reddening under his masterful mitt while my own bottom had been languishing in neglect. I remembered when I used to wear pleated cheerleader skirts—knowing how much an older woman in a pleated cheerleader skirt provoked him to madness—and then feigned astonishment when, in some public place but at a moment when nobody was looking, he would hoist the back of it and give me a terrific smack right on the heinie. I would go cross-eyed trying to stifle my yelp of delight and pain, stand there knock-kneed rubbing my ass, while he nonchalantly pretended that absolutely nothing whatsoever had happened.

God, it had been fun. And now he was a bastard, an absolute, fucking bastard. And she, the one the bastard was fucking, she was hot—no doubt about it. I didn't know whether this should make me feel better or worse. And she had good taste, I thought, glancing about the house, no doubt about that either.

My nemesis and I reached the home's expansive gallery: two stories tall with a breathtaking skylight and one wall that was all window. The snow outside reflected the pale light of the overcast day wonderfully, such that a clear and peaceful winter light permeated the indoors. A sad light, but a hopeful one, unlike whatever light was in myself just then.

The phone rang. "Excuse me please." She smiled, tapped her way in her green, tightly laced leather boots to a masterfully carved coffee table, and picked up the phone. I looked around the room while she talked.

I don't know much about art. Some of it was nice. Most of it was mystifying: abstract paintings on the wall, strange sculptures in plastic or steel on various little podiums. There was a painting of what I took to be a representation of Actaeon turned into a stag and hunted by his own dogs, and a very large, bold painting of the female symbol done in a kind of 1960s style. I liked that one. I wished I could feel that woman warrior spirit right now. There was also an oil painting of a woman ashamedly covering her naked breasts with her forearms and wearing a girdle. That one, I also liked. I felt like her: exposed, ridiculous.

Distracted, my mind went back for the umpteenth time to

216

the past. What had been the warning signs? Could it have been two years ago when he suggested a threesome and I said no? If I'd said yes, would he and I have gone through a series of third parties, including doing it with Miss Fancy-boots now? I hadn't wanted to share him with anyone. Was I wrong? Shit.

Two more art works in particular now caught my attention.

They seemed to have been done by the same artist. One was just a very large metal keg. In fact, it was a kind of simplified and stylized aluminum hogshead lying on its side, screwed to the floor.

Nearby was the other piece. It was an open-ended aluminum tube about three feet long and, I don't know, maybe a foot and a half wide. I'm not much for estimating distances. Each end of the tube flared out sharply, like the bell of a musical instrument. The tube rested horizontally on two U-shaped steel brackets, each held up by a vertical steel post about a yard high and bolted right into the floor.

"Bizarre," I muttered out loud to myself, "what is the point of this?" I wondered whether Hank had started his seduction of her by striking up a conversation on these very pieces. Rather, I suspected, she had started it. As if it mattered now.

She was right there at my elbow. I had not noticed her get off the phone.

"It is called 'The Trumpet of Destiny.' A brilliantly simple design, no?"

"It is that," I said.

We went over to it, and she gestured for me to look inside. I bent over. "Oooooh." Inside, there were subtle yet beautiful patterns of blue, purple, green, a kind of anodized thing. I found myself curiously attracted by it.

"Does it symbolize something?" I asked, standing upright again.

She blinked at me as if I were an idiot. "It is a yonic symbol, of course."

Ah yes, naturally. I think it would symbolize a cock just as well, I wanted to say, like the one my husband has obviously been stuffing your lah-de-dah avant-garde pussy with, but what do I know?

Something seemed to snap, gently, unexpectedly, inside me, leaving a kind of anger to uncoil slowly, very slowly.

"I prefer *that*," I said, gesturing to the oil painting of the woman wearing a girdle. "My mother used to own a lingerie and corsetry shop. I can see that the artist has her foundation wear just right."

She raised her eyebrows ever so slightly. "Has he? Personally, I don't think I've ever even seen one of those dreadful patriarchal contraptions up close. Of course, the fetish of 'realistic' representation dies hard. Nonetheless, a fine piece."

I wanted to tear her blonde hair out.

In the meantime, she seemed to want to focus my attention on the tube piece. She gestured impatiently for me to back away from the mouth of it and I did so. She stepped up to it and bent over. Looking down the narrow passage, she began to expound on its nature and meaning. I knew she had no idea who I really was, but I began to feel as if she intuited on some not-quite-conscious level the nature of our relationship here and despised me for it. This whole pompous art lecture on some stupid piece of metal was really just the poisoned icing on a very bitter, very judgmental cake. *What have I gotten myself into here?* I wondered. I came to encounter some full-of-herself chippy who's been boinking my husband and who ought to be on her knees begging for forgiveness. Instead, I'm treated like some kind of schoolgirl philistine.

"Of course," she said eventually, bracing herself with her

hands just above her knees and leaning so far forward her head was partly inside the tube, "the nature of the feminine passageway to destiny is such that one must bend over; that is," she seemed to say pointedly, "one must humble oneself to enter and to understand."

Some kind of light, or red flag, or whatever, went off in my head. I stepped behind her, put both hands on her green-leathered ass, and pushed her in until she was snugly muffled in the smooth aluminum tube from the waist up. I heard a baffled exclamation, a cry of surprise, then silence as she began her struggle.

From the shoulder to the elbow, her arms were pinned tightly to her sides. Her hands and forearms flapped about ineffectually and erratically from the bottom of the tube. She tried to back out. But the tube slid lengthwise a little on its cradles, rose slightly, then fell back in place. She tried again. The whole tube rose bodily out of its cradle (it didn't seem to weigh much) and she stood up, staggered back a couple of paces, and turned around once or twice, as if looking for me. This was stupid, because she could see nothing except maybe the distant ceiling through the top opening of the tube. She bent forward a little, and tried, in vain, to shake it off.

"Help! What's going on out there?"

"Oh my goodness! I *am* sorry!" My voice was sickly sweet with anger and insincerity. "How clumsy of me, Adrienne. Here. Let me help you out of that."

Impossible as it was for her to get herself out, it would have been easy enough for me to liberate her. But I had decided then and there I wouldn't. Not just yet.

I walked about her quietly as she struggled and demanded explanations.

That skirt, I thought, was deliciously tight.

With great difficulty, I undid the button at the back of it. I pulled the zipper down.

"Huh? What are you doing back there? Augustine! What the hell is going on! I demand to know the meaning of this!"

I gasped. But not at her indignation. "A girdle!" I cried. "You're wearing a fucking *girdle,* aren't you, Little Miss I-never-saw-such-a-patriarchal-contraption!" I grabbed the bottom of her skirt and pulled it down until the whole thing slipped over her fulsome hips and I let it drop about her ankles.

"You fucking maniac! What are you doing?"

The girdle was a longline, open bottom type, bright white and looking absolutely new.

I found one of my hands gently caressing her lower tummy, and the other sliding slowly up and down her highly compressed bum. "Oh wow! I mean, this is a really expensive, heavy duty rig you've got here, honey. And it looks like you took a longgg time to wriggle your lovely big ass into it, didn't you?"

"You get me out of here!"

"Out of what, dearie? Are you stuck in that 'Trumpet of Destiny' thingy? Or is it your girdle you can't get out of? I'll bet a certain someone helps you with that, doesn't he?" I stuck a finger in the lower edge of the girdle, pulled it out as far as I could, and let it snap loudly against her thigh.

"Ow! Barbarian!"

"So you like spankings, do you?"

"What? Get me out of here!"

"You'd have to if you're going out with Hank. He gives very good ones."

"Hank? How do you know Hank? What has he got to do with this?"

"I should know. He's my husband."

There was a quick gasp from within the tube.

220

"Tell me something. Did you know Hank was married?"

"No. I swear."

With my left hand carefully bracing her tummy, I wound up with my right and smacked her right on her girdled backside. She shrieked in painful indignation. "I don't believe you. Hank can't keep his mouth shut about anything. He let something slip—unwittingly, he still doesn't realize he did it—and that's how I found out about you, girdle girl."

"Please! Let me go! I...I'll give you some money."

"Money!" I smacked her three times in swift succession. "*You're* the ho here, honey-buns, not me. How *dare* you!" I steered her over to the aluminum hogshead and pushed her forward over it until her feet left the floor. I smacked her repeatedly while the studio rang with the sound of flesh on that complex mix of Lycra/Spandex/latex that gorgeous white girdle of hers was made of.

"Ow! Ow ow oowwww!" she yowled. I began to really enjoy myself. I had never spanked anyone before, let alone someone of my own sex. Strange feelings I'd had as an adolescent began to come back to me...memories of girls I'd had a crush on, on my way to straighthood, and I wondered if I was recovering something that had been pushed aside...

"You, my girl, are going to get the spanking of your life. And, I might add, having unfortunately acquired from my worthless husband a taste for bad puns, I have you over a barrel." I found myself laughing maniacally.

She was kicking ineffectively from below the knee only. Her thighs were so tightly bound in her foundation wear there really was nothing she could do with them. "You can't get away with this!" she cried and sobbed. I reached for the garter tabs at the bottom edge of the girdle and popped them open, disconnecting her expensive, retro, back-seamed stockings. I looked up at the wall which had the enormous painting of the female sign on it.

"Some feminist." I laughed at her. "You with your Cold War lingerie. Here. Let me heat things up for you." I slid her off the barrel and set her on her feet again. She wobbled and staggered in her boots.

"Wh-what are you going to do with me? This is outrageous! You cannot strip and spank me like this!"

"Shut up!" I commanded, smacking her ass sharply again. She squealed like a schoolgirl.

With both hands, I grabbed the lower hem of her immaculate white girdle and began to peel it up.

"Help! No! You...you bitch! How dare you!" She writhed, twisted, turned, tried to break free.

I was getting very turned on.

Eventually, her ass popped out. Foop! Fine, fat, and fulsome it was, and very firm even without the girdle, which was now rolled up to the waist.

I spun her about this way and that to have a good look at the goods that made my hubby pop his cork. Very nice. I loved the way those fulsome buttocks jiggled helplessly. And I hadn't seen so much bush since camping in Northern Ontario. I seized her hair with the left hand and she yelped as I made her bend way forward.

"You have a choice, dearie," I said, my right hand playing gently over her fat labia and her squeaky clean European asshole, "now that you are stripped of your patriarchal armor: spanking, or finger fucking. Which will it be?"

"Help!"

I smacked her. She squealed. "You should wear your girdle proudly or not at all, you bourgeois, hypocritical pseudo-feminist. Very well, I will choose for you." I began to finger her cunt lips.

"No! Spank me! Spank me!"

"Really? Well, since you insist, you ho, I'll spank you then."

I let her have it. One after another. Whap whap whap. One cheek, and then the other. She squealed, writhed, wriggled, danced on her heels, and begged for mercy. I felt something wet on my left hand. "You slut!" I cried. "You enjoy this, don't you? Steal my husband, eh?" Then I let go of her pubic hair and she stood up straight, whimpering, tottering knock-kneed. I chased her around the room then with spankings. Staggering blindly, she was directed by which cheek I smacked her on as a horse is directed with bit and bridle.

"I guess Hank thinks you're pretty hot, doesn't he?" I said between my blows and her confused, hysterical yelping. "Well, I'm going to ruin you for him, dear. When I'm done with your ass, his tepid little spankings will only bore you, love. Hold still." I seized her, bent her over the barrel again, and whaled on her with a cracking symphony of skin-on-skin blows.

I stopped to rest. She whimpered quietly, her cunt drooling all over the Hogshead of Doom or whatever it was supposed to be called. From outside the front of the house I heard a car horn. *Oh-oh*, I thought. *Company*. I left the studio and rushed to the front window.

It was Hank's car. And lo and behold, he was in it, too, and about to get out. I heard a barking sound behind me. For a moment I thought I had driven Little Miss Frenchie-Perfect crazy. It would have served her right. I turned and saw a friendly little white poodle, holding a long leash in its mouth. It barked merrily at me.

"Hoping to go for a walk, little fellah? I'm sure someone will take you presently." I rubbed him under the chin and he barked affectionately. "But in the meantime, I could use your serendipitous leash."

Back at the barrel, she begged me from within her tubular prison. "Please. Augustine. Why do you delay? Fuck my cunt with your masterful fingers. You can't bring me this far and not bring me off."

"Oh I can't, can't I? Miss Trumpet of Destiny? Beg me for it."

"Please, oh please. For you to fuck me is the only way I can accept this humiliation."

"Oh please. You know something? Loverboy is on the driveway. Does he have a key? Might he let himself in?"

"What? Hank? Oh please, Augustine, please! Don't let him see me like this. It's just too humiliating!"

I slid her off the barrel onto her feet, smacked her ass again, and she whooped. "Shut up, trumpet head. My goodness you look stupid." I grabbed the lower part of one buttock then and pinched it with all my might.

"OW! OW-OW-OW-OW!" She danced trippingly, her pussy-footing little heels beating a frantic staccato on the hardwood floor.

I stopped and fastened the leash about her waist. "You are now a bitch with a new mistress. But to complete the transaction, your old master will have to see something." I heard the front door unlock. "Perfect timing."

"Huh?"

I slipped two fingers of my left hand into her oozing snatch. "No! Please! Not if Hank is here!" With my right hand I smacked her ass.

"Ow!"

"Yes-no, yes-no, you can't make up your mind, can you, you silly French tart." Whap whap whap, I smacked her again. "Come, you bitch!" I smacked her yet again. She groaned and groaned.

And then Hank was just standing there, at the edge of the studio, dumbfounded. I gave him what must have been the most evil smile of our married life while a fat, oozing cunt, an ass, a pair of convulsing forearms, and writhing leather-booted legs sticking out of a giant trumpet danced to my groping and smacking.

"Look Hank!" I said, pulling my hand out of her honey pot and showing him how wet and gooey it was. "She likes it."

"Augustine! Don't stop! Hank! Please! Make her put her hand back!"

With my hands on my hips, I looked at Hank and shook my head knowingly. "Poor little thing can't make up its mind. Yes no yes no...I've hopelessly confused it." I patted her patronizingly on her red ass. "But watch this. I've taught it how to dance for you!" I pinched her ass as before and she really put on a show, her boots tap-dancing as she whined and begged Hank to save her. I let her go.

"What is all this?" Hank asked stupidly, and I handed him the leash.

"My first work of art, dear. I call this, 'The Strumpet of Destiny.' Do you like it?"

"Y-you mean, that's Adrienne?"

It was my turn to stare at someone like they were an idiot.

The trumpet whore squealed: "S-somebody f-fuck me! Spank me! Please! I-I'll do anything afterwards, just bring me off! Oh!"

"That's right, Hank. And I think she needs you, though I daresay you've probably lost all interest now, haven't you? As for myself, I'm through with her too. For today. And I'm through with you, asshole, forever."

My only connection with Hank after that was to see his lawyer from time to time. That went surprisingly smoothly. We had a divorce. I never saw Hank again.

Fortunately, I cannot say the same for Adrienne. She wears cheerleader skirts for me now, from time to time, and tight skirts and girdles and dog leashes whenever I tell her to.

Because her lovely, high-falutin', hoity-toity French ass is mine.

Richard's Reward

By D. L. King

The doorbell rang and Suzanne glanced at the time. He was a full fifteen minutes late. She opened the door to find Richard standing there, that sweet, slightly reticent 'you're not angry with me, are you?' look on his face.

"Hello, Richard, come inside," she said, standing back to let him in. "You always have that same look on your face every time you come to my door. Why is that, Richard?"

"What look?"

"That frightened look with the silly grin attached, that 'deer caught in the headlights but thrilled to see the car anyway' look. You're not afraid of me, are you?"

"No, of course I'm not afraid of you, I only—it's just that..."

"Don't worry about it, Richard. It's all right. You're my sweet boy," she said, kissing him as she ran her hand down the curve of his bottom. Suzanne loved Richard's bottom—so round, so sweet, so perfectly spankable. "Now why don't you have a seat and tell me why you're late."

Richard sat down on the couch and Suzanne settled in next to him. Her hand on his thigh, she used her fingernails to explore the weave of his blue jeans as the explanation of his morning and the obstacle-ridden journey to Suzanne's house began to flood out.

It seemed the entire city had conspired to make him late for his appointment with her. As he continued, she inched her way up to his crotch. Mmm, he was already hard.

His diatribe slowed as she approached his crotch, but when she gently squeezed his erection, all language abruptly ceased.

"Ah, it seems someone's happy to see me, at any rate. We'll discuss your habitual lateness a bit later, but for now, let's just relax a while. Would you like a cup of tea?"

As he followed her into the kitchen, eyes glued to her formidable rear end, she made sure to give him a proper show. She knew the effect her black leather skirt-encased rear would have on him. She added that extra wiggle. It was a move that never looked out of place and never looked contrived, but seemed instead to be a completely natural aspect to her walk. It was also a move guaranteed to have Richard salivating and ready to do anything she wanted.

The black-seamed stockings and black leather pumps added to the overall picture. Richard could become positively weak in the knees when given an up-close view of her seamed nylons running down into high-heeled pumps. Wanting to complete the picture for him, she had made sure the white silk blouse opened far enough to show the beginnings of her black lace bra hugging her breasts and accentuating her cleavage.

As she put the kettle on, he stepped up to her from behind and began to massage her shoulders while he pressed himself against her leather-covered rear. "Would you mind getting the cups out, My Sweet?" she asked pleasantly. When the tea was made, she had him carry everything back to the living room.

Settling back onto the couch, he dutifully rubbed her feet while the tea cooled. They chatted about politics and fashion over tea until Richard just couldn't stand it anymore. Putting his quickly emptied cup down, he leaned in and kissed her neck, working his way over to her mouth while his hands worked their way up to her breasts, first over her blouse, then reaching inside the neck and under her bra.

Knowing where this was headed, Suzanne decided to nip it in the bud. "Shall we move into the bedroom?" she inquired. Richard followed her lead as she stood. She took his hand, towing him along behind her. She could sense his eagerness; after all, many things took place in the bedroom, all of which managed to excite him to no end.

She took the small leather-bound book he'd given her from her bedside table. His eyes grew large and he began to splutter.

"But I've been good lately. I've really tried to be good."

"Yes, Dear, you have been good. You've been very good," she said patting his thigh as they sat together on the edge of the bed. "You're my very good sweet boy," she said, kissing the palm of his hand and nuzzling it. "But..."

Richard had given her the book so she could keep track of his bad behaviors and any infractions of the rules, large or small. This was her spanking diary. She thumbed through the last few pages.

Richard called every night to tell her about his day. This was something she'd insisted on from the very beginning. She would question him about his actions and behaviors, both private and public, and he would answer truthfully. When it was plain that correction was needed, she would write the infraction down in her book along with the date of the occurrence. As these conversations took place over the telephone, Richard was never aware what, if anything, was being recorded in the diary. But it was in this way, since they were not together daily, Suzanne was able to assure his disciplinary needs could be met.

"I see more than a few entries here, Richard," she said and tutted. Suzanne could sense his growing anxiety. A good spanking was what Richard needed. It served to ground him and focus his thoughts. It helped to relieve his tensions and stress and she knew he enjoyed it. But that didn't keep him from fretting about it before it happened.

"Now, you know I care about you. I wouldn't go to the trouble of keeping this diary and making sure you received the proper discipline you require if I didn't care. You're my very sweet boy and how will you ever learn if I don't care enough to take you in hand?"

She didn't believe in raising her voice; it was always gentle and soft. Regardless how stringent the discipline, her voice remained calm.

"Now let's see—on Monday, the fifth, you were very bratty." Richard looked at her. "Oh yes, you were. I remember it distinctly. Were you thinking about arguing with me about that entry?"

"But I..."

"Yes?"

"Nothing."

"All right. Then on Wednesday the seventh, you were late to several appointments. What on earth was the problem *there*, Richard?"

Richard hung his head. "I don't know."

"Lateness seems to be a recurring theme just recently. You need to center yourself, Richard. If you're centered, you'll find you're more punctual."

"Yes, Suzanne."

"I see that you haven't been sleeping much lately. That could have something to do with it. You really must take better care of yourself." She leafed through the pages. "Yes, hmm, you were very argumentative and actually raised your voice when speaking with me the following Friday."

"But I immediately apologized! You remember! You know I didn't mean to."

"Yes, I know you apologized and I know you really were very sorry, but that doesn't change the fact that you raised your voice to me now, does it? I know these things happened almost a month ago and that you've been very good lately." He looked up at her and she placed her hand on his cheek. "Yes, I'm well aware of how hard you've been trying and how good you've been, so I plan to reward you for your good behavior.

"But first we need to get your punishment out of the way for the bad behaviors. We can't simply forget about them now, can we?"

Richard slowly hung his head and shook it.

"So, if you wouldn't mind taking down your pants, there's a good boy."

Suzanne opened the cabinet and chose the implements she planned to use. She pulled the spindle-backed chair away from the secretary, placed it in the middle of the room, and hung her leather riding crop and her new leather strap from the back.

"By the way, Richard, thank you so much for bringing me this strap. It was such a thoughtful gift and it's exactly the right size." She ran the supple leather through her hand and tested the balance and heft. "Yes, I think this will do nicely."

She pulled her skirt up and sat down, exposing her nylon-clad thighs. She wore thigh-high black stockings, Richard's favorites.

"Let's have the shirt off. Come and stand in front of me so I can take your shorts down."

Suzanne eased the silk boxers over Richard's very prominent erection to just above his knees. "My, but you are a bit excitable today," she said, patting his balls. "Over my knees now."

As his skin came in contact with her legs, she guided his erect penis between her thighs and closed them, effectively trapping him against her lap. She noted his audible sigh and smiled as she placed her hand on his bottom and gently stroked it. "I'm afraid we've a bit of a marathon ahead of us as you've chalked up quite a list of infractions and general bad behavior, so you may as well get comfortable."

The first blow was delivered, barehanded, to the outside of his left cheek, which immediately reddened; a blow of equal strength closely followed with regards to his right cheek. She paused to admire the two small, red handprints before she began alternating sides. She covered the entire area of his pert bottom from the very top of his ass to the very bottom, where the crease of his thighs began.

He was beginning to squirm nicely. Suzanne gently stroked the red and warming skin, happy with her handiwork up to this point. Sliding her reddened and tingling palm between his legs and underneath, she massaged his balls and the back of his very stiff cock. She ran her index finger up its length, opening her thighs just enough to tease the head. "Very nice," she murmured.

Closing her legs again, and without warning, she began raining smacks in rapid fire on the left side of his bottom. "I'd like you to reflect on the error of raising your voice to me, Richard. That is something I simply won't stand for." She switched to his right side. "I think you know this and I'm sure you'll think twice before doing it again, won't you?"

He mumbled something.

The smacks stopped as quickly as they'd begun. "I'm sorry, what was that? I didn't hear you."

"Yes. Yes, Suzanne. I'm sorry."

Suzanne gently soothed his stinging skin. "That's it. Relax, no more clenching now." He wrapped one arm around her leg and began stroking her calf in time with the soothing attention she was giving his punished bottom.

"That's right. Now, let's move on to your recent problem with lateness." His body stiffened again. She lifted her crop from the chair back and gently slapped it from side to side between his legs. Knowing what she was after, he moved his legs apart and began to whimper.

Using the crop, she pounded first one cheek then the other, relishing the audible whistle as the downward motion of the crop sliced the air on each stroke. Suzanne liked to use her short, square-headed crop during over-the-knee spankings. It was much easier to control, and could therefore provide exactly the sensations she was looking for. Poor Richard had a difficult time keeping his legs apart and each time he'd bring them together and clench his bottom, she'd stop and gently tease them apart with the head of the crop.

She paid special attention to the sweet spot where his thighs met his rear end. The cropping went on until he was rolling uncontrollably against her lap and she heard him sniffle.

Satisfied with these results, Suzanne stopped and hung the crop back on the chair and gently brushed his exquisitely hot cheeks with the back of her hand. Leaning close, she murmured sympathetically to him.

"You're taking your punishment so well. I'm very proud of you. You're being a very good boy. We're almost done now and then you'll get your reward."

She gazed at his bottom, which for all the attention it had received, had really no more than a lovely red glow. But it was oh so hot to the touch. She could feel the heat coming off in waves. Suzanne had been very careful to cover every inch with her attentions, warming and waking up all the nerve endings in the area without leaving any welts or broken skin. Should she decide to stop now, he'd be sore for several hours, but wouldn't suffer any bruises and would have no physical reminders of the afternoon by bedtime.

"I've saved the most distressing of your recent behaviors for last. Stand up, Richard. Step out of your shoes and socks and your jeans and underwear. That's it; I want you lying on the bed. Place the pillow under your hips. It's so much easier when your bottom is a bit elevated, isn't it?"

Without a word, a naked and contrite Richard docilely complied. She noticed his face was quite red. It wouldn't be long now. She took the new strap from the chair back and crossed to the bed. Caressing his cooling bottom, she said, "Not sleeping is very bad, Richard. I won't allow you to take such poor care of your health. I insist that you go to bed at a reasonable time and get the proper amount of sleep." She let the strap trail gently, back and forth over his backside. "These last six strokes with your new strap will serve to focus your attention on the seriousness of my wishes in this respect."

Richard clenched his cheeks and groaned.

"No, no, no, dear." She let her fingertips play very lightly over his rose-colored rear. As soon as she saw the muscles relax, she brought the strap down hard across both cheeks just in the middle of his ass. A perfect image of the strap appeared immediately in deep red on his skin. It was exciting to watch. She ran a finger lightly across the stripe and felt wetness trickle down, between her legs.

Richard made her wet; there was no getting around that. The act of spanking him, first with her hand and then with leather, could become a religious experience. The scent of his arousal, the sight of his marks, and the feel when she ran her fingers lightly over them could almost cause her to climax, at times.

She brought the strap down again, just above the first stroke, and he bounced against the bed and grunted. Quickly she gave him a third just below the original stroke. This time he cried out.

Suzanne gazed at the three perfect red stripes on his rosy bottom and ran her fingertips over them lightly. She heard him wince.

"Please, please, please," he moaned.

"Open your legs for me," she said. She reached between them and fondled and massaged his balls until he groaned and sighed. "Just three more now. Are you ready?"

"Please, please, please," he whispered.

"Please what, Richard? I'm waiting. You need to tell me to finish your spanking."

"Please..."

"Yes?"

"Please, Suzanne, please finish my spanking," he groaned.

"All right then, if that's what you want...Close your legs for me now; we wouldn't want any accidents."

Suzanne quickly finished up with a vertical stroke on each side and a final stroke across his sweet spot. The last stoke wrenched a scream from him and he was actively crying when she put the strap down and gathered him into her arms. He came willingly and buried his face against her neck.

Suzanne sat next to him on the side of the bed, gently rocking and holding him close. Although shaking with sobs, she could tell he was much calmer than when he had arrived. A good spanking tended to relax him and relieve his stress. This particular spanking would hopefully keep him stress-free for most of the coming week.

She handed him a box of tissues and waited until he regained his composure. "There now, are you ready for your reward?" When he looked up, she was standing in front of him, holding silk scarves in one hand and a belt in the other. She watched the new understanding dawn on his face, along with a smile.

"Yes, I've been promising for a long time and you *have* been very good just lately, and you *did* take your punishment like a good boy." She handed him the belt. "Here, fasten this loosely around your waist."

Suzanne tied a scarf around each wrist and had him lie on his back, in the middle of the bed. She put a pillow under his head.

"Comfy?"

"Yes, Suzanne."

"Good." She could tell by the way he eased himself down that his bottom really was quite sore.

Richard put his arms above his head and smiled at Suzanne.

"No, Sweetie," she said. She tied his wrists to the belt around his waist. "There now, try to lift your arms."

Satisfied that he couldn't move his hands from his sides, she stood next to the bed, unzipped her skirt, and stepped out of it. She slowly unbuttoned her blouse and removed it, leaving the matching black lace bra and thong on as well as her stockings and pumps.

She knelt on either side of his shoulders and, grasping the bars of the headboard, lowered her lace-clad mound onto his face. He immediately began to lick the already wet lace of her thong.

"Everything all right, sweetie? You can breathe freely?"

He made a few muffled sounds, so she lifted herself up a bit. "Yes?"

"Yes, I can breathe fine, but I was asking why you tied my arms down. I could pleasure you better if I could use my hands."

236

"Yes, I know you'd like to be in control, Richard. But you're not. You'll reach what I allow you to reach," she said, knowing he couldn't reach anything. She lowered herself back onto his mouth, rubbing her mound against his mouth and chin.

Reaching down, she moved the fabric of the thong to the side, exposing herself completely to his oral attentions. Richard was very good at cunnilingus. But then, people are often good at the things they love most.

She felt his tongue enter her and, at the same time, she felt motion behind her back. She turned her head in time to see a freed hand beginning to untie the other arm.

She moved off his face immediately. "What do you think you're doing?" she bellowed, grabbing his freed wrist.

"I told you, I could do a better job if I could just use my hands!" he said.

"Well, Richard," she said, "you've ruined a perfectly nice reward, haven't you? You're so bad! If I'd wanted you to use your hands, I wouldn't have gone to the trouble of restraining them, would I?"

She quickly flipped him over onto his stomach and began energetically spanking his sore bottom as he writhed and yelped. "You're so bad! Absolutely incorrigible!"

She heard him begin to snicker and was unable to hold it together as she collapsed into hysterical laughter. Rolling off him, she lay breathless.

"Bad, bad, bad—naughty and bad! What *am* I going to do with you?"

What Jackie Gives Me

By Evan Mora

Jackie gives me a white dress, because I am a good girl. A pretty sundress with ruffles and lace, and tiny white buttons that fasten in the back. I twirl in a circle and Jackie smiles.

"Would you like to go on a picnic?" he asks, and I clap my hands excitedly.

"Oh yes, oh yes, oh please, please yes!" Jackie is so sweet.

He holds my hand as we walk through the fields, tall golden grasses tickling our thighs. Jackie's dressed in white too, a button-down shirt and soft linen pants. He's so very handsome with his alabaster skin, his brilliant blue eyes, and his coal-black hair. It's hard for me to watch where I'm walking, because all I want to do is look at Jackie.

We spread our blanket beneath a big beautiful tree and Jackie lies with his head in my lap, reading me love poems by Neruda. There is nothing in the world but Jackie and me; I am such a lucky, lucky girl. I listen to his voice and the rhythm of his speech, to the richness of language and sound. I feel the vibration of his words in curious places and giggle at the tingly warmth.

"Are you hungry, my sweet?" Jackie asks with a smile, setting the book aside and touching my cheek.

My tummy rumbles as if on cue and I look shyly at the basket and then Jackie.

"Go ahead," he gestures, "open it, please."

I am excited to see what treats are inside; Jackie takes such good care of me. I lift the lid and gasp with delight–crisp apples, rich cheeses, ripe succulent grapes, fresh crusty bread, and warm roasted chicken. A bottle of wine is nestled amongst these treasures, with a picture of a castle and foreign words on the front.

"We'll save that for later." Jackie tucks it aside. I am not normally allowed such things. I nod my head solemnly, for surely then, today must be special.

Jackie breaks off a small piece of bread and extends his hand toward me. I reach for the bread, but Jackie pulls back, shaking his head as he does.

"Let me feed it to you," he says. "We wouldn't want your dress to get all dirty, would we?"

He extends his hand toward me once more and I lean in obligingly, lips parted. He places the morsel in my mouth, and it tastes of such warm, yeasty goodness that I close my eyes and sigh. Jackie chuckles a little and my eyes pop open, warmth stealing into my cheeks.

"No–don't be embarrassed," Jackie says to me gently. "I think your reactions are delightful." I search his eyes, but they are clear and true, and I hesitantly return his smile.

"Here, try this." Jackie offers me a fat grape plucked from the basket beside him. My mouth is open in eager anticipation as Jackie places the cool globe on my tongue.

"Go on," he says, and I bite down on it then, sweet juices exploding in my mouth. I moan with pleasure this time, I can't help it; I'm not sure I've ever tasted anything so good.

What Jackie Gives Me by Evan Mora

I look at Jackie; he's watching me, and his eyes seem to have darkened, just slightly.

"Now this," he says in a husky voice, a piece of soft cheese between his thumb and forefinger. My lips close over his fingers as well as the cheese, and Jackie pulls back with a sharp intake of breath. I wonder at his strange reaction, but then I am lost in the rich creamy texture spreading over my tongue. I press my tongue to the roof of my mouth, sinking into and then through this rich treasure.

I look to Jackie hungrily, eager for whatever comes next. He's still for a moment, watching me silently the way men watch the bad girl who stands on the corner, whose dress is much too short, even for summer. Jackie's eyes are like stormy blue seas and the muscle in his jaw is clenching and unclenching. I'm worried that I've done something wrong.

"Jackie..." I whisper questioningly, and he comes alive again, with a smile that makes me shiver. It's the smile that I know, and yet it's not; it's different, though I don't quite know how.

"Forgive me," he says, reaching into the basket and tearing off a large piece of chicken. It smells so good that I forget his strange mood, and my appetite returns with a vengeance. I snatch up the morsel greedily in my mouth, nearly biting Jackie's fingers in my haste. Warm juice trickles down my chin and my tongue darts out to catch it.

"More," I say, though I know it's not polite, and hastily tack on a "please."

Jackie complies, then shifts positions on the blanket, a grimace flashing across his handsome face. I wonder if he is simply uncomfortable, or if my bad manners are the cause of his distaste. I lower my eyes just in case and try to act more ladylike, chewing slowly, my hands in my lap. When a moment has passed, I look cautiously at Jackie; he's got the apple in his hands.

"Would you like this, my sweet?" he asks, holding it out to me, his voice a low whisper I don't recognize. I nod silently, unsure of his mood, and offer a tentative smile.

"Go ahead," he says, and I lean forward, then hesitate, my eyes flickering from the apple to Jackie.

"Bite it," he says, and my teeth part its flesh, and it's firm and delicious and sweet. I try to stifle the moan that wells up inside me, but I can't, and it escapes into the space between us. My eyes fly to Jackie's, but they are unfathomably dark, and a flush stains his alabaster cheeks. Out of the corner of my eye, I spy a droplet of juice fall from the apple to Jackie's palm. It slides down to his wrist and I impulsively lean in and lick up the drop with my tongue.

Jackie makes a choking sound and drops the apple as though it burns. His chest is heaving as though he's out of breath and I freeze under his icy glare. I don't know what I've done wrong. I don't know why he's so angry. I look down and sit very still. After a moment, I hear movement, but I still don't look up; I don't want to do anything to make him angrier.

"Here," Jackie says, and I have to look at him then. He's holding a glass of wine out to me. I don't want to take it. Sometimes Jackie lets me have wine, but then he's always happy and we laugh together like we're sharing a secret. I don't want the wine now, not when he's so mad. I worry my lip between my teeth.

"Take it," he says, thrusting the glass toward me. I reach up with trembling hands, but I'm so nervous that it falls from my fingers. A cascade of deep red soaks the front of my dress, my beautiful white sundress with ruffles and lace.

"You've ruined it!" Jackie roars, and my lips start to tremble, tears prickle at the corners of my eyes.

Then Jackie's hands are on me, pushing me down, so quickly I can't voice a protest. I'm on my back on the blanket and Jackie is astride me, tearing at the dress with a fury.

"Wanton!" He spits. "Temptress—"

"Nooooo..." I moan, my head shaking back and forth in denial.

"—with your greedy mouth and sinful tongue." His eyes are alight with madness, and his body is hard where it's pressed against me. The seams of my dress give way beneath his hands, and in a moment, I am naked beneath him. He staggers to his feet, my ruined dress in his hand, and looks down at me contemptuously as I try to cover myself.

"Look how you try to hide yourself from me!" Jackie shouts, and I am miserable, crying in earnest because I don't know what to do.

"You are no sweet, innocent little thing," he says, throwing the tattered dress away from him. "You are a wicked, wicked girl." Jackie falls to his knees, and before I can guess his intent, his hand is wrapped around my ankle and he's pulling me toward him.

"You need to be punished," he says, and his eyes are bright like the Reverend Carmichael's are when he talks about God and the Devil. I try to scramble backwards, try to pull my leg from his grasp, but Jackie is strong, and no matter how much I struggle, he keeps on pulling me closer.

"No Jackie!" I cry when his hands grab my hips. "Oh, pleeease no!" I keep saying it over and over; I keep telling him I'm sorry, that I'll be a good girl, but it doesn't make any difference and soon Jackie's sitting on his heels and he's got me facedown across his lap. He's got one hand pressed hard into the small of my back to keep me from moving and before I can voice the plea that's on my lips, his other hand delivers a stinging blow to my upturned backside.

"Jackie!" I shriek, redoubling my efforts to escape, but everything I do only seems to spur him on and he spanks me again and again, the blows raining hard and fast on my tender flesh until my words dissolve into open-mouthed sobs pressed into the picnic blanket beneath my face. Even then he doesn't stop, and misery and hopelessness steal slowly into my heart, because I know that Jackie must be right; I must be a bad, bad girl. I deserve to be punished. I deserve to be hurt.

I stop struggling to be free. I want to tell Jackie that he doesn't have to hold me down anymore, that I won't go anywhere, but I can't make the words and he keeps on holding me and spanking me as though he's never going to stop. All the hurt in my body gathers together like a wave and washes over me, and it's so much I think that I might drown. But then somehow it changes—not how much it hurts, and not how hard Jackie hits me—but something inside me changes and opens up, and although I don't really know why, I start lifting my backside to meet Jackie's hand.

For a while, it continues like before, but then something in Jackie seems to change too, because he slows down a little and leaves a bit of space between one spank and the next, and then in between spanks, he squeezes my swollen bottom, or runs his hand across its surface. My bottom feels hot and prickly and very, very big. Each time my heart beats, I can feel it there, and in between my legs as well. And even though I don't say this out loud, Jackie seems to know, because the next time his hand smoothes over my skin, his fingers dip into that place and touch there too.

I make a tiny sound, but not of pain, and Jackie's fingers push into me. Jackie makes a sound too, and his fingers are moving in and out and he's not spanking me at all anymore. I'm

243

not sure how it's possible to feel good after hurting so much, but I do, and the more Jackie's fingers move, the more the hurting changes into something entirely different. My body feels heavy and empty and I want...I don't know what I want, but Jackie does, because with a muttered curse, he lifts me off his lap and lies me down on my belly on the blanket.

I can see Jackie out of the corner of my eye, and I watch him strip off his button-down shirt and open his white linen pants. He pushes his pants down over his hips and then moves between my thighs on his knees. He pulls my hips up to meet his, my shoulders and head still resting on the blanket, and then our bodies are joined together, and I can feel the heat where they connect. Jackie moans and is still, though not for long, and then he moves inside me. He feels so big and so good, filling up my emptiness, taking away my hurt, until all that's left is an ache in my belly that keeps churning and getting tighter.

I slip my hand between my thighs, press my fingers to the place that seems to pulse with a life of its own. It's small and slippery and hard, and it feels so very, very good when I rub my fingers over it. I circle it slowly once, then twice, pressing down on it gently at first, then more firmly. Something is building inside me, getting bigger each time Jackie moves and each time my fingers rub this hard little nub. I rub it faster, press down on it a little harder–

"What are you doing?" Jackie is suddenly still. My mind is racing, trying to find the right thing to say.

Silence stretches between us.

"I said, what are you doing?" Jackie's voice is ominously quiet.

I know he's waiting, waiting for me to say something innocent and naïve, something that will allow the fantasy to continue, but just that quickly, I've lost her–that candy sweet little girl Jackie Daddy likes to turn over his knee and punish.

There's nothing I can say. Not really. Nothing that will push us back into that suspended disbelief. I've blown it. Me and my hungry clit and my impatience to get off.

"Goddamnit!" Jackie's hand crashes down on my already tender ass with enough force to snap my jaw shut and drive my face into the blanket.

"Greedy little whore," Jackie snarls, fucking me now without any pretence of gentleness. "You just couldn't wait, could you?" He hits me again and again, his hands like hot irons on my burning flesh.

"Let's see it then," he says, his cock driving into me ruthlessly. "Get yourself off, you dirty bitch."

I moan then, already half lost in the crazy rush of pleasure-pain his words and his cock and his vicious, beautiful hands deliver, but grateful still for the permission he's given. He could have denied me any kind of release; Jackie can be cruel.

I pinch my clit between my fingers, then stroke myself in earnest, pushing my hips back to meet his angry thrusts, feeling the beginnings of my orgasm already pulling at my cunt. Jackie delivers another jarring blow to my ass, strong enough to push the air out of my lungs and derail my budding release. I whimper just a little and Jackie laughs, a harsh sound that sends shivers down my spine.

He doesn't tell me to stop, though, so I keep stroking my clit, and in a moment, I'm right back on that edge. Jackie's cock is long and fat, and he fills me like nothing in this world. Just when I think I'm about to explode, my fingers moving furiously, Jackie's cock pounding into me, he smacks me again, and then again. I cry out this time, breathless and frustrated and needing to come so bad that I'm crying all over again, hot tears spilling onto my cheeks and disappearing into the blanket.

"Don't you quit on me," Jackie growls behind me. "You want it so bad, you take it."

He settles into a rhythm then, fucking me and smacking me, until the sensations start to bleed together, until they are one and the same, until I'm flying and coming and crying and rolling on waves of pleasure so intense I'm sure my body will come apart with the force of it.

I'm still reeling when Jackie pulls out of me, my cunt still contracting on the space where his cock used to be, when he rolls me over and straddles my chest, supporting his weight with one hand and pushing his cock into my mouth with his other.

He's slow for a moment, letting me adjust to his size, pushing forward only a little and then pulling out, letting me breathe before he fills my mouth again, pressing deeper this time, until his pubic hair tickles my nose and I have to fight not to gag as he pushes into my throat. Jackie groans, and I feel his cock grow even harder. He takes his hand away from his cock then, bracing himself with both arms above me and fucking my mouth with a steadily increasing pace.

It won't be long now, I know. I'm still riding my own endorphin high, and I can feel Jackie's thighs tremble, hear the helpless sounds he makes in his throat. I moan around Jackie's cock—I know he likes how that feels—and I'm rewarded when I hear his bitten-off curse and feel the jerky way his hips move a heartbeat before his orgasm hits and hot fluid spurts down my throat.

Jackie collapses on his back next to me, his chest heaving and perspiration shining on his skin. With leaden arms he pulls his pants back up over his hips, and then pulls the zipper shut and fastens the button. He scarcely looks my way, and says nothing of what has transpired. We lie in silence on our blanket, beneath the canopy of the big beautiful tree. We lie there for what seems a long, long time.

Then Jackie moves. He reaches for the picnic basket. There is a small compartment on the side I hadn't noticed before, and Jackie unfastens the snap. He reaches inside and pulls something out, something small and bright and impossibly sheer. He holds it in front of me wordlessly, by a thin spaghetti strap. It seems almost alive as it unfurls from Jackie's hand; it seems almost to slither toward me. I smile at Jackie, an evil smile, because this time the game is different.

Jackie gives me a red dress, because I am a whore.

About the Authors

D. L. King is a smut writing—and editing New Yorker who lives somewhere between the Wonder Wheel at Coney Island and the Chrysler Building. She is the editor of two anthologies of erotica from Cleis Press: *The Sweetest Kiss: Ravishing Vampire Erotica* and the Lambda Literary Award Finalist, *Where the Girls Are: Urban Lesbian Erotica*. *Spank!* is her third anthology. She is also the publisher and editor of the book review site, Erotica Revealed. Her short stories can be found in anthologies such as *The Mammoth Book of Best New Erotica, Best Women's Erotica, Best Lesbian Erotica, Fast Girls, Sex in the City: New York, Please Ma'am, Sweet Love, The Cougar Book, Girl Crazy, Broadly Bound, Frenzy* and *Swing*, among others. She is the author of two novels of female domination and male submission, *The Melinoe Project* and *The Art of Melinoe*. Find out more about D. L. King at dlkingerotica.com and dlkingerotica.blogspot.com.

Also known to enjoy being spanked, **Cassandra Park** loves spanking miscreants. Ms Park has been writing for newspapers, magazines and journals for over 20 years. Her spanking and erotic fiction has been published by The Eulenspiegel Society and Scarlett Hill and her own collection of spanking stories, *It's Supposed to Hurt*, is now available. She writes about female dominance on her blog, *The Corporal Consultant* www.mscassandrapark.com. Cassandra lives with her husband in Queens, NY. Her corporal consultation is much sought after in New York City and around the country. She can often be seen at various venues with a recalcitrant young man or woman over her knee.

Lee Ash is a UK author who has published half a dozen erotic novels and novellas and countless short stories, all firmly set within the punishing genre of BDSM. He has written principally for the UK imprint Silver moon and was a regular contributor to the website, "Darker Pleasures."

Anna Black's erotic short stories have appeared in *The MILF Anthology*, *Cowboy Lover—Erotic Tales of the Wild West*, Zane's *Purple Panties* and *Honey Flava* anthologies, *Hurts So Good*, *The Mammoth Book of the Kama Sutra*, and *The Sweetest Kiss: Ravishing Vampire Erotica*. She writes for Ellora's Cave under the name Jenna Reynolds and her books, *Madison Avenue Vampire*, and *Kiss of Honor*, are both forthcoming. Her novella, *Sweet Spot* is available now. Learn more at her website www.jennareynolds.com.

Award winning author **Kathleen Bradean's** stories can be found in *The Best of Best Women's Erotica 2010*, *The Sweetest Kiss*, *The Mammoth Book of Best New Erotica 9*, Zane's *Sensuality – Caramel Flava II*, *Broadly Bound*, *Where the Girls Are*, *Coming Together Against the Odds*, *Haunted Hearths and Sapphic Shades*, and many other erotica anthologies. Read her reviews on EroticaRevealed.Com and Erotica-Readers.Com. Or let her seduce you 140 characters at a time on Twitter. KathleenBradean.Blogspot.com

Cervo is the pen name of a dedicated Brooklynite, He maintains his ancient brownstone where he writes screenplays and fiction, paints, acts, and directs. He does political columns and literary criticism for national and international publications. He is inspired in these sometime lurid pursuits by his two dogs and the solace of his flower garden. His work appears regularly on the Erotica Readers and Writers Association website and in several editions of The Mammoth Book of Best New Erotica and the erotic anthology, Cream.

A.D.R. Forte's erotic short fiction runs the gamut from contemporary to fantasy, sweet to kinky and everything in between. Her stories appear in various print and e-anthologies from well-known editors in the genre, including *Where the Girls Are* and *The Sweetest Kiss* also edited by D.L. King. http://www.adrforte.com

Sacchi Green lives and writes in western Massachusetts. Her stories have appeared in numerous publications, including seven volumes of *Best Lesbian Erotica*, four of *Best Women's Erotica, Best Lesbian Romance*, and *Penthouse*. She has edited or co-edited five lesbian erotica anthologies: *Rode Hard, Put Away Wet* (Suspect Thoughts Press)*; Hard Road, Easy Riding* (Lethe Press); *Lipstick on Her Collar* (Pretty Things Press); *Girl Crazy* and the Lambda Literary Award winning, *Lesbian Cowboys*, both from Cleis Press.

Roxy Katt (roxykatt.blogspot.com) lives in Canada and describes herself as a pornographer and cultural Bolshevik. She got started composing erotic stories in the genre of "VHF"

(Vaudevillian Humiliation Fetishism) because of being traumatized by certain supposedly normal cartoons as a child. Damn that Popeye and the hapless Olive Oyl! Roxy writes not only lesbian but also phallogyne (shemale) erotica, and often includes rubber, leather, armour, and science fiction settings as elements in her work.

Jessica Lennox's love for writing is rivaled by her love for poker and her addiction to video games, which she plays as often as possible. Jessica's other hobbies and passions include motorcycles (yes, she rides!), travel, sports, gender theory, and of course, books! Jessica's erotic work appears in *Where the Girls Are: Urban Lesbian Erotica*; *Hurts So Good: Unrestrained Erotica*; *Rubber Sex*; *Best Women's Erotica 2008*; and *Tales of Travelrotica for Lesbians: Erotic Travel Adventures, Vol. 2*.

Sommer Marsden is the author of *Sensitive, Lucky 13, Base Nature, Blank* and *Calendar Girl*. Sommer is the editor of the *Dirtyville Collection* and *Coupling: Filthy Erotica For Couples*. She currently writes erotica and erotic romance for Ellora's Cave, eXcessica, Pretty Things Press and Xcite Books. You can find her private releases all over the web and through her tiny, almost invisible epress SPASTIC GIRL PRESS. You can find her doing yoga, walking her fat wiener (dog!) or eating frozen blueberries in her small Baltimore home--when she's not watching reality TV, that is. Visit her at smutgirl.blogspot.com.

Sean Meriwether has been living up to his moniker as "The Naughty Harry Potter" by working his own brand of magic on the page. His immersive fiction has been transporting readers into the tumescent landscape of his imagination. His work has appeared in print and online including Best of the Best Gay Erotica 2 and Lodestar Quarterly. The Silent Hustler (Lethe Press Books) collects a decade of his fiction. One of his alter-egos is managing editor of VelvetMafia.com. Like what you see? Stalk him online at penboy7.com.

Evan Mora is a recovering corporate banker living in Toronto who's thrilled to put pen to paper after years of daydreaming in boardrooms. Her works can be found in *Best Lesbian Erotica '09, Best Lesbian Romance '09 & '10, Where the Girls Are, The Sweetest Kiss: Ravishing Vampire Erotica, Girl Crush*, and *Please, Sir*.

Maggie Morton lives on the coast of California with her lovely partner and their eccentric cat. Her erotic short story "Unexpected Gifts" is published by Dreamspinner Press.

Ever since **Tara S. Nichols** was a little girl she has had an affinity for romantic adventures. With crushes on the likes of Tarzan and Hans Solo, she grew up looking for the perfect gentleman rogue. When she is not writing romance, erotica, or paranormal fiction, she can be found tending her garden, keeping bees, or reading a spy novel. Tara roams free on the flat prairie land in Manitoba Canada where she lives with her young son and husband. She can also be found at http://tarasnichols.webs.com

Jean Roberta writes in several genres. Her other recent spanking stories include "Flaming" (M/m) in *Bottoms Up*, "Nightmare" (F/f) in *Lesbian Cowboy Erotica* and "The Taste of Salt" (M/f) in *Wicked Pleasures*. Her own collection of 14 erotic stories, *Obsession* is available in several formats. Her column, "Sex Is All Metaphors" (www.erotica-readers.com) changes monthly, and her reviews appear monthly on "Erotica Revealed" (www.eroticarevealed.com).
Learn more here: www.JeanRoberta.com.

Lisabet Sarai has been writing and publishing erotica since 1999 and has six novels, two short story collections, and two erotica anthologies to her credit. Her stories have appeared in more than two dozen collections including four straight years of the *Mammoth Book of Best New Erotica*. Recently she began ePublishing with Total-E-Bound, Eternal Press and Phaze. Lisabet also reviews erotica for the Erotica Readers and Writers Association and Erotica Revealed. Visit her website at http://www.lisabetsarai.com.

J.Z. Sharpe writes nothing but fiction; her efforts have appeared in various print and Internet venues, including The Mammoth Book of Best New Erotica 5, MOIST, and the Erotica Readers and Writers Association galleries.

Donna George Storey loves to travel to exotic lands. She is the author of *Amorous Woman*, a steamy, semi-autobiographical tale of an American woman's love affair with Japan. Her short fiction has appeared in numerous journals and anthologies including *Spanked, Bottoms Up*,

Swing, *The Cougar Book*, *Penthouse*, *Best American Erotica*, and *The Mammoth Book of Best New Erotica*. Read more of her work at www.DonnaGeorgeStorey.com.

Allison Wonderland has been writing erotic fiction and poetry since 2007. Her work appears in *Hurts So Good: Unrestrained Erotica*, *Sweet Love: Erotic Fantasies for Couples*, *Fairy Tale Lust: Erotic Fantasies for Women*, and several editions of *Coming Together*. Aside from erotica, Allison's indulgences include cotton candy, kitten heels, and Old Hollywood glamour. Find out what else she's into and up to at http://aisforallison.blogspot.com.

Beth Wylde writes what she likes to read; which includes a little bit of everything under the rainbow. Her muse is an equal opportunity plot bunny that believes everyone, no matter their color, gender or orientation is entitled to experience love, acceptance and incredibly HOT sex! She is currently published with Logical Lust Publishing, eXcessica, Torquere Press and Phaze, with projects pending elsewhere. She has a voracious reading habit and loves to chat online. You can find out about new releases and contests by joining her yahoo group at http://groups.yahoo.com/group/bethwylde/ or by contacting her directly at b.wylde@yahoo.com. To read excerpts and buy a book (or two) visit www.bethwylde. com.

Swing! Adventures in Swinging by Today's Top Erotica Writers

Whether you are a swinger, think about swinging, or just interested in reading about it, *Swing!* has something for you!

Another acclaimed collection by Jolie du Pré and featuring a line-up that reads like a *Who's Who* of the top erotica writers.

$14.99 US, £9.99 UK, $7.99 eBook download

Best S&M
Erotica Vol III

Logical-Lust is the publisher for the third in M. Christian's
series of "Best S&M Erotica" volumes. In these pages you'll find
light stories, dark stories, powerful stories, subtle stories, fierce
stories, and even romantic stories – but all of them dealing with
the basic idea of consensually giving up, or taking, sexual power
and control.

$11.99 US, £8.99 UK, $5.99 eBook downloads

www.logical-lust.com

**Books also available from Amazon, Barnes & Noble,
and all good online retailers.**